Pamela

The Burden of Choice

Second Son Chronicles - Volume 9

Black Rose Writing | Texas

ISBN: 978-1-68513-223-1
PUBLISHED BY BLACK ROSE WRITING
www.blackrosewriting.com

Printed in the United States of America
Suggested Retail Price (SRP) $20.95

The Burden of Choice is printed in Book Antiqua

*As a planet-friendly publisher, Black Rose Writing does its best to eliminate unnecessary waste to reduce paper usage and energy costs, while never compromising the reading experience. As a result, the final word count vs. page count may not meet common expectations.

For Marlo

The Royal Family

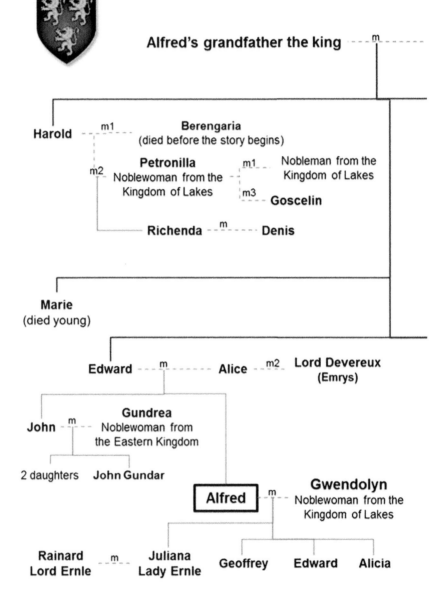

Alfred's grandfather the king ----m----

Harold ----m1---- **Berengaria**
(died before the story begins)

Petronilla
m2 Noblewoman from the
Kingdom of Lakes

m1 **Nobleman from the**
Kingdom of Lakes

m3 **Goscelin**

Richenda ----m---- **Denis**

Marie
(died young)

Edward ----m---- **Alice** ----m2---- **Lord Devereux**
(Emrys)

John ----m---- **Gundrea**
Noblewoman from
the Eastern Kingdom

2 daughters   **John Gundar**

Alfred ----m---- **Gwendolyn**
Noblewoman from the
Kingdom of Lakes

Rainard
Lord Ernle ----m---- **Juliana**
Lady Ernle   **Geoffrey**   **Edward**   **Alicia**

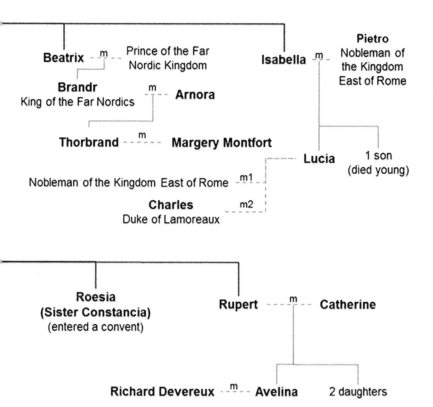

Juliana
Princess of the Kingdom Across the Southern Sea
(died before the story begins)

Beatrix - m - Prince of the Far Nordic Kingdom

Isabella m **Pietro** Nobleman of the Kingdom East of Rome

Brandr King of the Far Nordics — m — **Arnora**

Thorbrand - m - **Margery Montfort**

Lucia

1 son (died young)

Nobleman of the Kingdom East of Rome - m1 -

Charles Duke of Lamoreaux m2

Roesia (Sister Constancia) (entered a convent)

Rupert - m - **Catherine**

Richard Devereux - m - **Avelina**   2 daughters

The Nobility

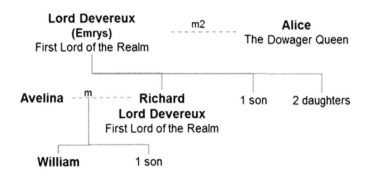

Lord Devereux (Emrys) First Lord of the Realm —m2-- **Alice** The Dowager Queen

Avelina --m-- **Richard Lord Devereux** First Lord of the Realm | 1 son | 2 daughters

William | 1 son

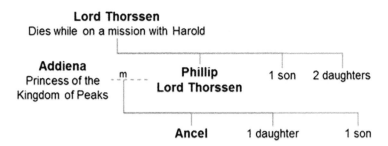

Lord Thorssen Dies while on a mission with Harold

Addiena Princess of the Kingdom of Peaks --m-- **Phillip Lord Thorssen** | 1 son | 2 daughters

Ancel | 1 daughter | 1 son

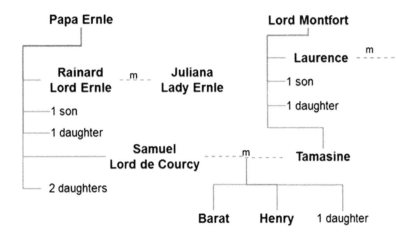

Papa Ernle

Rainard Lord Ernle --m-- **Juliana Lady Ernle**

1 son

1 daughter

Samuel Lord de Courcy --m-- **Tamasine**

2 daughters

Lord Montfort

Laurence --m--

1 son

1 daughter

Barat | **Henry** | 1 daughter

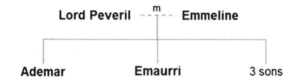

Lord Peveril --m-- **Emmeline**

Ademar   **Emaurri**   3 sons

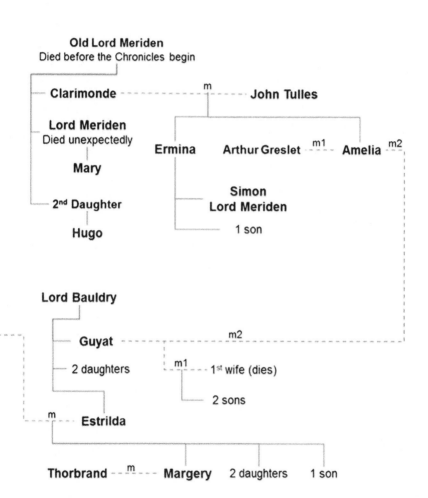

Old Lord Meriden
Died before the Chronicles begin

Clarimonde ------- m ------- **John Tulles**

Lord Meriden
Died unexpectedly

Mary   **Ermina**   **Arthur Greslet** --m1-- **Amelia** m2

2nd Daughter   **Simon**
                      Lord Meriden

Hugo   1 son

Lord Bauldry

Guyat ------- m2

2 daughters   m1 ---- 1st wife (dies)

                     2 sons

m --- **Estrilda**

Thorbrand --m-- **Margery**   2 daughters   1 son

Royal House of the Kingdom Across the Southern Sea

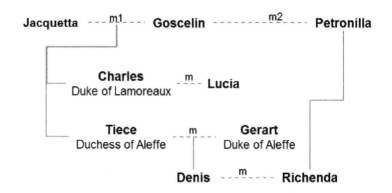

Lords of the Unorganized Territories

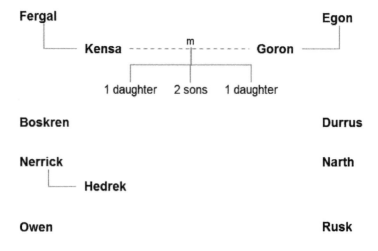

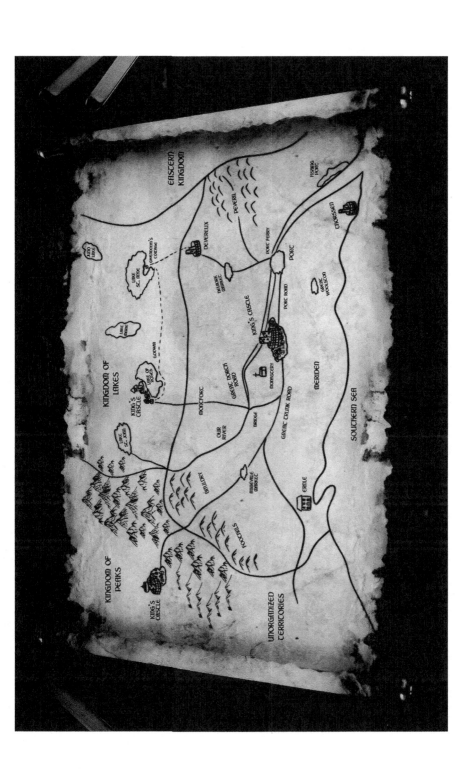

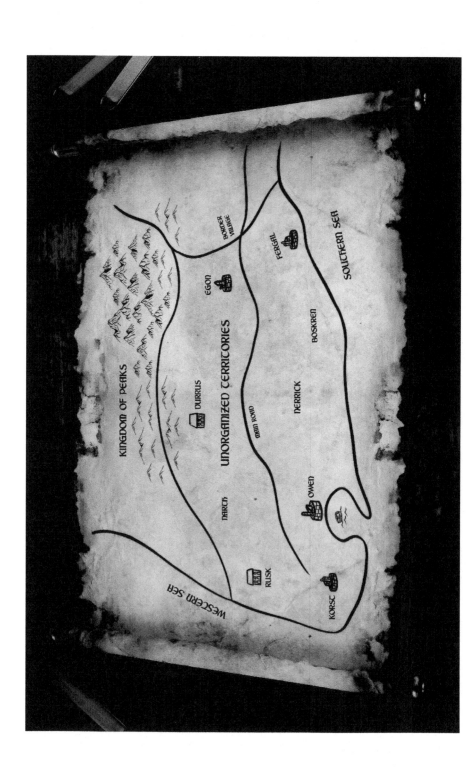

The Burden of Choice

"Alfred?" Samuel's voice jars me out of my trance. How long have I been staring at the words on the paper in my hand?

Now you must choose. Your kingdom or the boy's. It is time for the debt to be paid.

I've been vaguely aware of the guards taking charge of Gunhild . . . of Laurence admonishing them she can put up a nasty fight . . . of Cedric . . . or was it Carew? . . . asking about a scar on the stranger's face, looking to affirm that it was the Teuton king who sent the message. Of that, there's no doubt. But, of course, they haven't yet read his words.

Of all the scenarios Samuel and I postulated about what might happen when Denis came of age . . . all the discussions with Jasper and Evrouin and Carew about how we would respond . . . Even as we learned more and more about the brewing unrest in our neighboring kingdom and contemplated if or how it might affect us . . . or how we might come to the aid of a fellow monarch . . . Never did we imagine anything remotely like what we now face.

Has the Teuton been masterminding events in the Eastern Kingdom all along? Or did his spies simply uncover a situation he could exploit to his advantage? Either way, the anxiety that has nagged at my mind for so many months is now a reality that's descended heavily onto my shoulders in the space of three short sentences.

I hand Richard the message and gesture for him to pass it around to the others in the room. By the time Coliar has closed the door behind the guards, everyone has read the message, and I retrieve it from Peveril's outstretched hand as I resume my seat. All of them seem to be waiting for someone else to speak first. "Rather different from what we'd planned for, Jasper," I address the knight commander.

"Yes, Sire," he replies then, after a brief pause, adds, "Yes and maybe not so much. The presence of the Teutons does alter what we thought we might face in the east. But I think what it means is adjusting our plans – not starting over completely."

"Is that possible?" asks Richard, his tone one of incredulity.

"It's not out of the question, my lord. Thanks to the king's insistence that I humor his visceral unease with certain modifications to the construction of the eastern garrison, we may be in a better position to respond to this new threat than we would've been otherwise. That doesn't mean we don't have to alter some things, but—"

"How quickly can you be ready to bring the Council – in fact, all the lords – into the picture?" Richard interrupts Jasper's temporizing.

"Don't rush them, Devereux," says Samuel. "Plans concocted in a hurry can be full of more holes than a butt used for archery practice. Besides, my brother and Thorssen aren't yet back from their errands." Something of an understatement of their missions to prevent hostilities breaking out between the Peaks and the Territories by revealing it was Teutons, not Peaksmen, who'd sabotaged Korst's tin mine. Phillip has the added task of finalizing the contract for Geoffrey's marriage to the Peaks king's daughter, Eirwen. This may put paid to Geoffrey's hope of traveling to the Peaks for the betrothal announcement. On the other hand, that announcement might very well work to our advantage in this new conflict – something to challenge the Teuton's assumptions.

"We may have to fill them in when they return." Richard's comment brings me back to the current discussion.

"I understand," says Samuel. "But consider this. Whatever Gunnvor and the Teutons are up to, they feel in control of the situation. They've positioned their forces – here and across the sea – and can bide their time. The Teuton king will want to watch our reaction before deciding on his next move. And he no doubt has numerous tactical options already worked out with his field commanders."

"Very well," Richard acquiesces. "Let me rephrase the question, Sir Jasper. When is the *right* time for me to call the lords together?"

"Tomorrow afternoon might be best, my lord."

"Let's say two days hence. I think we should take de Courcy's advice to heart."

"With respect, your lordship, tomorrow might be better. You see, while you and Lord de Courcy have been talking, I've come up with an idea. Some might say it's hare-brained . . ." Smiles all around the room acknowledge my own propensity for such things. ". . . but I think it could be what we need to change the balance of power. And time may be of the essence. I just need to work through it with Sir Evrouin. Sir Samuel too, if I can have a few moments of your time, my lord?"

"Would half an hour from now suit your needs?" Samuel asks.

"It would indeed. Permission to go get things underway, Sire?"

"Of course, Jasper," I reply. "In truth, I'm looking forward to hearing anything that might help us out of this dilemma." He bows quickly and hurries out the door. "The other part of the dilemma, gentlemen, is how to get word to Denis. Thanks to Peveril, we know Denis's situation and his deployments, but he's undoubtedly expecting us to be poised to come to his aid straightaway."

"Any chance the Teuton king sent him an equally cryptic message?" asks Carew.

"Quite likely. And all the more reason we need to get word to him about how we intend to handle our own situation and still fulfill our commitment to him."

"I can return, if that's what's needed," Peveril offers.

"I've no doubt you would . . . and I'm grateful for the offer. But it seems to me that would be precisely the sort of move the Teuton would be watching for. Stealth is what we need. The longer we can keep him guessing about what we might be up to, the more we can tempt him into showing his own hand."

Laurence recognizes my meaning straightaway. "I suspect you'll also want the messenger to have the skills to help Denis work out how to mesh our plans with his own. And you'll want someone you trust completely." I nod in reply. "In that case, if Sir Cedric is willing to maintain his current state – maybe even add a touch of the smell of the sea that most fishermen can never seem to shed – I can get him in. What I can't promise, in these circumstances, is when or how I can get him out."

All eyes turn to Cedric, who hasn't had the opportunity to shed the worn peasant clothing or the scruffy beard and unkempt hair of his scout's disguise. My raised eyebrows convey the implicit question. "If Carew can spare me, Sire."

"Are you certain, Cedric?" Carew asks. "You'll be on your own . . . on a rather uncertain mission."

"We've worked too hard getting that boy safe on his throne to just abandon him now, sir. Permission to join Sir Jasper, Sire? If I'm to know how to help King Denis, I'd best learn everything I can."

"Learn it well, Cedric," Laurence chimes in. "Whatever you carry will have to be in your head if we're to get you in safely."

"Permission granted, Cedric. And you should be present when Jasper briefs the lords. I trust you've no objection, Devereux?"

"Would it matter if I did?" Richard chuckles and Samuel grins.

"Very well, Cedric. Off with you and cram that head of yours full. We'll talk privately before you leave. And Cedric?"

"Aye, Your Grace?"

"Thank you." A quick bow is his only reply.

"Perhaps I'd best see to arranging the guards for our prisoner, Sire," says Carew, "as it seems I'm to be deprived of my deputy for who knows how long." The smile on his face tells me this isn't a complaint.

"I know guarding Gunhild is an added burden, Carew, but until we figure out what to do with her, it's necessary. Get someone strong from among the kitchen maids to search her thoroughly for anything that could be used as a weapon – I don't want her screaming rape if the guards do it. Just be sure whoever you get is up to the task if she puts up a fight. She should get decent food – and make sure she eats. We don't need her starving herself."

"As you wish, Sire."

Carew's departure leaves the rest of us alone with the burden of knowing we're soon to be embroiled in another fight – and that there's absolutely nothing we can do to prevent it. The best we can hope is to somehow find a way to preserve both kingdoms.

"I'm sending for Lady Mary and Simon," I announce. Richard nods his assent, but no one else offers a comment. "If anyone objects to having a woman in the Council chamber, Richard, then we'll just meet elsewhere. The library perhaps. Or Jasper's office. I simply refuse to send the men of the Meriden estate to war without the Meridens having a say in the matter."

"I have a better idea," says Richard. "Let *me* send for them. That will send a stronger message to anyone who thinks to object." This time it's Peveril who nods. "She can't be here for tomorrow's meeting though."

"I'm guessing what Jasper has in store for tomorrow," says Samuel, "will just be the bits that can't wait. He'll want to present the bigger plan only after he has all the adjustments completed."

"In which case, Phillip should be back in time for the full plan," says Richard. "What about Rainard, Alfred?"

"Hard to say. A couple of days or a week or more, depending on where he found Goron and if he had to travel all the way to see Korst in person."

"Let's hope for sooner," says Richard.

"As for you and Ademar," I address Peveril directly, "I'll leave it to the two of you to work out how you want to prepare your lands for what's to come."

"I'll talk with my son this evening, Alfred, but I suspect he'll be anxious to get home to shut down the quarries properly and move his family into the castle. Besides, I think I may yet have some influence should anyone venture to object to your inclusion of Mary and young Meriden."

·   ·   ·   ·   ·

When Gwen and I climb into bed this evening, I tell her everything Peveril reported about the threat to Aleffe province and Denis's port, as well as what Cedric discovered about the Teutons on our border, before showing her the message. She crumples the paper in her hand, snuggles close, and lays her head on my chest. "I had *so* hoped we'd finally put fighting in the past." Her tone is wistful . . . melancholy.

"No more than I, my love." I take the crumpled paper from her and drop it on my bedside table, to be smoothed out in the morning and placed in safekeeping with the chronicle. If only destroying the page could obliterate the threat! I hold her close. "There's something you should know. It was Gunhild who brought the message."

"So perhaps it really *was* her I saw that day in the market."

"Perhaps." I'll say no more. There's no reason for anyone else to know Laurence has been using Gunhild as a spy for more than a year now. A spy whose reliability we've always treated with some skepticism, never completely certain if she was a double-agent for her brother Gunnvor. And now, we have to wonder if it was the Teuton king stoking the fires in the background all along.

"How could you possibly choose?" Gwen asks softly.

"There *is* no choice. Both kingdoms must survive. And if the Teuton thinks I would choose otherwise, he's made a grave error of judgment. The question we have to answer is not which, but how."

She caresses my hand then brings it to her lips. "I assume you have some ideas for how?" She phrases it as a question.

"Jasper's been working on plans for months. We've known all along we might have to come to Denis's aid. What he's been working on most recently was based on the fact that we couldn't be sure if Gunnvor's ambition would be aimed at his own king or at us. An upstart Gunnvor we could deal with rather expeditiously. And even if a threat from Gunnvor coincided with the need to support Denis, Jasper had plans to deal with both simultaneously. It's the presence of Teutons on our border that changes things. But Jasper's not entirely pessimistic, so we just have to wait and see what he has in mind."

"Will you include Geoffrey in the Council meetings?"

"I'm still trying to decide. For tomorrow though, no. Samuel told me secrecy is key to what Jasper wants to do, and that's a burden I don't feel comfortable imposing on a young man who's not yet of age, even if he is the heir."

She laughs softly. "I suspect he's actually up to it, Alfred. But let's not throw water just yet on the flames of his impending betrothal."

"He'll have to know eventually."

"So will Edward."

"So will everyone."

To a man, the faces around the table are grim. Richard, Peveril and his heir Ademar, Samuel, Papa Ernle on behalf of Rainard, Rupert, Guyat Bauldry, Sir Jasper with Sir Evrouin and Sir Cedric seated just behind him, Laurence, and Montfort. The Bishop's seat is empty by design.

At midmorning, I'd made my way to the church in search of the wisdom or solace that often comes from quiet time spent alone at the tombs of my father and grandfather – and now, even my mother. Their voices in my head may be fading with the passage of time, but I can still feel their presence in that sacred place – a presence that calms my mind and brings clarity of thought in even the most troubling circumstances.

Somehow, the bishop always seems to find me there just as I'm ready to leave, and thankfully, this morning was no exception and served my second purpose well. I found him waiting at the foot of the stairs from the crypt up to the east transept. "I trust you found the peace you were seeking, my son?" His most frequent greeting on these occasions.

"For myself, perhaps, but sadly, not for the kingdom."

He allowed me to precede him up the steps. "Why so ominous, Alfred?" he asked.

When we reached the top, I asked him, "Father, will you hear my confession?" He and I long ago reached an accommodation to use the seal of the confessional when extraordinary circumstances require we speak freely but with assurance of absolute secrecy. I first used it to discourage him from attending a war council when we learned of Charles's planned invasion and couldn't risk that he might be compelled by ecclesiastical means to reveal our plans to the wrong people. He used it two years ago, when he thought it necessary to ensure that neither of us could be implicated in the papal inquisition launched against me. Now I've no choice but to use it again. I know the hold that the Teuton king has over the Pope, but have never revealed the secret. What I don't know is how widely that might be known within the Church hierarchy. And though I know what threats the Pope has already made to keep the Kingdom East of Rome from intervening on Denis's behalf, I don't know what orders he may already have issued to archbishops and bishops to prevent any attempt to thwart the Teuton's ambitions. So the risk, should our bishop learn anything of our plans, is unimaginable.

Nothing further passed between us until we were seated in the confessional. "Father, forgive me for I have sinned," I began. "It's been many months since my last confession."

"What's troubling you, Alfred?" came from the other side of the screen. His direct question told me he already understood my purpose.

"It seems my destiny is to rule at a time when threats to the peace arise far more frequently than I'd like."

"And what new threat do you now face?"

"From the east. I'm sure you recall the challenge from that quarter on the day of my coronation."

"I do indeed. But it was my impression that was put to rest on that day and has troubled you no further."

"A belief I shared. And yet it seems the failure of that day has festered in the mind of the brother of the young woman whose child was the claimant – the man who is now head of the family and lord of the estate. We've learned he's recruited other lords in the Eastern Kingdom to his cause and intends to try once again to lay claim to our throne by force." It felt more than a little unsettling to withhold from him the information about the Teuton's role since he was so forthcoming with me about how to deflect the papal inquisition. But I must. Everything you've said is true, Alfred, I reminded myself. And it has to be enough to make the case for discussing war plans without the bishop's presence.

"And so you must once again take up arms to defend your kingdom," came the voice through the screen.

"Something I would avoid if there were any way. But Gunnvor's armies are already being positioned on our border. And our information tells us he's hot-headed and fueled by ambition to claim what he believes was wrongfully denied to his family. That leaves me no choice but to call a gathering of the lords and our military leaders to prepare."

"We've been here once before, Alfred. At that time you suggested a man of the cloth might not be well pleased to be part of planning how men might kill their fellow men. That showed wisdom then . . . as it does now. And why can you not gather your lords at any time for any purpose outside of formal meetings of your Council?"

"I would far prefer to do so for celebrations than for such grim tasks."

"I've no doubt you would. But you must follow the path the Lord has set for you, and I will pray that you do so with the wisdom of your father and your grandfather . . . and that you will seek God's counsel as well."

"All I can do is whatever is my best."

"And that is all God asks. But know that I'm here to help you understand His will and you need only ask for whatever guidance you may require. *Ego te absolvo a peccatis tuis in nomine Patris et Filii et Spiritus Sancti. Amen.*" He paused then added, "Now I think you should go about your task of protecting your throne and your people."

I left feeling both relief and disquiet. What did he mean by that remark about helping me understand God's will? Was that a hint that we were both holding back something of what we know? That perhaps instructions from the Pope have already come? Or was I once again – as I did with Brandr's generosity last summer – reading too much into what was merely intended as kindness? In any event, he gave me a gift with the phrase "gather your lords." I must remember to share that with Richard.

Richard had delayed the meeting until midafternoon to give Rupert time to come from the country manor, so my uncle had only just arrived when everyone took their seats, grim faces and all.

"Sir Jasper," Richard wastes no time on formalities, "I believe this is your meeting."

"Aye, my lord." He pauses, as if gathering his thoughts. "So to begin, my lords, the success of the plan I'm about to reveal depends on two things – swift action and absolute secrecy. To that end, I need a decision before we leave this room on whether to proceed or not. And regardless of that decision, I need your words of honor to each other, to my men, and to the king that nothing we discuss here today will be spoken of outside this room. That means we must do our best to get all questions answered here and now. And whatever decision is taken, I must ask you – if you have any question after we leave this room, direct it only to me or to the king." He pauses to let everyone consider.

Richard wastes no time. "You have my word, Sir Jasper. Gentlemen?" He goes around the table, asking each man in turn, finishing with Montfort.

"And you have my word of honor as well, Sir Jasper," I add. Not really necessary, but something I want known.

"Very well," Jasper resumes. "The essence of this plan is something Lord Goron and I worked out some months ago as a way to provide an unexpected reserve force should we be called on to support King Denis against the Teutons. I think we can adapt it now to support him without the Teutons suspecting what we're up to. But, as I said, we have to act swiftly so they don't get wind of what's afoot.

"We'll use Lord Owen's fishing fleet to transport men from Goron's army across the sea, landing them in the small port where

Owen trades in the summer. The fishing boats can only accommodate foot soldiers and their arms, and they'll also transport some initial supplies. Owen will captain the first boat himself. He's well known in the opposite port and will be able to convince them this isn't an invasion but men coming to support their own king. He'll also hire wagons for the supplies. We'll provide the money to hire the wagons and to buy more supplies as the soldiers advance.

"They'll be under Hedrek's command and will move through the countryside in small groups, so they don't appear to be an organized force until they all come together at a point just west of Denis's castle town."

"Sending foot soldiers is something, I suppose," says Guyat, "but will they really be much help?"

"An unexpected reserve force of any kind is always helpful in a fight," says Jasper. "But that's not everything. I want to use the cove below Ernle Manor as an embarkation for cavalry. Two of our troops from the western garrison and as many of Goron's horse as can be accommodated. We believe we can load horses onto a ship from the jetty there at high tide. Only one ship at a time, and we may have to blindfold the horses to get them on board since the water won't be as calm as the river, so it will be slower going, but I'm convinced it can be done.

"And that's where I need your help, Lord Laurence. I need two ships, and I need them to look to all the world like they're departing on a trading mission. To that end, I need some trade goods loaded onto each ship. Hopefully, you have something in your warehouses that you can do without for a while. Don't load each ship fully – just enough that people see some goods going aboard. We'll be unloading them at Ernle's cove to make way for the cavalry. And not the new, larger ships. Ordinary trading vessels that people will have seen come and go often. Everything needs to look painfully mundane."

"We can do that," says Laurence, "but the minute they turn west beyond the mouth of the river, anyone watching will know something is up."

"Which is why they won't do that. Next week – and it will take that long for me to get word to Goron and to get everything in place – the tides and the moon are in our favor – the tide begins to ebb late afternoon and the waning moon doesn't rise until well after midnight. The ships can sail on the late tide and proceed south, like an ordinary trading expedition. As soon as it's good dark and the captains are certain no other ships are around, they turn west and make for Ernle Cove. We'll have a few beacons lit along the coast to help them with their bearings and with avoiding the cliffs.

"Once they're off the cove, they'll wait for the next flow of the tide and one ship will anchor off the jetty, unload the trade goods, and load the cavalry. They'll have to be quick about it – and my garrison commander will be in charge on the land side to make sure things are well organized – because they'll have to depart with the ebbing tide to avoid foundering. They'll sail to the fishing port across the sea. Owen assures us the jetty there can accommodate one ship at a time to get everything offloaded, and the water's deep so the tide is of little concern. Owen himself will organize what's needed at that end. The second ship will use the next high tide at Ernle Cove to follow suit."

"So then what happens when these ships are seen returning from the west?" asks Laurence.

"They won't be," says Jasper. "They'll sail on to the western port in Lamoreaux to be on hand in case they're needed for an evacuation. Which brings me to a question we've been unable to answer. Do we know, Lord Peveril, how well that port is defended?"

"That was perhaps the most difficult decision for Denis and his commanders. They know it's their escape route and needs to remain secure. But they don't have enough men to protect both the Teuton border and that port, so they had to make a choice. The port is guarded only by the duchess's men. It's a huge vulnerability, but they gambled that the Teutons would have to sail past their main port in order to get there, so they'd have some warning."

"I suspected as much. Which means that's another way we can help out. Only one of our troops will disembark with Goron's cavalry at the fishing port. The other will remain aboard and go on to Lamoreaux to reinforce the protection there.

"Like the foot soldiers, the cavalry will advance in small groups to the rendezvous point. It being summer, there should be plenty of grazing for their horses, so they should be able to make the journey with the food the men can carry in their packs. Cedric will meet them there with Denis's instructions for when and how they're to deploy, but Hedrek will remain in overall command." He turns to Evrouin and Cedric. "Have I forgotten anything?" Both shake their heads in the negative.

"Questions for the commander?" asks Richard.

"It's ambitious," says Montfort, "and most impressive if you can actually pull it off. What do you see as the risks?"

"The loading of the horses at Ernle Cove. They'll never have done anything even remotely like this. If the men there can keep them calm, all will be well. But if even one of them gets spooked and throws a fit, he'll infect all the others, and we'll have to abandon the operation and try again with the next high tide. That's why my orders are that we blindfold them before leading them onto the gangplank and that each man lead his own mount aboard. If the horse is with someone he already trusts, he'll be more likely to go willingly. And if the ones still on land see their stablemates go on board without incident, it'll minimize the chance of fear spreading through the herd. Oh, and Lord Laurence, wider gangplanks than usual wouldn't go amiss."

"So assuming all this goes according to plan," says Ernle, "it sounds to me like you'll be largely depleting our defenses in the west. Does that mean you'll have to steal from the forces in the east to replenish the western garrison?"

"We won't do that, sir. Goron will take on that mission for us. This was part of the original scheme. He'll leave a small force in the west to protect Owen's port, but it can be a very small force since Owen has both the rocks and his cannons to repel any threat there. Goron will move his forces to the border, where he can be positioned to protect us in the west or to pivot and protect his own lands in the event someone comes against them from the north. But we both believe the latter threat is unlikely unless the Lakes and the Peaks have already been overrun."

"Could the Lakes be overrun from the north?" Ademar asks.

"We don't know, sir, but that's something we'll discuss when I walk you through the full defense plan in a few days' time."

"De Courcy, you've been conspicuously silent," says Richard. "Of all of us, you have the best skills to assess what Sir Jasper is proposing."

All eyes turn to Samuel, who takes a moment before replying. I can feel the tension rise. "Jasper told me what he had in mind, so I've had a few more hours than any of you to think about it. The Teuton king thinks he's backed us into a corner such that we can't go to Denis's aid. And even though he knows we'd have allies in that fight, he'll expect to have eyes on whatever any of us are up to by watching the sailings from our port.

"Since his spies in the Territories managed to get themselves killed . . . and it's entirely possible he doesn't even know that yet . . . he no longer has eyes there. He probably is also not wasting spies in the western reaches of Denis's kingdom other than perhaps near the Lamoreaux port, so the comings and goings around an obscure fishing village will likely come under little or no scrutiny.

"In the meantime, our actions here will signal that Alfred intends to vigorously defend his kingdom, leading the Teutons to think he's made a singular choice. Until we've dealt with the direct threat here, our only option to support Denis is stealth. To that end, what Jasper and Goron have come up with is, to my mind, brilliant. And I think there's a quite reasonable expectation that the Teutons won't realize what's happening until Hedrek's forces are assembled and deploying into Denis's defenses." He pauses. "But I'm also in complete agreement with Jasper. Success depends on swiftness and secrecy."

"And what say you, Your Grace?" asks Richard.

"I've thought of little else since I first read that message. And I may have found a chink in the armor of the Teuton king's strategy. I think his intent is to use Gunnvor's ambition as a diversion, to prevent us from mounting the kind of response that thwarted his plans once before. And he's committed enough of his forces to that endeavor to be sure we can't ignore the threat . . . but no more than he's willing to lose trying to keep us occupied." Samuel and Jasper look across the table at one another and nod.

"For whatever reason," I continue, "the Pope has intervened to prevent a second front being opened across the sea, leaving Denis apparently on his own. So it's now our job to be that second front. With our allies, we have to mount such a vigorous resistance in the east that the Teuton *cannot* ignore that fight, lest we quickly demolish our opponents and sail immediately to Denis's aid.

"But we have to assume the Teuton has eyes within our kingdom. For now, any direct support for Denis must be entirely by subterfuge, and the farther away we can keep it from here and from the fighting in the east, the more likely it will succeed. I'm grateful, Sir Jasper, for your inventiveness. It's a bold plan, but one that's likely to disrupt the Teuton's calculations."

No one says a word. The faces around the table are still grim, but it seems now to be a grimness of determination rather than of dread. At long last, Richard speaks. "Do we have any other questions for Sir Jasper, gentlemen?" A long, silent pause. "Then, I believe, Sir Jasper, you have our concurrence. Is there anything else before we leave this room?"

"You'll get word to me, Sir Jasper, when the ships are to sail?" asks Laurence.

"If you'll come with me when we leave here, my lord, I can show you our time line and you can take that information with you when you return to the port. And, my lords, Sir Cedric departs on the morrow to be infiltrated into Denis's kingdom so Denis will know what's up before the reinforcements arrive."

"Godspeed, Sir Cedric," says Richard as heads nod around the table. "And I assume you'll tell me, Sir Jasper, when we should gather again to hear the rest of your plans."

"I will, my lord."

"In that case, I think we're finished here for now."

We all leave the room together, and I hang back to walk with Cedric. "I'm headed to the stable in half an hour to see how Regulus is faring. Perhaps you could meet me in the paddock."

"As you wish, Sire." And we go our separate ways.

The grooms have already fed the foals and turned them back out into the paddock by the time we arrive. I still do a double-take each time I see Cedric in his scruffy disguise. "Nice foals, Sire," he says as he climbs over the fence to join me.

"See one you particularly like?"

"Haven't really had a good look at them."

"Maybe you should do that when you get back." We walk to the opposite side of the paddock, to be sure we're out of earshot, and sit on the grass, our backs to the fence. "I promised we'd talk before you left, Cedric, and didn't want to take the chance you'd be off before I'm up in the morning."

"Actually, Sire, I'm leaving tonight. It's only two days since the full moon so there should be enough light for me to get well away from here before I need to camp for the night. More of the subterfuge. I'm headed for Great Woolston first, to be seen around the market square. Then I'll vanish from there in the middle of the night, headed to the port where I'll wait in a tavern on the dock until Lord Laurence's man contacts me. It means an extra day, but we judged that was the best way to prevent anyone getting wind of what I'm up to."

I can't help but chuckle. "How did I get so lucky that the men I trust most possess such a streak of deviousness?" He smiles. "I'm grateful, Cedric. I know how risky this is, but you'll be in good hands with Laurence's people. My greater concern is the difficulty you might face actually getting the chance to speak privately with Denis. His guards are naturally going to be quite reluctant to let someone who looks like a vagrant and smells like a fisherman into his presence."

"I've worked that out already, Sire. I'll just tell them to give him a message from me."

"A message?"

"Aye. They should tell him I still haven't learned how to fish with my bare hands. That should be enough to remind him of that day on the stream bank when Carew amazed us all."

"It should indeed. I trust you have all of Jasper and Evrouin's plans committed to memory?"

"Aye, Sire."

"Then there are some other things I want you to tell Denis . . . and tell him it comes directly from me. Tell him my thoughts about our role being a second front. And it might actually be useful for you to tell him that in the presence of his commanders and his advisors. Reassurance, of sorts, that we have no intention of abandoning them in this new conflict."

"As you wish, Sire."

"The rest, you should tell him only in private. First, that I intend to bring *all* our allies to bear in the fight against the Teutons. Be sure to emphasize the word 'all.' It will have significance for Denis, though he's no more likely to reveal what that significance is than I am here and now." Cedric nods.

"Then tell him that I understand he has no choice as a new king but to take the field. But he *must* remember that his job, first and foremost, is to stay alive. He should let his commanders lead in battle, under his banner, while he watches from a safe location, surrounded by his most trusted guards. No banner. No coronet. No indication of his identity. It must look to the enemy as if he's a reserve commander, observing but waiting to see if he's called into the fray. In fact, he shouldn't wear his coronet at all after his arrival in the field. And his observation post should vary from skirmish to skirmish – to keep the Teutons guessing about where a reserve force might be and what the battle plans are."

"You're worried about him being taken hostage, aren't you, Sire?"

"Precisely, Cedric. We know the Teuton has no hesitation about hostage-taking nor would he have any compunction in offering Denis's life in exchange for the port. So Denis shouldn't draw attention to himself in the camp. No elaborate king's tent. In fact, he should probably move around the encampment, sleeping in different places from night to night, and alternating which guards are with him at any given time. He has to do everything possible to avoid making it easy for the Teutons to find and kidnap him. Tell him also that, if things go badly, he must have the resolve to leave the field. In disguise if needed. He can seek sanctuary in the monastery north of Aleffe Manor."

"I recall the place, Sire."

"If that should become dangerous, then he should retreat to another stronghold – or even go to ground as his mother did in the civil unrest – and let his commanders continue the fight. The thing you'll need to help him see, Cedric, is that there's no dishonor in doing this. That he's a prize in the eyes of the Teuton king and that the honor is in denying his enemy that prize."

"I'll tell him, Sire. And I'll do whatever I can to help him."

"You have my complete trust, Cedric. But remember this. Your job, too, is to stay alive. When this is all over, I want to see you back here in this very spot choosing the colt that you want for your own."

"Any objection if I choose a filly so I can breed my own horses when I retire?"

I laugh and clap him on the shoulder. "None at all, Cedric. Just so long as you're here to make a choice."

We cross the paddock and exit through the gate then go our separate ways. Godspeed, Cedric. Your great-uncle would be very proud indeed.

Phillip arrives the next day in high spirits, placing his papers on my writing table with a flourish. "Geoffrey's marriage contract. Everything you wanted. Seems the Peaks king is quite enthusiastic about this alliance. All that remains to be done is your signature." From his demeanor – and the fact that he's still in his traveling clothes – it's obvious he came straight from his carriage to my private reception room without speaking to anyone along the way.

"So how did the negotiations go?" I ask, glancing quickly through the two pages of dense writing.

"Easiest thing I've ever done. Well, there was one small hiccup. Lady Morfyl was determined that it should be specified that whatever title her niece held here would also include 'and Princess of the Kingdom of Peaks.' The king tried valiantly to dissuade her but finally gave up – just to get her out of his hair, I think. As you might imagine, I was . . . shall we say, disinclined . . . to accept that.

"It was Eirwen herself who resolved things. The king and I were debating the point in his study one afternoon when she came in unannounced. 'I finally wheedled out of Aunt Morfyl what she's been haranguing you about, Papa,' she said, 'and I don't want any part of it. It isn't right that people should think I have divided loyalties. Yes, it's known this is an alliance, but my title should reflect my loyalty to my husband. Please tell me you'll take that out, Papa.'

"'You're sure that's what you want?' her father asked her.

"'Absolutely,' she replied.

"'So what do I do about your aunt?'

"'Aunt Morfyl can style me any way she wants when I visit here,' Eirwen said. 'We both know there's nothing either of us could do to stop her. But no one else should. Please, Papa.'

"The king looked at me with his eyebrows raised in question. 'I think your lovely daughter's just given us the way out of this conundrum that we've both been looking for,' I told him. The only thing I can say is that I'm glad *he* was the one who had to break the news to Morfyl and not me." He pauses for a moment then adds with a chuckle, "And even more glad that I didn't have to tell *you* such a thing was in the contract."

"Gwen's favorite way to broach such topics is to ask me not to fly into a rage."

He laughs out loud. "I'd best remember that in case something like this ever comes up again. In any event, it came right in the end. And we were both grateful for your message that those renegades in the Territories were actually Teutons. Not having the worry about conflict between the Peaks and the Territories hanging over our heads allowed us to have a little celebration for Eirwen the evening before Addiena and I left to come home. But Teutons, Alfred? What were they doing there?"

I rise and gesture to the chairs before the hearth. "You'd better sit down." By the time I finish bringing him into the picture about what's happened in his absence, his exhilaration has completely vanished and he's donned the grim expression that everyone else has been wearing as standard attire.

"So what can we do?"

"We bide our time, leaving the Teuton king to wonder how we'll respond. Jasper will bring his plans to a gathering of all the lords in a couple of days, so I'm glad you're back. In the meantime, you should go to Jasper's office for a private conversation with him. I'll say no more than that here. When you speak with him, you'll understand why."

"Dear God in Heaven." Phillip shakes his head. "Aren't we ever to get a lasting peace?"

．　　．　　．　　．　　．

When we finish this evening's supper, I ask Geoffrey and Edward to join me for brandy. Well, brandy for me . . . small ale for them. I'd delivered the news of Geoffrey's marriage contract over the meal, much to the delight of everyone present. But now it's time for news of a very different sort. Having reached the decision that, if Simon Meriden is to participate in the next gathering of the lords, it would be wrong for me to exclude Geoffrey, I now must tell my sons what lies in our immediate future.

They both sit quietly as I describe the situation with all the calm I can muster, telling them everything about what we're facing. Everything, that is, except the secret plans that are even now being executed. "I suppose," says Geoffrey when I finish, "it was too much to hope for that things would just go on as usual once Denis came of age. How much danger will he be in, Papa?"

"I can't say with any certainty. What I do know is that his commanders will do their utmost to keep him away from the heart of the battle."

"It seems the Teuton king outwitted everybody," says Edward.

"He's been clever . . . there's no doubt about that. But now that we know his game, it's our turn to be just as clever."

"But how can we do that, Papa?" asks Geoffrey. "How can we support Denis when our own kingdom is under threat?"

"There's more than one kind of support. You're right that we can't just send our army across the sea to join Denis's forces. But we *can* keep the Teutons so occupied here that they can't just ignore us and focus all their attention on Denis."

"You mean like a two-front war?" asks Geoffrey.

"Precisely. And that's exactly the sort of plan Sir Jasper will bring to the lords in a couple of days. I think, as the heir, you should be there to hear it Geoffrey. To listen and learn. But this time, if you have questions, save them for me."

"Aye, Papa."

"Edward, I'm sorry to have to exclude you from hearing Sir Jasper directly."

"It's alright, Papa. I know there'll always be things Geoffrey's part of that I'm not." I can tell he's sincere . . . but he's also a little sad.

"You may not be in the thick of it, Son, but that doesn't mean you and your brother shouldn't talk about it between yourselves. For that matter, maybe the three of us should get together just like this from time to time so we can talk about what's on your minds."

"I'd like that," says Edward.

"What about our mates?" asks Geoffrey.

"Their fathers will have told them we're about to be at war once again. But, Geoffrey, this is one of those times where being the heir starts getting difficult. It's not out of the question that Sir Jasper's plan may include some elements that need to be kept secret. He'll be very explicit about that when he meets with the lords, so pay close attention to anything he says shouldn't be discussed outside the room. And be very careful not to reveal what you know to anyone – not even your mother.

"Other than that, it occurs to me this might be another opportunity for you lads – you and Henry as well, Edward – to discuss things with Sir Tobin. You've already seen how complex figuring out the new defenses was. This will be a very real war strategy problem – not just the made-up exercises you've worked on so far."

The three of us sit quietly for a few moments. And in those moments, I recognize it's become as important for me to have these postprandial conversations with my sons as with the adults. Finally, Geoffrey breaks the silence. "I suppose this means I won't get to go to the Peaks to celebrate our betrothal announcement with Eirwen."

"I'm not sure. The announcement of your betrothal is actually something we can use to put the Teuton king on the back foot. It sends an indisputable message about the strength of our alliance. We'll just have to assess how risky the journey is . . . and we'll announce it here regardless."

"Alright, Papa, but I really want to go."

•   •   •   •   •

Lady Mary and Simon arrive the next afternoon. Richard and I meet with them together and share the burden of breaking the news. By the time I tell them, "I could not, in good conscience, send men from the Meriden estate to war without the Meridens knowing why I have to do so," their faces are as grim as everyone else's.

"So what must I do?" Simon asks. "I don't know if I have the skills, but should I lead our men in the fighting?"

"No, you needn't fret about that," I tell him. "The men from every estate will come together into a single army under Sir Jasper's command, and they'll fight under the leadership of Jasper's experienced captains. Your job, along with Lady Mary, will be to help your people understand why we have to do this – what's at stake if we don't – and why they're being asked to sacrifice yet again. Normally, I'd do much of this myself, in the towns or at the great manor houses. But we don't have the time for that – the threat is too immediate.

"After the men leave and the war is well and truly underway, then your job will be to help keep people calm – to give them reassurance while they wait to learn their loved ones' fates. And should a catastrophe happen, you'll have to prepare them for what's to come."

"I remember, Simon, watching my father do this when King Charles invaded," says Mary. "He said it was hardly a pleasant task, but it was a very important one. I think he even wrote in his journal about some of what he did. We can find those journals and emulate him."

"I hope so," says Simon.

"I think we've finally overcome all damage Hugo did, Your Grace," says Mary. "Simon's made himself well-liked, so I think he'll be trusted if we do this carefully. But I'd be grateful, Lord Devereux, if you'd give us some of your time before we leave here to tell us just what you plan for your own domain. I think it wouldn't hurt for us to emulate that as well."

"It would be my pleasure," says Richard.

·　　·　　·　　·　　·

By the time Rainard arrives just before sundown, I've grown weary of being the painter of grim faces. He can hear the news from Samuel and his father. But first, I want the news from his trip.

"Rusk, Narth, and Owen were pleased. Narth, in particular, seemed to feel vindicated by his assessment of the two strangers. And Korst was satisfied," Rainard tells me. "But he insisted I remind you that you promised to visit him and drink a toast to his lost son."

"Something I fully intend to do just as soon as it's possible."

"Truth be told, sir, I think it was Goron who was most relieved of all. You could almost see him shed a mantle of worry as I recounted what we'd learned."

"In a way, that doesn't surprise me," I reply. "When we saw him at Korst's fortress, it was obvious he was uneasy about the notion of leading an army into the Peaks to exact one man's revenge." As yet, only Samuel and I are privy to Egon's grand plan to unite the Territories and Goron's role as the linchpin in that plan. Goron was between a rock and a hard place while Korst's fury raged. If he'd failed to respond to a call for help from one of the Territorial lords, he'd lose all he'd built toward that long-term future. But attacking an ally of mine risked rupturing everything Egon and I have so carefully nurtured over the years.

"Naturally," Rainard continues, "the conversation turned rather quickly to the question of what Teutons were doing in their land and how they got there. I couldn't offer them much other than the fact that we were still trying to work that out. That seemed to be enough for them in the moment."

"They'll find out soon enough – just as we have over the past few days. Samuel and your father can tell you everything we've learned. You should speak with them tonight, since there's a gathering of all the lords tomorrow. I'm glad you're back for that. And one other thing, Rainard. Find some time before the meeting for a private conversation with Jasper. That will complete the picture for you."

"If there's nothing else, sir, I'd best be off then. I should break the news to Juliana that she'll have to wait until later in the evening to have my undivided attention."

Finally something I can actually smile about. "Nothing else at all, Rainard."

·   ·   ·   ·   ·

As before, Richard wastes no time turning the meeting over to Jasper. "When the Teuton king's message first arrived, my lords, my initial thought was that we could modify our plans to quash Gunnvor's ambition to deal with the new threat. But what the king said about launching a true second front in the Teutons' fight against King Denis led us to expand our strategy. It still relies on all the elements we'd planned to support Denis or to suppress Gunnvor, so none of that goes to waste. We just do things differently. I'll start with the two foundation plans and then describe how we tie it all together.

"First, what we'd agreed with the commanders of our allies for supporting Denis. Much the same as when we came to Charles's aid a few years ago. All three kingdoms and the Territories united with Denis to repulse the Teutons. But it would be easier because we wouldn't have to worry about who's loyal to who in Denis's kingdom. That's all pretty straightforward.

"The plan to send Gunnvor home with his tail between his legs relied primarily on our forces, but included small contingents from each of our allies as a demonstration of the much stronger force that could be brought against him if he didn't capitulate. Once again, rather straightforward and unlikely to require much time to achieve our ends." He pauses to look around the table for questions and seems to realize something.

"Lord Meriden, Lady Mary. I know this is all new to you. Ask questions if you have them. No one will take offense. But I must remind you that what you're hearing today is war plans. Information that cannot fall into the wrong hands or onto the wrong ears. For that reason, it's customary that we don't speak of these things outside this room. You'll have to prepare your people for war, of course, and support them for however long the fighting goes on. But you can't reveal any of the specifics of what you learn here today. Is that agreeable?"

Simon looks to Mary, who merely nods, encouraging him to be the Meriden voice in the room. "We understand, Sir Jasper. And we plan to seek Lord Devereux's advice on what we should do."

"Very well," Jasper resumes. "So, my lords . . . my lady . . . this is our new strategy. It relies on full participation by all our allies. And unexpected tactics that we hope will allow us to dispense with the problems in the east quickly so we can turn our attention to joining Denis's fight. We have to do just enough to protect our rear, and that job falls to Lord Goron and to the Kingdom of Lakes. With the exception of a small force to prevent anyone coming ashore at Lord Owen's cove, Goron will amass all his forces along our border, putting him in position to support us – even to ride to the assistance of the Lakes if need be – or to pivot to protect his own lands in the event someone manages to stage an incursion there. We all believe that's extremely unlikely unless the Lakes port falls, so Goron's force is primarily our final reserve in the rear.

"At the outset, we do nothing to supplement our defenses at our port. Our cannon emplacements there are robust and can easily repel a test of their effectiveness. Besides, we know the Teutons aren't really after our port and would try to take it only as a way to attack our rear. But we have that contingency covered, as you'll see later.

"The Lakes will split their forces, sending enough to their port on the Western Sea to thwart any landing attempt there and the rest to defend their border with the Eastern Kingdom and that section of our border down to the point where the stream turns east. We throw all our strength at the central portion of the border. I'll come back to that later.

"The Peaks also split their forces. Half join up with ours, but only after the real fighting has begun. The other half camp south of our port, ready to defend the port if any serious assault on it should be attempted, but otherwise held in reserve for one of two purposes, which I'll also come back to later." He pauses and looks around the table. "Any questions so far, my lords?"

When there are none, he proceeds. "Right now, I have four troops at the eastern garrison. Not enough for Gunnvor or the Teuton to think it's our final disposition, so one of the gambles in this plan is that they keep waiting to see what we'll do and don't charge across in full force before we're ready. I acknowledge it's a big gamble, but it's one we've no choice about.

"Since we have to move more quickly, we can't afford for the ferry to become a choke point. I've designated one of my senior captains to be in charge of all the men coming from Bauldry, Montfort, and de Courcy's estates. They'll cross the river on the Great North Road and then turn east toward Neukirk Market. The Devereux men will join them there, and they'll continue through the hills on the north side of Peveril's valley toward the border. Lord Peveril . . . Lord Ademar . . . I need to position a hidden force in your easternmost quarry. They will either then serve as a decoy – to draw some of Gunnvor's forces into a trap – or a reserve force we can bring to bear when and where they're needed. I won't know which until we see how things unfold in the field. I'll do everything in my power to ensure the fighting stays well away from the quarry, but it's an ideal hiding place to keep the enemy from knowing our full strength. That's why I hope you can evacuate all your workers to another location.

"Another senior captain will be in charge of the men from Ernle, Meriden, and Thorssen's estates and the Crown lands. They'll follow behind the cavalry and the archers and foot soldiers of our standing army, who'll be under my command. This force will cross the river by way of the ferry and march along the usual route through Peveril's valley to set up camp just west of the garrison. The supply train comes last, by way of the ferry, since it can travel faster on the better roads. Oh, and yes, the King's Own Guard become the castle defenders.

"Now all the pieces are in place. There'll be no parlay. I'll refuse any offer. Whether Gunnvor attacks straightaway or whether we sit there in stalemate for some time remains to be seen. In truth, a stalemate probably suits the Teuton king's purposes best because the longer our armies have to simply sit there, the more time he has to wreak havoc across the sea."

"Surely we're not simply going to play into their hand," says Phillip.

"Not at all, my lord," Jasper replies. "Something the king said the other day gave shape to an idea I'd been toying with. His comment that the Teuton king had committed only as many forces as he was prepared to lose. Based on where those forces are deployed, I'd take that one step further. What the Teuton really hopes is that those men ultimately aren't needed. But he's prepared, if Gunnvor and his cronies prove inept, to use those men either as a reserve or as a flanking force to keep us pinned down. So our first order of business is to change that plan – to go after the Teutons first. An initial stalemate along the border would, in fact, suit us quite well.

"Once my main force has passed Peveril Castle, I intend to divert a highly specialized group to the south, across the fields. Their role will be harassing raids on the Teutons. We'll start with a surprise attack from the wooded hills north of those meadows. Longbowmen on foot, infiltrated during the night. The number I have in mind, firing from the shadows of the forest, should be able to take out a couple hundred men and animals in very short order and then vanish before the Teutons can organize a pursuit. We'll have to assume we get only one chance for that since any decent commander would then post men in the hills to prevent a second raid. At night, we launch fire arrows into their tents from the Roman wall – concentrated fire into a couple of groups of tents that are in close proximity, with the idea of getting the fire to spread so they have to deal with it, giving our archers time to escape.

"We lay low the following day while we move to new positions in the fens. The next attack comes from the south – longbowmen and crossbowmen both this time – and we keep up the attack until we see signs of an organized attempt to find us. With any luck, we can deplete their numbers by another couple of hundred. Then we retreat into the marsh, where their horses will be of no use and foot soldiers will need to be exceedingly cautious.

"Half our men stay in the south and the rest return to our original positions. The next day, we try to set up a cross fire, from the south and the west. Always very fast, short attacks with our men disappearing before the Teutons can get organized. Fire arrows from a different location every night.

"Our purpose is to get the Teuton commander so angry about the continuing depletion of his forces that he makes his own decision in the field to ride out and track us down, regardless of what his previous orders might have been. And we retreat toward the garrison, leading his men into the mouth of our cannon fire and cavalry positioned on both his flanks."

"What's to prevent Gunnvor's forces from thwarting your plan?" asks Montfort.

"At the same time we start harassing the Teutons, the Lakes forces start rolling up Gunnvor's cronies from the north, driving them south. When they get to the point where the stream turns east, our men join up with the Lakes army and keep driving them south. My main force repositions south and east of the garrison, to drive whatever's left of the Teutons toward Gunnvor's forces as the Peaks army moves in from the center, their men fresh for the fight since they haven't been engaged prior to that time." Jasper pauses once again, looking around the table for the third time.

"You should know, my lords, this will be hard fighting. We'll have casualties. Quite likely, a lot. And though we have a battle plan that I believe accomplishes what the king wanted in terms of creating a true second front for the Teutons, battles rarely play out exactly to plan. But if we can achieve our goal of depleting the Teuton forces and making them play *our* game, then it's quite likely the Teuton king will have little choice but to give more attention to the fight here than he'd expected to. As soon as we have this threat contained, the Peaks forces waiting at the port sail immediately to Denis's aid with most of our own following as soon as it's practical. We'll leave the Lakes and the remainder of the Peaks to keep things subdued in the east. Assuming all's still quiet in the west, Goron will then move his army into our territory to be ready to respond if any new threat appears.

"If for any reason, we find ourselves at risk of losing control of the situation in the east, the Peaks forces cross the river and rush to reinforce us.

"That's it, my lords. The speed of our success relies on depleting the Teuton strength. But if my assessment of the Teuton king's strategy is correct, our harassment will be utterly unexpected and will work to our advantage. And I remind you once again my lords . . . my lady . . . secrecy is essential."

As usual, Jasper's plans are both thorough and inventive. And if our gambit in the west also succeeds, then we may just be able to preserve both kingdoms intact.

At long last, Samuel breaks the silence in the room. "This is well conceived, Sir Jasper. Creating a pincer where the enemy expects a head-on battle along an extended line greatly increases our odds. And the repeated infusion of more men into the ranks will absolutely confound an enemy who believes he's taken the measure of our strength when he observes our initial positions. I hope you also have a plan for containing their scouts."

"Rest assured we do, Lord de Courcy."

"I think you have another advantage as well," Samuel continues. "From what we've heard, Gunnvor is something of a hothead, and it wouldn't surprise me if his cronies are of the same ilk. Men like that are always quick to rush into a fight, confident they'll prevail. What I know of your senior captains tells me they'll keep their heads about them and make short shrift of wild, ill-conceived actions by their opponents.

"Speaking for myself, gentlemen," Samuel gestures around the room, "I think we should give Jasper's plan our unequivocal support."

"Aye-aye's" and "hear-hear's" all around the room.

"Your Grace?" asks Richard.

"When do you expect to march, Sir Jasper?"

"My captains are ready to move immediately to collect men from the estates, Sire, and my fast couriers are poised to depart as soon as I give the word to convey my message to the commanders in the Peaks and the Lakes. My contingent will march from here a week hence. That should ensure proper timing for all the arrivals."

"Very well, Sir Jasper, it's in your hands."

"There's one other thing, Your Grace."

"Yes?"

"I ask that you not take the field, Sire. We'll fight under your banner, of course, and we'll engage in a bit of deception to make it seem to the casual observer as if you're with the main force but commanding from the rear. We know the Teuton king is an inveterate hostage-taker, and we mustn't give him that opportunity. The best way to prevent that is for you to stay here under Carew's protection.

"I've already told you I'll refuse any parlay. And if the Teuton king should insist on meeting you face to face, then I'll just find a way to delay while we get word to you, Sire."

"You needn't delay, Jasper. If you get such a request, let me know, of course. But the only answer you need give the Teuton king is that he's broken my trust and the only meeting I'm interested in is one that guarantees the peace and the integrity of both my kingdom and the boy's." Jasper bows his head in acknowledgment. "And, Jasper, use those exact words – 'my kingdom and the boy's.' Echo the words of his threatening message back to him. Leave him in no doubt of my determination."

"Is there anything further?" asks Richard. When no one speaks, he adds, "Very well, we're finished here. God go with you and your men, Sir Jasper, and those of the Peaks and Lakes as well. And God grant we can finally put paid to the Teuton ambitions."

The faces that leave the room are still serious – particularly those of Simon and Geoffrey, who actually look a bit bewildered, having heard more today than their young minds ever expected they'd be privy to. But what was once grimness on every face seems now to be conviction that we have a way through this mess.

Mary and Simon go with Richard. I'm grateful he's taking them under his wing. I waylay Samuel and his father briefly in the corridor. "A word with you both this evening?"

"Of course, my boy," says the elder Ernle. That he still refers to me that way warms my heart and removes a tiny bit of the weight from my shoulders.

Geoffrey's been hanging back to walk with me. "Can we go talk, Papa?" he asks.

"I rather thought you might want that. Shall we go to the paddock?" He nods and we make our way down the stairs to the entrance hall and out into the courtyard.

Jasper's plan has also removed a tiny bit of the weight from my shoulders. Samuel's approval of it, a tiny bit more. But these little bits make barely a dent in the enormous responsibility I feel to make the Teuton king regret he ever tried to force me to make a choice.

We lean on the fence, elbows propped on the top rail, watching this year's foals at play. "Everything has changed, hasn't it, Papa." Geoffrey makes it more a declaration than a question.

"For now, yes," I reply. "But not for always."

"That assumes we prevail against the Teutons here and that Denis does as well."

"Do you doubt that we will?"

"I really have no idea." He shakes his head sadly. "Everything Sir Jasper described . . . it sounds good to hear him tell it. But it's ever so complicated with so many things that could go wrong."

"That's just the nature of a fight like this. You have to start with a plan – and hope that the assessments you've made about how to catch your opponent off guard are good ones – but then you have to keep a keen eye for how things are playing out and be ready to change your tactics completely if necessary. If you think about it, it's rather like a sword fight but on a much grander scale."

"I never thought about it like that, but I suppose you're right." He pauses for a moment, brow furrowed in thought, then continues. "What Sir Jasper described though. It has to play out over long distances, and he won't be able to know in the moment exactly what's happening anywhere except what's right in front of him. If Gunnvor's forces should break through unexpectedly somewhere, he'd have a big problem on his hands. And if the harassment of the Teuton encampment doesn't produce the results he expects, then what?"

"You remember him talking about hiding men at the quarry? That's his safeguard against a breakthrough. As for the Teutons, it would be strange indeed for any commander to watch his forces being depleted day after day and just sit there. I doubt even the Teuton king would give orders to simply allow that many men to be slaughtered needlessly while the main body of our army is elsewhere. And in any event, the battle plan you heard is just a starting point. Jasper and his senior captains will be adjusting it every day.

"There's something else Jasper didn't mention in the meeting with the lords. Think you can handle one more secret?"

"I suppose so, Papa."

"You'll like this one since you played a part in making it possible. Jasper's going to use those new horses we got from Denis – the ones from across the Roman Sea – for his fast couriers. He thinks doing that will improve his communications by as much as an hour – maybe more – in any direction, meaning he'll be able to get information faster than Gunnvor or the Teuton king. If that proves to be the case, it gives him a significant advantage as the fighting ebbs and flows."

Geoffrey manages a half smile. "I've heard from some of the knights that those horses are remarkably sure-footed besides being fast."

A couple of foals that had been romping nearby decide to interrupt their fun to check out what we're all about. When the others see the curious ones are getting their muzzles or necks stroked, half a dozen more wander over and it becomes a competition to see who can monopolize the available hands. Eventually, we have to move away from the fence to preclude the bickering that seems about to break out among the more aggressive ones. Geoffrey takes a seat in the grass and I join him as we watch the equine jealousy dissolve into playfulness once more.

"You know, Papa, all the time I was listening to Sir Jasper describe the battle plan, I was thinking it was probably going to be my duty to join a troop and demonstrate my commitment to defending the kingdom."

"You're not yet of age, Son. That won't be necessary."

"Well, I couldn't help but wonder if maybe things are different for the heir to the throne. But anyway, when he came to the part about hostage-taking, I suddenly realized something. Sir Jasper is concerned about you being taken hostage, but in reality, I'm the one who's more in danger. The Teuton king would know he could get you to agree to anything to gain my release. So now I understand what you meant about having to assess the risk of my traveling to the Peaks."

"That's very astute, Geoffrey. The Teuton will have no doubts about where I'm most vulnerable. You and Denis . . . perhaps even Edward, though that's somewhat less likely."

"Does Denis know to be wary of becoming a hostage?"

"I'm sure he does. It was his mother's concern about him being used as a pawn in their civil war that caused him to disappear for a year." To this day, only Gwen and Warin know my role in the young viscount's disappearance. Now is not the time for anyone else to learn that. "And he and his advisors are keenly aware of his uncle's time as a hostage and the fate that befell him as a result. I'm confident those around him will be especially vigilant for his safety." There's also no need to burden my son with the knowledge of Sir Cedric's secret mission. Geoffrey has enough to grapple with as it is.

We sit in silence for quite some time. There's clearly a lot more on Geoffrey's mind, but it will take him much more than these few moments to absorb all that's about to unfold. At long last, he says, "I guess I can't discuss any of this with Edward or my mates, can I?"

"Not everything. Certainly not the details of Jasper's battle plan. Which means this is your first *real* experience of the meaning of kingship. With William and Ancel and Barat, you need to be guided by what they know from their fathers. Don't discuss anything they don't bring up directly. And don't succumb to the temptation to answer any question that might hint at what must be kept secret. I know that sounds like you're going to be shutting them out, but that's sometimes necessary. They'll make it easier than you expect though. They'll know their fathers won't have told them everything, and they'll understand you're bound by the same strictures that apply to everyone who was in the room. They're unlikely to press you – only to stumble into a question or comment that shouldn't be pursued.

"What you can and should feel free to discuss with them is how this is affecting all of you – what's going to be different in your lives until we get this business resolved – even to the point of your awareness of the possibility you might be kidnapped. I don't know if they'll stay here or go with their fathers to their estates. Either way, if they know you're at risk, they'll be vigilant to help protect you."

"I hope they stay here, but I know they might feel their duty lies with their people, since they'll be the lords one day."

"Not an easy choice for their fathers or for them. But I have to admit that having them here would provide extra protection for you. It has to be their decision though – I won't interfere with the lords' rights, especially since I'm having to depend on them for helping people with what's to come."

"I understand, Papa."

"As for Edward, let's take that one step at a time. You can speak as freely with him as you wish about how each of you feels about all this. But be circumspect. Keep those conversations limited to times and places when you know no one is around to overhear. At times like this, we have to assume information could easily fall into the wrong hands.

"As for specifics, let's see what Edward feels ready to handle before we put too much on his shoulders. My chat with Samuel and his father this evening won't take long, so I'll come to your room afterward and the three of us can talk."

"I'd like that, Papa. I'm sure Edward would too."

"There's actually something *you* can do for *me*."

"Really?" He seems quite surprised.

"Spend some time with Simon Meriden when he and his aunt finish with Richard. Help him cope with what's facing him."

"In what way, Papa?"

"Remember the visits you and I made to Abbéville Market and Great Woolston when people were so angry about the last campaign? Remember their fears and their frustrations and how we helped calm them?"

"Aye."

"Tell Simon about that. Give him some idea what to expect when he goes home to prepare *his* people. I think he'd relish hearing your experience rather than just having those who are so much older simply tell him what to do."

Finally, there's a smile on Geoffrey's face. "I can do that, Papa. And can I tell him he can write to me if he has questions while all this is happening?"

"I think that would be a splendid idea."

· · · · ·

"Looks like you're finally going to get that long-delayed meeting with your estate manager," I tell Samuel when he and his father join me after our separate family suppers.

"Hardly the way I'd imagined it," he says, unable to muster much enthusiasm for my attempt to lighten the mood. "When is it going to be our turn for a long stretch of peace and prosperity, Alfred?"

"None too soon for me. Looks like it was your generation, sir," I nod to Papa Ernle, "that got to enjoy that."

"These things ebb and flow, my boy. Your turn is coming. The Teuton is testing your resolve . . . hoping to find a chink somewhere that he can push his own ambition through. He either doesn't know . . . or he's conveniently overlooking . . . how strong-minded you can be when the whole world seems arrayed against you. The lad who walked home from the ends of the earth won't be defeated by a bully who wants to remake the world to suit himself."

Inspiring words from the man who identified me and saw what a state I was in when I showed up at the western monastery after months in captivity. Who took me into his home and helped me recover from near starvation. Who, ever since, has been like a second father to me. Do I still have that strength and determination? It's going to take that and more to match wits yet again with the crafty bastard who's willingness to play a long game has brought us to this point.

"Which is precisely why," Ernle continues, "I don't think you requested this conversation just to hear me ply you with encouragement. What is it you need, Alfred?"

"I need Samuel's help."

They both smile. "And why should this time be any different from all the others?" Samuel chuckles.

"Because it seems like there's no end to the number of times I ask. And I've run out of ways to repay you."

"Well, then, you're a lucky man because, unlike the Teuton king, I don't keep a tally of favors performed and debts owed. How can I help, Alfred?"

"I know you need to prepare the people on your estate, but then I need you to come back here as soon as you can. So I need your father to stay with Tamasine to help her reassure everyone that you're not abandoning them but merely serving the kingdom."

"You needn't ask twice, my boy," says Papa Ernle. "It would be my pleasure to do something useful."

"Anything else you want to tell me about what's on your mind?" Samuel asks.

"Not right now. Go take care of your people, but get back here as quickly as you can. By then, I should have worked out how we can do what needs to be done."

As always, Samuel doesn't press. He trusts I'll tell him everything at the right time. "In that case, I'd best go make sure Timm has the packing well in hand."

When they've taken their leave, I waste no time making my way to my sons' room. They're in their nightshirts, ready for bed, but the candles haven't been doused. "We've been talking while we waited, Papa," says Edward. "Geoffrey says Sir Jasper has his battle plan ready and that the lords think it's a good one."

"And I agree. But a lot of its success depends on our opponents not getting wind of what's about to happen, so we all have to be even more circumspect that usual."

"You're saying there might be spies around, even here in the castle, aren't you, Papa?" Edward's tone seems remarkably calm for such a perceptive comment from a lad his age. Have he and Geoffrey been discussing this?

"Well, between servants' gossip and all the people who come and go from here, it's all too easy for information to fall into the wrong hands. Even here in your room – you can never be completely certain there might not be someone listening at the door."

"That's why," says Geoffrey, "we've decided to keep our voices low when we talk about anything important."

"A good idea," I tell them. "But it's just as important that you act perfectly normal when you're going about your usual business. If people don't think you're being wary, then they'll be less likely to eavesdrop."

"That's going to feel strange." Edward wrinkles his nose. "Having to work to act normal."

"It might at first because you'll be aware of what you're doing. But after a few days – when this isn't all so new – all your usual habits will fall into place and it'll feel natural again. There are some things that *will* have to change, though, until the war is finished. Carew will be in charge of protecting us, as always, but he'll also be responsible for all the defenses of the castle. That means we won't be able to go about as freely as we usually do, which is probably going to be more difficult for me than anyone. I'll have to curtail my morning rides and not go anywhere without a contingent of guards. Same for your mother – she won't be able to go to market days without guards."

"I guess that means no visits to the hut or rides in the woods for us," Geoffrey opines.

"I'm afraid so."

"Well, we wouldn't want a bunch of guards hanging around while we were at the hut anyway," Edward offers. "And if our mates stay on their estates, there's not much reason to go there anyway. Do you think they'll stay or come back here, Papa? Geoffrey says every lord has to decide for himself."

"Your brother's right, so I really have no idea. And in truth, what happens depends a lot on how long this war lasts."

"Can we carry on training our horses?" Edward asks. "They're two-year-olds now, so we really should start riding them this summer."

"I think that depends on how you're feeling about things. I'm going to forego riding Regulus for the first time until this is all over. There's so much weighing on my mind right now that he would pick up on my anxiety – he'd become anxious himself about everything I ask him to do – and he'd never forget that, so he'd always be a nervous mount. But if you lads are in good spirits and feel calm and easy-going around your colts, then working with them might be a nice bit of normal in your lives. Ask Elvin to observe how things are going, and if he thinks a first ride would be successful, then give it a try. Just remember that you won't be able to take them out into the meadows without a full complement of guards. Elvin can give you advice on when the youngsters are confident enough that all the guards won't spook them."

"All the guards," says Edward. "Is that because Carew thinks someone might try to kidnap one of us?"

"Is that what Geoffrey said?"

"No, I only just thought about it. I remembered the Teutons kidnapped King Charles so they might try to kidnap you too."

"In war – particularly when things aren't going well for one side – those who are losing sometimes try to change the game. Like you said, that's what happened to King Charles. And that's why Carew is going to be more serious even than he usually is about how he protects us. We *want* the fighting to go badly for our opponents. We just have to be extra careful when that happens. I'm putting my trust in Carew – he's very, very good at what he does."

"Then we should too," says Geoffrey. "But we can talk about it if we're anxious, can't we, Papa?"

"Between yourselves and with me, of course. Just remember to have those conversations where you're reasonably certain no one is listening."

"But how can we do that if we can't go to the hut?" asks Edward.

"Go where I go when I need to have a completely private conversation – the old library. The room's made entirely of stone and the door's twice as thick as any of the others. It was the Treasury room a long time ago, so it's the safest room in the castle."

"I never thought about that," says Geoffrey.

"Just remember you'll need to have something with you to light the candles before you close the door. Otherwise, it'll be blacker than midnight inside."

"I feel better now, Papa," says Edward.

"Good. Just remember to be more vigilant than usual for now, and we'll get through this as quickly as we can."

I bid them goodnight and head for my own bed. Gwen is already leaning against her pillows, the covers pulled up to her waist. "I'll only be a moment," I tell her as I disappear into my dressing room.

"How are the boys?" she asks when I return and climb into bed beside her.

"A bit overwhelmed. Trying to work out what it all means for them. And doing their best to avoid seeming apprehensive, though I know they are."

"I told Alicia this afternoon. Didn't want her hearing a random comment from a servant and making up her own stories about what's afoot."

"And?"

"She turned very serious then asked if you were going away to fight. It was good to be able to reassure her that you aren't, Alfred. Her next question was, 'Does this mean Geoffrey and Edward and I have to go away to the cottage like we did last time?'"

"What did you tell her?"

"The only thing I *could* tell her – that I don't know. But she made one thing abundantly clear. Her exact words were, 'Well, I don't want to go anywhere unless I can take Dog and Snow with me.'"

I can't help but chuckle. My youngest daughter is nothing if not opinionated, and the thing she's most opinionated about is her dogs.

"I know you haven't had time to really think about it, Alfred, but we probably should consider what's safest for the children sooner than later."

"Aye. One thing I do know is that the cottage *isn't* safe for them this time. It's much too close to the border with the Eastern Kingdom. In fact, you might want to send a message to Hamon and Agnes to take precautions – even evacuate to the village across the lake for a time if need be."

"I was thinking about that this afternoon. Do we have any messengers at our disposal? Or has Jasper conscripted them all into the army?"

"Oh, he won't take Coliar's cadre of couriers. But it's probably best to send word to Hamon quickly, before all the armies are on the move. In fact, there are messages I need to send straightaway as well."

"Oh?"

"I'd originally planned to let Geoffrey take the signed marriage contract with him when he went to the Peaks to celebrate Eirwen's birthday and their betrothal. But now I think I need to get that document to the Peaks king without delay, as a sign of my firm commitment to our alliance. I should probably send a brief letter to the Lakes king as well."

"So back to the question of the children," she says.

"I actually have given it a bit of thought. My dilemma is whether they're safest here or elsewhere. If all of us are in one place, does that make us safer or more vulnerable? Jasper's concerned about the Teuton king trying to take me hostage. But Geoffrey went straight to the heart of the matter when he said the bigger risk was to the family – and to him most of all – because I'd be inclined to accede to any demand as a condition of his release."

"And would you?"

"Heaven forfend I should ever have to face such a choice." She squeezes my hand. "Truth be told, Gwen, the looming choice is for the boys' safety. Should things turn sour, you and Alicia could easily take refuge with Sister Madeleine in the convent."

"Couldn't our sons do the same at the monastery?"

"Perhaps. But something about the Teuton king tells me that, while he'd be unlikely to threaten a convent, he'd have far fewer scruples about honoring the sanctuary of a monastery. So I have Warin and his brothers to consider as well."

"Well, you don't have to decide tomorrow."

"No, but we have to know before the need becomes urgent. That said, Carew's opinion is going to weigh heavily."

"Good. For now, I'll tell Alicia she's staying here, but there'll be more guards around wherever she goes. I anticipate some protest, but she'll get used to it."

"Tell her the guards are to protect the dogs, and I'll wager her protests vanish in an instant."

The exodus begins just after sunrise. Those who have the longest journeys – Guyat and Amelia, Rainard and Juliana – depart first, making way for the next two carriages to be loaded with traveling trunks. The Devereux and the Peverils will travel together as far as the ferry, going their separate ways once they've crossed the river. By midday, the entire court has departed. A week later, when the final elements of Jasper's column disappear in the distance, a stranger might be forgiven for thinking the castle had been abandoned.

The day before the army marched, I'd insisted Jasper and I ride alone to the meadow. Though Carew questioned the wisdom of such a move, he also understood the need for final instructions to the man who bears full responsibility for whatever happens over the coming weeks. After a gallop around the meadow to let the horses expend some energy, we stopped in the middle of the field and let them graze while we talked.

"I hope this goes without saying, Jasper, but I'll say it anyway. You have my full confidence for this operation. Make whatever decisions you must in the field, and I won't question them."

He bowed his head. "Thank you, Your Grace."

"I also won't question whatever you have to do to put an end to this quickly. Our past strategies have always been to let the other side be the aggressor. It would be nice if they'd oblige us by doing just that, but I'm not holding my breath since the longer they do nothing, the longer we're delayed in going to Denis's aid. So take the fight to them. Leave them in no doubt that they've miscalculated."

"That's what we plan, Sire."

The horses started to move slowly away from one another as they grazed, so I pressed my leg against Altair's right side, encouraging him to turn back.

"Truth be told, Jasper, for a very brief moment, I actually considered calling the Teuton's bluff. Ignoring the threat in the east and sailing immediately to intervene in his plans across the sea. In the end, I decided he probably wasn't bluffing."

"How did you come to that conclusion, Sire?"

"Cedric was absolutely certain he hadn't been seen. If that's the case, the Teuton still believes we don't know his forces are there, either as a reserve or a flanking force. Or – and this is what I've come to think might be his real purpose both in having them there and in where he's positioned them – to deploy them as his lead element should I make the choice that doesn't suit him. They would be brutal and our people would suffer. And I won't allow that."

Not far away, a hawk circled near the hedgerow, hoping something might be adventurous enough to emerge from the safety of the hedge to become its next meal. Having no luck, it took off for the nearest tree to bide its time, a luxury I don't have.

"So we play the game by his rules, Jasper. No hesitation. Make Gunnvor and his cronies wish they'd never succumbed to the temptation that was dangled before their eyes. Obliterate the Teuton forces. Don't hesitate to take the battle into the Eastern Kingdom. Drive them into the sea if you have to."

"You know that will cost men, Sire," Jasper said quietly.

"The faster we do it, the fewer of our men it will cost."

"Aye, Your Grace."

"I know these aren't the kind of words you're accustomed to hearing from me. They're not words I ever thought to be uttering. But we have to show our strength . . . and our resolve that we won't be forced into a contrived choice."

It was time to soften my tone. "But know this, Jasper. The only reason I can say these things to you is because I trust you to keep your head – to out-think as well as to out-fight our opponents. This kingdom could not be in better hands. I only wish I could be there to see the shock and confusion among the Teutons when you go after them first."

"Surely you're not thinking of —"

I smiled and held up a hand to interrupt him. "Calm yourself, Jasper. I agree the threat of hostage-taking is quite real, so I'll stay here and behave myself and follow Carew's orders . . . and devour your dispatches whenever you have the time to send them."

The horses seemed to have figured things out and remained side by side, their muzzles almost touching as they cropped the grass directly in front of them, now and then taking a step forward to the next fresh patch. I extended my arm to Jasper in the warrior's greeting. "God go with you and all your men, Jasper. Put paid to this absurd business so we can get on with lending a hand across the sea."

Now, all that remains is for us to do our best to carry on as if things were somehow normal. The servants and stable boys have less to do – a respite I don't begrudge them from the seemingly endless work of providing for the entire court, a full complement of knights and trainees, and all the animals that accompany them. The sentries and guards, however, are on higher alert than ever.

My morning ablutions are anything but normal. Robin – the young man we chose for Osbert to train as Geoffrey's squire – arrived as planned right after Whitsunday. Since then, he's become Osbert's shadow, meaning I have two attendants for even the smallest of needs. For the first few mornings, he seemed exceedingly embarrassed, never expecting, I'm sure, that his training would include watching the king take a bath. By the end of the week, after observing Osbert go about his business matter-of-factly, he appeared somewhat more comfortable that this was nothing more than part of the job of serving a great lord. That said, he's still a bit on edge in my presence. "That be a good thing fer now," Osbert assures me. "It mean he dinna' want to do aught wrong lest he be losing this chance. Mayhap it take him a few more weeks to be calming down, but if he learn to do things right fer ye, then he be perfect when he start serving Lord Geoffrey."

"No doubt you're right, Osbert. Just be sure he's calmed down a bit more before you let him attempt my shave."

Osbert chuckles. "Ye can count on that, m'lord."

Morning rides are far less satisfying than usual. The presence of half a dozen guards – more when Geoffrey or Edward or both accompany me – seems to drain the joy from a spirited romp around the meadow. The first time I jumped the hedgerow, the vigorous rush to circle around me on the far side brought to mind a sheriff's posse comitatus in pursuit of an escaped prisoner. At any other time, I'd probably find it amusing. Maybe I should just fall back on that now.

Every ride begins the same way, with instructions from the leader of the guards. "First sign of anything unusual, Your Grace, you're to gallop off at full speed and leave us to deal with it. No stopping at the stable. Ride straight into the inner courtyard and order the sentries to close the gates." After five days of this, I was severely tempted to stop the man short and tell him I already knew what was expected, but I bit my tongue. They're only following orders . . . doing their job. Everyone is on edge. Not surprising until we know more about what's happening in the field.

But it's time for a chat with Carew and Tobin. With all his trainees, except the sons of the nobility, in the field with Jasper, Tobin is filling in for Cedric. They're using Jasper's office as their command post. "Looks rather stark in here," I tell them when I arrive, "without all of Jasper's plans and diagrams adorning the walls."

Tobin chuckles. "Just what I said the first time I walked in, sir."

"So why do I suspect you're here to ask me to ease up a bit on our precautions?" asks Carew.

"Because you know me too well." They both grin. "So today, I'm going to surprise you."

"Nothing new about that," Carew chuckles.

"Actually, I want your advice. It should be pretty obvious since I didn't go with Jasper that I think his concern about hostage-taking is well founded. And truth be told, I'm more concerned for my sons than for myself. What I'm wrestling with is the best way to protect them. Does having all three of us here in one place increase the risk? Does it put more burden on the guards than their numbers can reasonably support?"

"I'm glad you recognize your sons – Lord Geoffrey in particular – are the most likely targets," says Carew. "Unfortunately, that means they're going to be under far more restrictions than they're accustomed to."

"They understand that. Geoffrey acknowledged his own risk without my ever having to mention it."

"Where else would the three of you be," asks Tobin, "except here?"

"Well, you'll remember I sent the children to safety in the Kingdom of Lakes when Charles invaded. Of course, the queen's cottage isn't a viable option this time, being so close to the eastern border."

"With respect, a lot of things are different this time, sir," says Carew. "If you were to send either or both of your sons somewhere else, then I'd have no choice but to split my forces in two locations. As it is, I have enough to keep intruders out or even to thwart a limited attack on the castle itself, but if those numbers were reduced . . ."

"He's right," Tobin agrees. "We have responsibility for all three of you regardless. Here, at least, we have a fortress and a full complement of men to do the job."

"Hear me out," I tell them. "This is something I've just been mulling over – nothing I've made up my mind about as yet." Though they both keep their expressions passive, I've no doubt that the fact neither looks at the other is a purposeful effort to avoid rolling their eyes at the idea of another hare-brained scheme. "It was always the plan that Geoffrey would travel to the Peaks court for the celebration of Princess Eirwen's birthday and the announcement of their betrothal. The betrothal will be announced regardless, but it would send a stronger, completely unmistakable message if he were actually alongside the Peaks king when it happens. I haven't broached the subject with Geoffrey yet – just told him we'd have to assess the risk when the time comes. What I've been wondering is whether it might be possible to get him there and have him remain there under the Peaks king's protection, as far away from any hostage-takers as one could get."

Now they look at each other. It seems like an eternity before Carew finally speaks. "I suppose . . ." he begins slowly. "I suppose we could get him there with some kind of ruse."

"I'm thinking of a disguise," says Tobin.

"Traveling as ordinary people?" asks Carew.

"Someone might still recognize him. What if he were to travel disguised as a woman . . . in a carriage? The lead guard as the driver, dressed as such. Two more guards in the carriage with him. Two more dressed as a rich man's retainers riding behind. All the guards armed to the teeth but not obviously so. We'd organize the journey so we were well away from any town at the end of each day, meaning we'd camp rather than use an inn. The 'lady' would sleep in her carriage."

I can't help but laugh out loud. "Who's the one with the hare-brained schemes now, Tobin?" They both join in my laughter. "It shouldn't surprise you that I rather like it."

"It's . . . almost plausible," says Carew. No surprise he's uncomfortable with anything that takes one of his charges away from the safety of the castle. But at least he didn't reject the notion out of hand.

"That's all I wanted to know for now – whether I should spend any more time considering the possibility or simply put it out of my mind."

"My suggestion, sir," says Carew, "is to get the queen's opinion sooner than later. I don't fancy the notion of her thinking I'm advocating something she disapproves of."

"Nor I," Tobin chimes in.

It turns out Gwen doesn't object outright. "Truth be told, my love," she tells me in bed that evening, "I don't know if it's a good idea or not. What I care about is that our son doesn't become a hostage. If it turns out the best way to prevent that also serves your purpose in sending a message to friends and foes alike, then I can understand why you'd make that decision. But, Alfred, is it really any less likely the Teuton king could smuggle a kidnapper into the Peaks than it is here?"

"Distance, for one thing."

"Didn't stop him from smuggling saboteurs into Korst's domain."

"I know. Which is part of why this decision weighs so heavily."

"Do you know what Geoffrey will think?"

"I know he's been disappointed about his plans being disrupted, and he's keenly aware that he's likely the prime target for abduction. Beyond that, he hasn't said much."

Which is why I'm somewhat taken aback when Geoffrey takes the decision out of my hands after I suggest the idea to him the following day. Knowing the only place we can get any privacy from the guards is in the old library, we've retired there with Osbert standing outside the door to forestall a sudden interruption. "Is that really a good idea, Papa?" he asks when I describe Tobin's plan to him. "What would people think of you sending their sons off to war then sending your own son to safety?"

I'm actually quite pleased that he's thought about this but need to test how far this line of thinking goes. "Isn't it possible they might see I'm trying to protect the succession?"

"Some might. The nobility, of course. Rich merchants. But the common people? They care about what gets them through each day. And if their sons and fathers and brothers don't come back from the war, each day is incrementally harder than before." He pauses for a moment. "Besides, Papa, what would they think of me? That I'm a man of no honor who hides from the dangers we expect them to face head-on?"

"Denis stayed in hiding an entire year to protect the succession across the sea."

"I've been thinking about that. It was different. He was much younger – not on the verge of coming of age. And he was caught in the cross-fire between rival nobles, each wanting to use a child for their own advantage or to blame him if they failed. The ordinary people didn't much care about squabbling nobles so long as it didn't disrupt their daily lives."

He rises, takes a turn about the room, then resumes his seat. "Truth be told, Papa, there's nothing I'd like more than to join Eirwen's birthday celebration and stay with her until all this is over. I could even put up with Lady Morfyl." He pauses briefly before adding, "I think." We both chuckle. "But remember your concerns during that papal inquisition? How you worried that if it succeeded, you'd lose all your moral authority?"

"Aye."

"I think if I don't show the courage to stand by your side now, I'm at risk of losing my moral authority as your heir."

What a change has come over him in just the past couple of weeks! It would never have been my choice that he should have to come to grips at such a tender age with all that it means to be a king. But like Denis before him, he's rising to the challenge. When this is all over, he deserves to enjoy his carefree youth. For now, though —

"If you're still concerned about protecting the succession," Geoffrey's words interrupt my musings, "maybe it's best to find a safe place for Edward."

"I'm not even sure where that might be."

"Then I suppose the three of us will just have to stay here and look out for each other."

"Something tells me Carew won't have any objection to that." And something tells me that I will continue to worry about the succession.

The restrictions on movement that we've no choice but to accept for the moment combined with the absence of the court make for a sameness about daily life that's quite unfamiliar. Is this what every day of every life is like for common folk with little means? No wonder then, that they relish even small diversions and that the grand spectacles of royal celebrations bring them such joy.

No wonder, either, that a certain excitement ripples through the castle when the lead elements of the Peaks forces are spotted on the road. It takes an entire day for the column to pass, and everyone from the turnspit to the king takes time out to watch and to cheer them on. As we make our way down from the battlements where we'd observed their progress, Gwen asks, "Fancy a turn around the garden?"

"Why not?"

She takes my arm as we make our way into the inner courtyard then through the hedge into the garden. Perhaps Mother Nature knows we need a bit of cheering up. The profusion of blossoms is more lush than I've ever seen it. It's hard to imagine anyone could gaze on this array of colors against the green foliage and not feel refreshed and renewed. As we reach the far corner, I ask her, "What is it about flowers that can lift a man's spirits even when there's so much on his mind?"

She smiles. "Maybe we should do this more often. I was even thinking it might be nice to take our midday meals here from time to time."

"Of course. If Matthias has no objection."

"I think he'd quite like it. It would give him something different to organize."

"Then dining in the fresh air it shall be, my lady." I bring her hand to my lips and bow as I kiss it. She giggles.

We resume our walk, pausing beside a mound of pink and white peonies. "I should ask Letty to cut a few of these for Alicia," says Gwen. "They'd cheer her up, I'm sure."

I pull my dagger from its sheath and lop off half a dozen of the largest blooms. "Why don't you take them to her yourself?"

"That's sweet, Alfred. I'll tell her they're from you." She says nothing more for a few steps then surprises me with, "You know, Alfred, there's someone else who hasn't had any fresh air for two weeks now."

"Oh?"

"Gunhild. Have you decided what you're going to do about her? You can't just keep her imprisoned for the duration of the war."

"Well . . . I *can* . . . and that might actually be the safest thing for all of us, Gunhild included." I pause to let her think about that. "On the other hand, Carew might be grateful not to have to divert some of his men to guarding her. Truth be told, I've no idea *what* to do with her. That's Laurence's domain."

"Then why don't you pay Laurence a visit and find out?"

"And ask Carew to divide his men?"

"It would only be for a day. With the long summer days, you'd have plenty of time to ride to the port, visit with Laurence, and be back before sundown. It would give you something to do, Alfred, besides fret about what might be happening elsewhere." Not for the first time she's right that doing something useful relieves my anxiety.

It takes some persuasion, but I finally convince Carew that three guards are ample for the short journey and that any more would simply draw attention to my comings and goings. We make straight for Laurence's home, and Estrilda sends a servant to fetch him from the Port Commissioner's office.

"Alfred!" His greeting, when he arrives a quarter hour later, is expansive. "To what do I owe this great honor?"

"To my feeling like a captive in my own castle. There are always guards around, I know, but these past two weeks they've felt more ominous than deferential."

Laurence laughs out loud. "Well, you're welcome to escape here any time. But even here we're starting to feel besieged. We're still working to get the Peaks forces across the river. Those that are going. The rest are already setting up their encampment just south of town."

"Actually, Laurence, it was the other captive in my castle I wanted to talk with you about."

"You mean Gunhild?"

"Aye. What are we going to do with her?"

"Well, I won't send her back home – they know what she's been up to, so she wouldn't last long there. And she's of no further use to us either, since they're onto her, so she's just going to have to embrace her new life as a nun. I've already put things in motion. My men will come for her once everything's arranged."

"It's a bit sad, really. She's been ill-used all her life."

"Don't feel too sorry for her. She made her bed when she lay with your brother. Everything else has been a direct consequence of that."

"You're right, of course. A bit sad for you too. You put all that work into grooming her and now that's all wasted."

"Hardly wasted. We got some good information out of her, even if we couldn't piece together the whole picture. But I got the biggest prize of all."

"Oh?"

"I now have an agent who can move about freely in that part of the world without anyone suspecting what they're up to."

"Gunhild's minder?"

"Precisely. And when things settle down a bit, I intend to visit Warin and thank him for his part in making it happen." Abbot Warin had initially been reluctant to allow Brother Nicholas to become involved in Laurence's shadowy world, but he relented when he discovered that one of his revered predecessors, Abbot Francis, had once done a bit of spying for my grandfather. Nicholas knows the language of the Eastern Kingdom and his initial undertaking was to teach Gunhild enough of our tongue that her minder could communicate with her and her brother would find it plausible that she'd been able to glean, on her own, the kind of information she was bringing him. In the process, her minder, who apparently has a keen ear for such things, became proficient enough in the Eastern tongue to undertake a couple of missions to help verify what Gunhild was telling us.

Laurence has revealed nothing about this minder – even whether it's a man or a woman. And I'm happy to keep it that way. I learned my lesson by getting too close to the operational details around what he was doing with Gunhild. Perhaps re-learned is the better word. Both my father and Abbot André had cautioned me about the value of a certain detachment from the trees if I wanted a clear picture of the forest. But I can't fault Laurence for involving me in his use of Gunhild, given that she'd been the source of more than one threat to my family and to our kingdom.

When it's time for the midday meal, I get another reminder of the constraints on my movement. "No chance for some ale and food at that nice tavern we've been to before?" I ask Laurence.

"Not a good idea today. It's still pretty chaotic anywhere near the docks with the remainder of the Peaks forces trying to board the ferry. Remind me I need to have two or three more ferries built before you decide to go to war in the east again."

"How about I save you the trouble and just not wage any more wars?"

He chuckles. "If only it were all under your control."

We join the rest of the family for the meal, then retire back to Laurence's study for a bit more conversation before it's time to collect my guards and return home.

At one point, I ask, "Has there been anything more on that stranger that was found in the collapsed barn where Mother died in the blizzard?"

"The sheriff never had any luck turning up anyone who knew anything about him. After all this time, there's almost no chance of figuring it out."

"I remember you saying something about an amulet he was wearing. Do you think the sheriff might still have that?"

"No." Even *I* can feel the disappointment settle across my features. Then Laurence adds, "But *I* do. The sheriff was going to discard it, but I had this peculiar feeling it might still be important." He rises, crosses the room to a small chest, lifts the lid, and retrieves a metal box, rather like a miniature strong box. From a drawer in his writing table he takes a key and opens the lock, then retrieves something from inside and returns to his seat by the hearth, handing me the object.

The amulet hangs from a chain made of gold. Two concentric metal circlets surround a round purple cabochon mounted in the same metal. Four similar cabochons in the shape of rounded triangles sit at the points of the compass, their narrow ends toward the center. Crossed swords, their tips pointing down, lie atop the circlets and behind the center stone. The gold chain and the type of metal make this a piece of jewelry, but the image formed by the purple stones I've seen before.

I shake my head slowly and Laurence asks, "What is it, Alfred?"

"I suppose I should've asked to see this sooner. The purple stones – their shape and color and the way they're laid out . . . identical to the emblems on the tunics of the Teuton saboteurs at Korst's mine. Identical to the emblems on the tunics of the Teuton king's guards. The dead man was a Teuton. And judging by how fine a piece this is, I'd say he was someone of very high rank, perhaps even close to the king himself."

"Well, that certainly explains why no one could identify him."

"Doesn't help answer the question of what he was doing here though."

"Now you've got me wondering if he was the one who led the travelers to the barn or if he was just another random victim of the storm. We'll never know, though, so wondering may be pointless."

"What *I* wonder is if the Teuton king knows this agent, too, is dead."

"It's been over a year, Alfred. Surely the Teuton would have expected some sort of communication in that time, and when none arrived . . ."

"A fair point. But what if the man's assignment was to insinuate himself into our society. Blend in. Gain friends and earn trust. Bide his time until he could use that trust to our disadvantage. Given what we've learned about the Teuton's patience to play the long game, it's not out of the question."

"If that were the dead man's mission, then what better way to start it off than trying to ingratiate himself with a noble family by helping them find shelter from a storm. That would have been serendipity, of course, but a man with such a mission would have recognized the opportunity and seized it without hesitation."

I can feel the bile rising in my throat. "If I find out the Teuton king is responsible for my mother's death—"

"Whoa, Alfred," Laurence interrupts me. "Don't get yourself all worked up. This is all just speculation. Somewhat plausible speculation, I agree, but speculation nonetheless. And we have no way to prove it since the man in question can't be questioned."

"You're right. But if nothing else, it reinforces my determination to make the Teuton wish he'd never gambled against me." I hold up the amulet on its chain. "Can I keep this?"

"You're the king, Alfred." He grins. "You can do whatever you want."

And just like that, he lightens my mood. "You were right to save it from the sheriff. And I have a feeling in my bones that it *is* going to be important. I just don't know how at the moment."

Jasper's first dispatch bears testament to the fact that even the best-conceived battle plans must be altered in the face of the reality in the field.

Your Grace,

I'm pleased to report that our harassment of the Teutons was as effective as we'd hoped. The surprise allowed us to inflict even more casualties in the first attack than we'd counted on and our archers escaped unscathed. We had some success with the fire arrows as well. Even with the protection of the Roman wall, ensuring the archers weren't captured limited their time in position, so it wasn't possible to get a large fire spreading throughout the meadow. Nevertheless, they did manage to fire multiple tents in three different locations and set a couple of supply wagons ablaze. The urgency to suppress the flames delayed the organization of any pursuit, so our men easily vanished into the darkness. I doubt many men or animals succumbed to the blazes, but as a harassing tactic, it seems to have succeeded.

By the time we approached from the fens, frustration had escalated to the point that they quickly pursued us into the marshes. Again, the result was even better than we'd hoped for. Our men had scouted a safe path out to solid ground and so were able to retreat as planned. Those charging headlong after us weren't so lucky, with many falling victim either to quicksand or to the random deep pools of water that can quickly swallow a man weighed down by armor. The pursuit was abandoned once they realized how many men the marsh was claiming, but not before they'd lost another fifty or so in addition to those our archers had dispatched.

Their commanders were, by then, sufficiently riled up to pursue our little group back toward the garrison. There, we were lucky as well. The scaffolding that had been used in construction of the final cannon emplacements hadn't yet been dismantled, so we leaned it back up against the garrison wall, as if construction were still ongoing. The Teutons fell for the ruse and charged blindly toward what they thought was an unfinished portion of the fort. We let them get well within range of the cannons, so we'd be firing into the middle of their ranks, before we kicked over the scaffolding and fired all four cannons simultaneously. Again, surprise caused a break in discipline as the lead elements pivoted to retreat back through those following. In the chaos that resulted, our archers and crossbowmen inflicted significant casualties and, of course, we continued firing our cannons until the Teutons finally managed to get out of range.

What's left of that force is now encamped just beyond the reach of our cannon fire. We estimate their numbers have been reduced to about three hundred. What we don't know until my scouts return is if this is all that remains of the Teuton forces or if they left some behind in the meadow. Those that are here have made no attempt to engage us in any way. Perhaps with their fury now spent, they're once again observing orders to hold position and wait. Now and again I allow the archers to harass them, and the screams that reach our ears tell me we've inflicted yet more damage. But so far, they've refused to mount another attack.

The operations in the north, however, are proceeding much more slowly than I'd like. Gunnvor's cronies in that area are as heavily armed as we'd been told, so pushing them south is becoming a bit of a slog. I may have to release the reserve forces from the quarry sooner than I really want to but am holding off on that decision for the moment.

The scouts report that Gunnvor's own forces are sitting astride the road at the border with a cannon positioned just outside each of the stone markers such that they can be pivoted to fire in any direction from which we might approach. Again, it's no surprise that he has the cannons. But how he's chosen to use them limits our options for a frontal assault. We're therefore adjusting our plans for the pincer such that we drive the cronies' forces into our lands, into a position that their only retreat will be straight into the face of Gunnvor's deployment with us at their backs. We already have the Teutons in the right position and must only hold them there . . . and hope there's no reserve Teuton force still waiting in the meadow.

Once I have the answer to that question, I can decide if we can afford to divert the Peaks contingent to help in the north.

Jasper

Why is it that all we've accomplished so far is to deal with the hidden Teutons and the north end of the battlefront? If this is really to be a second front in the Teutons' campaign, shouldn't we be more aggressive in our attacks all up and down the line? Didn't I tell Jasper "no hesitation"?

Didn't you also tell him, I remind myself, that you trusted him to keep his head and out-think the enemy? What seems like delay here, far away from the command tent, is likely no more than Jasper doing just that. Don't forget, Alfred – by the time you read these dispatches, things have already moved on. The army may be in the thick of battle by now.

And that's the hardest part of being so far distant from events as they're actually happening. Decisions must be made in advance of need since, by the time the need is apparent, it might be too late for a decision to affect the outcome.

Which brings my thoughts back to protection of the succession. I've broached the subject with Gwen a couple of times since Geoffrey declared his resolve to remain by my side, and so far, she's favored temporizing. I doubt Jasper's latest news will change her mind, but I show it to her anyway during our bedtime conversation. She reads silently then folds the page and returns it to me.

"If you were to send Edward somewhere for his safety, have you thought about where that might be?" she asks.

"A bit."

"He could go to my parents or even to the Lakes king's court. I'm sure that's safer than here, and he'd be with people he knows. In fact, Carew could probably use the same ruse they'd thought about for Geoffrey as a way to get Edward there."

"I've thought of that."

"He'd have more guards around for protection at the court, but Father's manor might actually be safer. Strangers snooping around would certainly be more obvious there."

"You do have a point, but . . ." I hesitate. "But, without casting any aspersions on Godwin or the care he'd take for his grandson's safety, might your parents not be a bit too old to be thrust into the middle of such a potentially dangerous business?"

"If it were them alone, I'd agree. But my eldest sister's family is living there now. Their son will inherit when Father dies, so they decided it was best he learn directly from his grandfather. And that would also give Edward someone nearer his own age for companionship."

"Very well. Let me think about it."

She snuggles close. "While you're thinking, Alfred, don't forget to think about how important it might be for the boys to see this thing through together. It might actually strengthen the bonds they already have."

And that, my dear, goes straight to the heart of my dilemma. What I need is something to tip the scales in one direction or the other – preservation of the succession or brothers relying on one another in a crisis.

Four days later, another dispatch arrives.

Your Grace,

The scouts report that the meadow has been abandoned. Nothing there except the rotting carcasses of men and horses and the scavengers picking them apart.

Such desecration of what had been a totally wild place is infuriating. What happened to the deer who once grazed that meadow? Were they all slaughtered to feed the Teutons? Even if some escaped, they'll have learned a fear of man that will stay with them for generations, even after the rotting flesh decays and nature reclaims the meadow. It's heartbreaking to think they may have forever lost their pristine home – if they even venture back there at all. But back to Jasper's missive.

The news doesn't shed any light on whether the only remaining Teutons are those now camped across the field from our garrison or if others left the meadow by another route to join with Gunnvor's forces elsewhere. It does, at least, answer the question of whether we have to be on constant alert for an assault from that quarter.

The fighting in the north continues, but the results are not what we wanted. The enemy is suffering greater losses than we are, and there's no evidence of reinforcements being added to their ranks, but their retreat is stubbornly to the east and we've been unable to coerce them to move either south or west, as I had hoped. I've released our forces from the quarry and diverted a rather large group from the Peaks army to hide in the quarry for later action. Our men will now begin a retreat toward the garrison, in hopes of getting the enemy to smell blood and pursue them. The Lakes forces will remain in place as a bulwark at the rear.

Once our men are within range of the main road, they'll turn and fight. And that's when I'll release the Peaks men from the quarry to attack the enemy flank.

The remainder of the Peaks forces have been diverted to a position well south of the garrison but out of sight of the Teutons. Their job is to prevent the Teutons from leaving their current positions to try to encircle us and then to serve as a reserve force for the central battle to come.

I've conducted what, in other circumstances, might be called practice drills by staging some forays toward their front lines. What we're trying to determine is how quickly they can reposition their cannons to react to attacks from varying directions – and what we need to do to respond to their changes

– what's the right timing to shift the direction of our charge so that we stay out of the path of their cannon fire and force them to expend their efforts repositioning the cannons rather than actually firing them. We've taken more casualties than I would have liked, but that's unavoidable if we're to learn their capabilities. I can only hope what we're doing looks to the other side like confusion and indecision.

Be careful, Jasper. If you're only dealing with Gunnvor, he's unlikely to think of anything other than repelling the attack. But if the Teuton king is in the command tent, he'll be onto you in a heartbeat.

By the time you read this, we'll have the measure of their cannon tactics and will be preparing an initial assault.

There's one piece of good news I can deliver. Those horses from across the Roman Sea that I'm using for my couriers are proving themselves invaluable. Never have I known such speed of communications along a battlefront this long. We must breed or acquire more of them.

Jasper

So the battle has been joined. And all we can do is wait.

I'd allowed Geoffrey to read the first dispatch. Should I show him this one as well? Perhaps I'll just borrow a page from Gwen's book and temporize – wait and see if he's curious enough to ask. A wait that lasts less than twenty-four hours.

We don't ride together every morning, much as I'd like both my sons to join me during this time when our activities are, of necessity, curtailed. In fact, we're careful to avoid any sort of pattern about when Geoffrey, Edward, and I might be outside the castle walls at the same time. But today, Geoffrey's joining me. And the first words out of his mouth as we walk toward the stable are, "Any further news from Sir Jasper?"

"A courier arrived yesterday afternoon. Come with me when we finish our ride and I'll let you read the report."

Later, in my private reception room, he reads with his brow furrowed, finally handing the pages back to me. "Is it always like this, Papa? Getting news only of what's long since happened?"

"When you're not with the army, I'm afraid it is. Even with the fastest couriers and a dispatch every day, it's not the same as when you're watching the battle unfold with your own eyes."

"So why doesn't Sir Jasper send a dispatch every day?"

"Commanders get busy. When they're not actually in the throes of a battle, they have to be anticipating what their opponents will do next and planning their own tactics. Sometimes they have to make a choice between an hour or two of sleep and sending a message. And if the fighting is moving rapidly across the landscape, there may not be time to set up all the accoutrements of a command post – as when Carew was pursuing Charles's army back to the east. I remember how impatient for news Samuel and I were, stuck back at Peveril Castle with our injuries while Carew prosecuted the war. And every courier sent away from the field is one courier who's unavailable for battlefield communications. All we can do if we're not with the army is trust our commanders."

"I think maybe what you're telling me is just how important it is to make a good choice of commander."

"That certainly makes it easier to trust. And in the long run, I think it probably leads to better outcomes. God knows we have a striking example in your Uncle John's case of how badly wrong things can go when a king runs roughshod over the men he's ostensibly put in charge of his army."

"But what if you make a bad choice, Papa? And how do you know if you've made a bad choice or if the things that go wrong would have been out of anyone's control?"

Yet more evidence of how quickly he's maturing in the face of the things playing out around him. "Sometimes you have to rely on your gut, Son. But there's plenty you can do to hone your gut instincts. That's precisely why we have a tradition of the heir to the throne spending time as a knight captain."

"But if peace prevails while I'm a captain . . ."

"Developing those instincts is at least as much about understanding men as it is about learning tactics and strategy. There'll be plenty of practice drills to help make the tactics second nature. If I were you, I'd take advantage of the fact that Carew and Tobin are both cooped up here with us for the time being. They're two of the best I've ever known, and you can talk with them as the heir and not just as a trainee."

"Maybe I'll include Edward too, if he wants to."

"I think that's a fine idea."

"So will you let me know, Papa, when the next dispatch arrives?"

"Of course. You know they may not all be good news, don't you? Some will be grimmer than others."

"I know. But I think I should know what's happening." He pauses, looking pensive. "I just wish there were some way we could let Denis know what's happening here. It feels strange not being able to write to him."

"Just remember that's temporary. Concentrate on hoping Jasper can prevail in the east quickly so we can go to Denis's aid."

"Do we have any news from there?"

"No. For the time being, all we can do is trust *his* commanders to hold the Teutons in check."

And that, at the moment, is the uncertainty that weighs on me most of all.

A soft knock on the door interrupts my routine affirmations of the sentences handed down by the magistrates, and I look up as Coliar steps inside. "A message from Carew, Sire. He wonders if you'd join him in the commander's office."

"Of course, Coliar. Won't take me long to finish up here."

"It seems, Sire, there might be some urgency. The lad who brought the message actually said Carew wants you to come straightaway."

I put down my quill, rise from the chair, and make my way toward the door. "Then it best be straightaway. Carew's not the sort to use that word lightly."

"Indeed not," says Coliar as he follows me out of the room.

The office door is closed – rather unusual when someone's inside – so I knock and hear hurried footsteps crossing the floor. Equally unusual – why not the normal "Enter" or "Come in"? Tobin opens the door a crack and peeks out, then puts a finger to his lips and opens the door just barely enough for me to enter. What are these two up to that requires such secrecy?

I get my answer when Tobin closes and locks the door. Hiding behind it is someone I certainly never expected to see. "Cedric?" I ask, keeping my voice low. "How on earth did you get here?"

"Sneaked into my quarters in the wee hours of the morning," Carew replies. "Damn near scared me out of my own skin, if I'm honest. He's lucky I didn't stab him first and ask questions later."

"Only way I could think of," says Cedric, "to sneak into these precincts without alerting the sentries."

"Yeah, well, I just may have to start posting a guard outside my *own* door," says Carew. The smiles on all three faces tell me there's no real animosity here and that Carew's actually rather pleased with Cedric's inventiveness.

"So why all the stealth?" I ask.

"Because I'm not staying . . . I'll be sneaking out again when it's pitch dark tonight."

"How did you get back?"

"I made a deal with the fishing boat captain who took me over in the first place. There's this tiny beach behind a big headland. You can't even see it if you're sailing east to west . . . and even when you approach from the west, you have to know what you're doing to find it. That's where he put me ashore the first time. We agreed he'd come back four weeks later, and if I was ready to come home, I'd be at the beach. He'll take me back as soon as I return to the fishing port."

"Any chance you were followed from there?" asks Tobin.

"I can't be completely certain, but it's pretty unlikely. I stayed hidden on the fishing boat until midnight then sneaked off and made my way here. I've gotten pretty good at traveling by night – it's actually rather fast once you get used to it."

"How'd you manage the ferry crossing?" I ask. Our fishing port is on the other side of the river, downstream from the commercial port.

"Joined up with a small group headed to the port to look for work, then just faded away while they were trying to work out where to go first. You'd think that might be the trickiest part, but somehow no one pays much attention to peasants – not even other peasants. Anyway, I was pretty sure you'd be hungry for news from across the sea, so it seemed worth the effort to get here."

"Indeed I am, Cedric."

"Well, sir. Hedrek's forces along with our own troop arrived exactly as planned. Seems they got ashore and made their way to the rendezvous without raising any alarms. Denis's commanders decided to use them to protect the border and bring their own men back into the main army. Their logic was that it would be better to have a common language in the middle of a pitched battle, and Hedrek would then have the same advantage should there be any attempted incursions farther south. Made good sense to me.

"The last message from Hedrek was that it's mostly been quiet on that front. When Denis's forces were pulling out to make way for Hedrek's men, there were a couple of skirmishes near two Teuton villages that sit right on the border. Hedrek quickly made an example of them, leaving no doubt that further attempts would be met with the same resolve."

"You know, Cedric," I tell him, "I'm actually quite pleased with that deployment. Based on what I saw of the Territorial armies in my brother's stupid war, they'll show no mercy in repelling any Teuton raids to test the border defenses. It'll take far more men than I think the Teuton king would want to divert from the main battle to actually breach Hedrek's lines."

"That's what I thought too, sir. And that's the good news. The rest isn't quite so heartening. Denis's commanders are good. They've had a lot of success anticipating what the Teutons' next moves will be. But they're outnumbered, sir. And no matter how big the Teuton losses are in any fight, they seem to have an endless supply of reinforcements to replace the fallen – men and horses alike – it doesn't seem to matter."

Carew and Tobin both look grim. Everyone knows we should be there to even the numbers. "How much ground have they lost?" asks Tobin.

"A couple of miles along the entire border between Aleffe province and the Teuton Kingdom. We think the Teuton strategy was to gain a firm foothold in Denis's territory before choosing a path to concentrate their main force for a drive up through the middle of the province to the port. Denis is convinced their first objective will be Aleffe Manor, so they've heavily fortified the area around it with cannons."

"I think Denis is probably onto something with his thinking," I remark. "It would be hugely symbolic for the Teutons to capture the country seat of the enemy king's family – and hugely demoralizing to Denis's people. But how is it you're privy to all this?"

"Denis invited me into the command tent. At the outset, his commanders left me in no doubt of their disapproval of my presence, but Denis left *them* in no doubt of his wishes. He's treating me as your emissary, sir, and encouraged me to attempt this journey. I think he wants both news from here and your advice, sir. And though he didn't say as much, I know he wants more fighting forces."

We spend the next hour discussing our deployments and what we know so far about the fighting in the east, at the end of which there's a dispirited lull in the conversation. "I suppose it's no surprise," Cedric finally breaks the silence if not the gloom, "that the Teuton king is trying to drag that fight out as long as possible. It may be an impertinent question, sir, but surely with all the men Jasper has at his disposal, he *must* have the advantage of numbers. Might it not be possible to go ahead and release the Peaks forces from the port to go to Denis's aid? Or even more of Goron's men?"

"I've asked myself that very question, Cedric, and have tried to get inside Jasper's head. Every fighting man we have is with Jasper at the moment – well, with the exception of Carew's guards. That leaves Goron as the last line of defense for us if our opponents should break through in the east. Same for the Peaks and, to a lesser degree, the Lakes. So I'm disinclined to deplete his army further. As for the rest, I suspect Jasper thinks supporting Denis half-heartedly would leave the final outcome in question."

"That would be my thinking as well," says Carew. "I know it means initial losses for Denis, but think about this. Once we've subdued the enemies here, the Teuton king will turn his full attention to the fight in Aleffe province, and he'll throw everything he has at trying to capture the port. If we commit forces to Denis piecemeal, those forces could easily suffer the same kinds of losses, and there'd be little left to counter an all-out Teuton offensive. Better to wait until we can bring a combined army into the fray with lots of fresh men from the Peaks and the Territories who haven't seen any fighting yet."

"There's logic to that," says Cedric. "Even if it'll be of little immediate comfort to Denis and his commanders."

Tobin's been quiet through most of this discussion – rather out of character for him. What's on his mind, I wonder? When we seem to have exhausted second-guessing Jasper, he changes the topic. "There's something I want to come back to – something you said earlier, Cedric, about the cannons around Aleffe Manor. That seems strange to me – that they'll only be using their cannons in retreat? And their army will be retreating with their backs to their own cannon fire? That sounds like a recipe for a potential catastrophe."

"That was my first reaction as well," says Cedric. "And I still don't have the whole picture. What I know is this. They decided they didn't want to be dragging their cannons all over the countryside or risk having to abandon them, in which case they'd likely fall into Teuton hands. So they staged them at a strategic location. They've also staged a huge quantity of supplies just north of the manor, so repositioning the army doesn't depend on the slow pace of the supply train. Plus, those supplies could easily be moved south if they were repulsing the Teutons or north if they had to respond to an assault on the port from the sea.

"The repositioning *does* depend on a lot of deception – like moving men under cover of darkness to give the impression they've sustained greater losses than they actually have. It also depends on a lot of things going just right. Things like judging the timing so they leave as little as possible for the enemy to capture and making sure the foot soldiers are moved early enough that they don't end up behind the final cavalry retreat. What are the chances of all that coming together entirely under their control?

"The plan was devised long before any actual threat materialized, so there's been no need for much talk of it in the command tent. I just hope there's more I haven't heard about that makes it less risky."

"Well, at least it sounds thought-out rather than relying entirely on chance," says Tobin. "Let's just hope they can execute it if they have to."

"When are you going back, Cedric?" I ask.

"I shouldn't stay here long, sir. Someone might see me, and word would get out that I've been here. My plan is to leave tonight."

"Can we keep him hidden for one more day, Carew? My gut tells me we might get another dispatch from Jasper tomorrow."

"I think so. He'll have to sleep in my quarters, but at least that means he won't be sneaking up on me in the middle of the night." Carew grins.

"I'll have to admit some good food wouldn't go amiss," says Cedric.

"Oh, so now I have to smuggle food for my own deputy?" Carew is clearly enjoying this. In truth, we all are. Light-heartedness is a rare commodity at the moment.

●　　●　　●　　●　　●

My gut proves prescient. Jasper's courier arrives just after the midday meal. I almost wish he hadn't.

Your Grace,

We've had some success. But at great cost.

Our planned retreat was met, just as we'd hoped, by Gunnvor's cronies chasing headlong after us. It was our intention to stay at least half a day ahead of them so there was time to form our lines when we turned to fight. We didn't anticipate that the cronies would keep their men on the move throughout the night, so we barely had time to pivot before we had to engage what by then was a poorly organized, bloodthirsty mob. Our discipline held, but there was far more hand-to-hand fighting than might have occurred had we been able to organize our ranks before any clash of arms.

Despite already being tired from their forced march, the enemy's men had been whipped into such a frenzy that they showed no sign of giving up the fight. In the end, we prevailed, but not before I had to release the Peaks fighters from the quarry to attack the enemy's rear.

We lost some two hundred fifty men – ours and the Lakes'. That's in addition to the losses the Lakes have already incurred. I only hope the price was worth it for what we've achieved. The cronies' forces have now been cleared from the north all the way to about half a day's ride south of where the stream turns east. Those that weren't killed in the battle – and most of them were – are now our prisoners, locked securely in the cells of the garrison. The Peaks soldiers have taken up position an hour south of the stream, to prevent anyone from reoccupying the area we've cleared. Since the Lakes have taken the brunt of the fighting so far, I've sent half of them to the quarry for some well-deserved rest. The remainder are being incorporated as a unit into our main force.

Having to release my reserve showed more of our hand than I would have preferred. Gunnvor will likely be concerned only with numbers and may fall for the ruse of my diverting some Lakes men to the quarry. I'm under no illusion, however, that the Teuton king isn't keenly aware that I have more men than they knew about and a hiding place for the reserve that he hasn't yet discovered. Assuming, that is, that he's still here directing Gunnvor's actions.

I actually have reason to think that's the case. Throughout the battle with the cronies, there was absolutely no move from Gunnvor to provide reinforcements. Those men were utterly sacrificed. Left to his own devices, Gunnvor would almost certainly have rushed into the fray to help his friends. Someone with a different motive is giving the orders.

Despite having to show some of my cards, I remain hopeful that the Peaks reserve south of the garrison hasn't yet been detected. Enemy scouts have ventured in that direction. But we maintain far more spies and scouts and sentries between the border and the Peaks position than I normally would. If we capture a scout before they've seen any indication of the reserve, we march them toward the Teuton camp and "throw them back," as it were. Any scout we suspect might be getting an inkling of what's up lands in a locked cell in the garrison. I wish I could lock them all up and deplete the Teuton's scouting assets, but if some of them didn't make it back, he'd grow even more curious about what we might be hiding.

We collected our dead on the morning after the battle, but there's as yet been no sign of the enemy doing likewise. If they're leaving it to us, we'll pile their dead near the border, where Gunnvor's men can see, and set them ablaze. Not a task I like assigning to anyone, but the field must be cleared and the warning sent.

Finally, Your Grace, we now know why the meadow by the Roman wall is deserted. If any Teutons stayed behind when the group pursued my men, they've apparently been incorporated into the enemy forces. The captain supervising the collection of our dead reported sighting several among the enemy casualties with the small Teuton symbol on the upper left of their tunics. So we know there are more. We just don't know how many or how they've been dispersed – or even if those in the meadow were the only Teutons here in the first place.

By the time you read this, we'll be preparing to take the battle to Gunnvor's main force. The current debate among my senior captains is whether to first try a night raid to capture Gunnvor's cannons or to rely on the tactics we've developed to try to prevent his using them effectively. We must reach a conclusion soon, though I haven't yet formed an opinion as to what that conclusion should be.

Jasper

I fold the page and make straight for the commander's office, where I find Cedric alone enjoying a veritable feast. "Going to be a long time before I get decent food like this again, Sire. A man's got to relish it when he gets the chance." He grins.

"But all in one sitting, Cedric?"

He laughs aloud. "Hardly. Not sure *anyone* could eat all this at once. Carew outdid himself, but I'm pretty sure he's not going to let me forget this. Anyway, I'll take some of it with me. Maybe save those sweet cakes to give to the fisherman. What brings you here, Sire?"

"News from Jasper."

I hold out the message and he wipes his hands on his trousers before taking it. "Adds to the disguise," he remarks before unfolding the page and reading. Finished, he hands it back. "Sounds like Jasper has as much of a fight on his hands as Denis does. How much of this can I tell Denis?"

"I see no reason to hold back any of it. It's important for him to know we're as fully engaged as he is – that we're not playing the Teuton's delaying game."

"Aye. Makes sense, though I'm not sure how much comfort it'll be."

"The most important thing for Denis to understand is that we're convinced the Teuton king himself is still on our shores. I've been thinking about Jasper's reasoning and agree it's sound. The Teuton knows we're the biggest threat to his ambitions. He also knows he can't rely on Gunnvor to neutralize us, so he has to oversee that himself. Gunnvor's only purpose is to provide men. This is Denis's best opportunity to keep the enemy field commanders off balance, even if he loses a little ground in doing so."

"How long do you think the Teuton king will stay here, sir?"

"He's played a long game to get what he wants. One that started shortly after Goscelin's death – when he recognized the instability and weakness that gave him an opportunity. First came proliferating black powder and new weapons, attempting to drive wedges between kingdoms. Then, when Charles dangled the prize before him, it looked like he might get his way with very little effort. We changed the game, but then so did he – taking a careful measure of the new players, offering inducements to trust, biding his time. He's used the Pope to neutralize any threat from the south. And he knows the Southern Nordics won't challenge him because they know he'd simply overrun them once he has Denis's port under his control. At the moment, he's single-mindedly focused on taking me out of the game and not particularly concerned what happens elsewhere so long as he can still see a clear path to his prize."

"Then I'll be on my way tonight, as soon as it's dark."

"Think you might be able to convince that fisherman to fetch you back here again from time to time?" I've no doubt the fisherman is on Laurence's payroll, but best to keep up the façade for Cedric's benefit. Whatever conclusions he may draw on his own, I can count on him to be circumspect.

"I think so, Sire. He seems to be something of an adventurer – seems to thrive on taking risks and outwitting the danger."

"Then I'll look forward to your return – and hope we both have better news. Godspeed, Cedric. Take care of yourself."

Samuel is back. Tamasine too. In truth, I was surprised she didn't remain at de Courcy Manor . . . until I recalled her reluctance to marry Samuel when he was a knight until his father promised she could always be at court when Samuel was there. At least Gwen will have some company.

"Sending men off to war is pretty disheartening," he tells me when we finally sit down to talk in the old library. "Especially when you've always been the one the men were sent to and not the one doing the sending."

"You sent men from your estate on the last campaign."

"Yes. But that all seemed more benign – it felt like they'd all be coming home. This feels different. More dangerous somehow." He pauses. "I don't know why, Alfred. I've sent men into battle without a qualm. But . . ." He pauses again then shakes his head slowly. "Maybe I'm just getting old."

"When you did that, the men were already in the field and you had a job to do. That's very different from watching men leave their families behind and seeing the anguish of those families firsthand. What you're feeling is the weight of responsibility on a lord who truly cares about his people."

"Well, whatever it is, it doesn't feel good." Then he sits up straighter in his chair, as if to shake off his melancholy. "Anyway, I'm here now. You said there was something you needed me to do."

"There is. But first, you should know what's happened while you were away." I hand him Jasper's dispatches to read. Finished, he returns them without comment, so I relate the news Cedric brought from across the sea and my conviction that the Teuton king is personally in charge of the enemy forces in the east.

"I wonder if Gunnvor has figured out yet just how dispensable he is." Samuel chuckles. "He and Gunhild deserve each other. Speaking of whom, what have you done with her?"

"Had a message from Laurence yesterday. He's sending men to collect her at the end of next week. Her destination, I'm told, is somewhere very far away in a cloistered convent."

"Or at the bottom of a very deep well somewhere, more like."

"Wherever it is, I don't want to know."

"So what is it you want me to do?"

"I need to get word to Brandr about all of this."

"Don't you think he's probably heard things from his own people?"

"Whatever he may have heard won't be the entire story. And he needs to know that. But there's more at stake. When Denis made his state visit here, the spring after he was crowned, he and Brandr made a firm but secret alliance. They both could foresee the value of an unexpected ally in a future conflict. I'm the only other one who knows about it."

"Not even Petronilla?"

"Not Petronilla. Not Greville. Not Denis's commander. And, of course, I've told no one until this moment. That means it's up to me to get word to Brandr that includes everything we know about what the Teuton king is up to and what we're facing."

"Including that business at Korst's mine?"

"Absolutely. And including another bit of business that only Laurence and I are privy to." I retrieve the dead man's amulet from my pocket and hold it up by the chain.

Samuel gasps. "Where did you get that?"

"It came from an unidentified extra body found in the barn where my mother died."

"Holy mother of God! You're saying there was a Teuton spy in the barn with them?"

"Precisely. Though how he got there, where he came from, if he led them to the barn . . . all those are unanswered questions. Unanswerable, Laurence thinks, since the man is dead and we've found no one claiming to recognize either the man or his amulet."

"One thing's certain. He must have been someone of rather high rank to have such a fine emblem of his king."

"My thoughts exactly. Especially since Laurence says he had it concealed beneath all his clothing." I return the amulet to my pocket.

"And you want me to be your messenger to Brandr."

"Samuel, there's no one in the world I trust more."

"Have you arranged a ship with Laurence?"

"No." Samuel looks at me quizzically. "Because this has to be done in complete and utter secrecy. However Brandr chooses to act must be a complete surprise to the Teutons if it's to be the kind of disruption that will shake their strategy to its core. A ship emerging from our river and turning north would grab their attention – they'd likely follow it and then the game would be up."

"Why do I feel a hare-brained scheme coming on?"

I chuckle. "Maybe not so hare-brained. Not without risk – I acknowledge that – but logical . . . and unexpected."

"Go on, then."

"Do you remember what Brandr told us about the Northern Kingdom? About how they're totally dependent on the Far Nordics for fuel?"

"Aye."

"Well, this time of year would be when all that wood is being transported, so there are surely ships sailing back and forth constantly between the two kingdoms. If you can make your way through the Lakes and the Northern Kingdom to where those transport ships dock, you should be able to get passage on a returning ship and then travel onward to Brandr's court without anyone being the wiser."

"Well, it's logical – I'll grant you that. But, Alfred, I know nothing about those lands and don't speak a word of their language. How do you expect me to make that kind of a journey with any hope of success?"

"How did you get to Egon when we were trying to outsmart John?"

"As a monk? Surely you're not serious."

"A monk on his way to a monastery in Brandr's kingdom. What better way to explain lack of language and needing help finding your way? You could even take shelter for the night in any monastery you encounter along the route."

"Logical, maybe, but my Latin's not what it used to be – and it never was great."

"I imagine Warin can provide something in writing that explains your journey when he arranges your disguise. I could write it, but Warin will know the right words to use that wouldn't be suspect by another abbot or prior."

"So you're going to bring Warin in on this?"

"Not every detail of the war. But certainly enough for him to understand the need for your journey. He may even turn out to be quite helpful. And we know we can trust him with secrets."

"I don't know, Alfred. Let me think about it. And talk with Tamasine."

"I'm not sure that's such a good idea."

"Well, it's non-negotiable." His tone borders on stern. "I swore an oath to her when we married that any time I had to go away, I would tell her where I was going and why – I'd never leave her wondering why I had just disappeared. The only time I came close to breaking that oath was when I took the news of John's war to Egon. All I told her was that it was an errand for you. And that was only because we were both committing treason, and I didn't want her caught up in that. So, if you want me to undertake this mission, Alfred, I *will* tell Tamasine where I'm going and why." He pauses, then softens his tone. "Come on, Alfred, you tell Gwen whenever you go off on one of your risky adventures. Don't deny me the same thing."

"You're right, Samuel. I'm just . . . anxious, I guess. There's so much riding on this. If anyone were to get wind of it . . ."

"I understand. What I would tell her is that you need me to take a message to your cousin and that it's riskier because of the war. But we're going to mitigate that risk by having me travel as a monk. I rather suspect, after her reaction to seeing my tonsure when I returned from Egon's, that will draw her attention away from wanting to know any details of the mission."

"Probably also means she'll want a piece of my hide for shaving your head yet again," I chuckle, "but *that*, I can deal with."

"Then let me think about it – see if I can find any holes in your plan. When would you want me to leave?"

"As soon as you can. But a day or two from now would be fine. We might even have further news from Jasper by then."

The next morning, I return from my morning ride to find an enormous commotion in the outer courtyard. Half a dozen guards marching two men, their hands tied behind their backs, toward the entrance to the prison cells. Carew barking orders to the sentries to double their vigilance. Servants scattering to get away from whatever's afoot. When Carew notices me watching, he shouts, "Get indoors, Your Grace. Now!"

Reluctantly, I turn away from the scene and obey his instructions. No doubt he'll come to report once the immediate threat is dealt with. In less than half an hour, Coliar announces his arrival. "Something up, Carew?" I ask him.

"You could say that, sir. The sentries saw two men wandering up the path from the town yesterday. As soon as someone shouted at them, they quickly turned tail back into town. Earlier this morning, the sentry spotted the two we captured skulking in the high grass on the hillside, trying to get close to the castle walls without being seen. We think it may be the same two, though no one got a close enough look at the ones from yesterday to be absolutely certain. They're locked in a cell now and being questioned."

"Tell your men 'good work.'"

"We think they were trying to find a way to sneak in, sir, so I'd rest easier if you and your family would agree to stay indoors until we're sure we've dealt with the threat. Especially your sons."

"It's likely they're already on their way to the stables to work with their horses."

"Then I'd best go find them straightaway." He makes for the door.

"Try not to scare them, Carew. Just tell them I want them both here now. I'll take it from there."

"Yes, sir."

He's already halfway across the outer chamber as I call after him, "And let me know later what you've learned."

Geoffrey and Edward arrive looking a bit flustered. "Carew said you wanted to see us, Papa," says Geoffrey.

"He said it was urgent," Edward chimes in, "so we left the horses with Mervyn Lightfoot."

"Carew's just a bit concerned at the moment. There were two men acting very suspiciously not far from the sentry gates earlier this morning. The guards took them into custody so they could be questioned. Carew just wants us to be especially careful and stay indoors until he gets to the bottom of things. Probably not a bad idea for us to go along with that. One less thing for him to worry about."

"We can do that," Edward says. The implications of strangers acting suspiciously haven't quite sunk in for him yet.

But Geoffrey's brow is furrowed. "Does Carew think they might have been saboteurs or kidnappers?"

"In truth, he doesn't know at the moment. That's why he's worried. Let's just give him time to sort things out and not jump to any conclusions."

"Alright, Papa," says Geoffrey. "But you'll tell us when we can go back out to the stable, won't you?"

"Of course. Now off you go and find something to amuse yourselves indoors."

I seem to have succeeded in diverting them from thoughts of immediate danger. As they walk through the door, I overhear

Geoffrey telling Edward, "Let's go down to the kitchens. Maybe Cook has some more of those fresh berries she gave us yesterday."

I, myself, am not so easily diverted. When Carew returns midafternoon, I feel justified in my concern. "We've had no luck getting them to talk, sir," he reports. "They won't say any more than that they were passing by and were curious to see what the sentry towers looked like up close. When asked where they're from, it's some vague village east of here that doesn't seem to have a name. They were even less specific about their destination – just headed west to try to find work. The only explanation they had for why they weren't on the main road was that same nonsense about wanting to see the towers.

"We've tried to probe about their families. Apparently they have none. About what work they used to do. Whatever came to hand. They claim to have no money, though the guard that searched them for weapons took a purse full of plain coins off one of them. Each of them had a rather nice dagger. They put up a howl of protest when those were confiscated. They'd have us believe they only had them to kill small animals for food. But the weapons were well polished and nicely sharpened – no indication they'd been used recently to clean a rabbit or squirrel."

"Any idea if they have accomplices somewhere?"

"If they do, they're not giving them away. To hear the prisoners tell it, they're just two dreadfully poor peasants who've been thrown in prison for nothing more than being curious."

"I want to see them, Carew."

"There's nothing to see, sir. Two scruffy-looking men with nothing to say for themselves in rough clothes that aren't very clean."

"Well, we know they've lied about at least one thing."

"Sir?"

"The money. Humor me, Carew."

"Very well, sir. If you insist. But I doubt you'll be able to get any more out of them."

"Then wait here just a moment." I go through the bedchamber and into my dressing room where I retrieve the amulet from my strongbox. Pocketing it, I rejoin Carew and we make our way to the prison cells.

They're exactly as Carew described. Probably twenty-something years old. Unkempt. Hair uncombed. Rough clothes looking like they've been slept in. Boots that have had some wear but don't appear in danger of developing holes any time soon. They're chained to the wall on opposite sides of the cell by a manacle around one wrist. No way they can gang up on the guards or run out the door when food is brought or the piss bucket changed out.

I start with simple questions about how they came to be in this predicament, to which they reply with protests about the unfairness of it all. They persist in their story that they're nothing more than poor travelers who wanted to get a glimpse of what a real castle is like. I didn't expect to hear anything different, but my purpose is to get them back into the familiar rhythm of telling their hard-luck story.

One of them finally asks, "Can't you help us get out of here, sir? We'd be ever so grateful."

"I doubt it," I reply, turning to leave. But at the door, I turn back, reach into my pocket, and produce the amulet, once again holding it up by the chain. "Have either of you ever seen anything like this?"

They can't resist the instinct to look straight at one another. And then, realizing that was the wrong thing to do, they look at the floor, the ceiling, the corners of the room, their hands, the ring on the wall to which they're chained – anywhere but directly at me. When I ask again, "Well, have you?", one of them takes a quick glance at the amulet then mutters, "Can't say as I have." The other echoes, "Me neither."

I pocket the amulet, and Carew knocks on the door for the guards to let us out. In that misbegotten glance, they told me everything I need to know.

Neither of us speaks until we're back in my private reception room. "Where'd you get that, sir?" Carew asks.

"It doesn't matter for the moment. What matters is their reaction."

"Teuton spies," he says. "Would-be kidnappers? Those daggers certainly say they meant business and were prepared to kill if necessary."

"Or at least threaten to kill. What's your next move?"

"Send for the sheriff. Get him to double his patrols in and around the town. The guards are already on high alert, but Tobin and I will make sure they all know who those two are and that the threat is real and immediate. Everyone to stay indoors until we're satisfied there are no more of them in the immediate vicinity."

"Very well, Carew. You know you have my complete trust."

"With your permission, sir, I'd really like to get this all underway."

"Of course. And I need a bit of time to think and to talk with the queen." His bootsteps, as he leaves and crosses the outer chamber, echo the determination I saw in his face.

In truth, I don't need more time to think. My mind was made up the moment I saw that ill-advised gaze. The choice is no longer whether I need to protect the succession but which son to protect.

I go in search of Geoffrey and find him – alone, thankfully – in his room. Before I can even finish closing the door he asks, "Has Carew figured out what was up with those two men?"

I take a seat on Edward's bed. "We have, Son. They were working for the Teutons. We don't know if they're just ordinary spies sent to determine the lay of the land or if their assignment was hostage-taking. Truth be told, it doesn't matter. Whatever their mission, we discovered them before they could cause any harm. Carew and his men are now trying to determine if they had accomplices who might still be lurking around or if the threat's been quashed for the time being."

"They'll remain our prisoners, won't they?"

"Absolutely. But the fact that they got this close forces me to re-examine how I best protect the succession. And that means I need to offer you once again the chance to go to the Peaks until this is all over. Even though Eirwen's birthday celebration is past, visiting your bride-to-be is still a perfectly legitimate reason for you to go there."

He walks to the hearth and stands with his back to me, apparently deep in thought. The silence lasts so long I feel the need to contribute to whatever is going through his head. "There's no dishonor, Geoffrey, in changing your mind. The idea of possible hostage-takers is very different from the reality of knowing they're already in our midst. I'll tell you something I wouldn't admit to anyone else other than your mother – I'm pretty unnerved by it as well. So if you want to guarantee the succession by spending the rest of the war with your betrothed, under her father's protection, I will move heaven and earth to make that happen."

The silence continues. At long last, he says, "You could order me to do that, but you haven't. Why?"

"Your reasoning when you first told me you wanted to stay here. You had clearly thought about it very carefully, and it showed a maturity I've only ever seen in one other young man of your age."

"Oh?"

"Denis. You two are having to embrace the reality of kingship much earlier than should have been necessary. I was exceedingly proud of you for how you reached your decision. And I'll be no less proud if you now make a different choice. Part of kingship is assessing the facts on the ground in the moment and knowing that changing course is often strength of mind rather than weakness of spirit."

He finally makes his way back to sit on his bed facing me. "If you insist I leave, Papa, I will. But I don't think I want to change my mind. Denis is having to face even worse. If he can do it, so can I. So if you'll let me, I'll stay here with you." He pauses, looks down at his feet, then looks back up to meet my gaze. "I can't promise I won't be scared – especially if more of these Teuton operatives show up. But if you'll help me, I'll do my best to see it through."

I stand and extend my arm, and he stands to grasp it. The first time we've exchanged the warrior's greeting. And then we embrace – father and son committed to facing the future together, no matter what happens.

When I tell Gwen everything in our bedtime conversation, her eyes glisten with moisture as she takes in what all this means for those she loves. "I still have to protect the succession," I tell her quietly as she comes into my arms.

"I know."

"I'm following your lead, you know."

She almost manages a soft laugh. "I know. But that doesn't make it any easier to accept that one of my sons will be going away for who knows how long."

"Nor does it for me. But I have a plan. Hear me out. I think you might like this." And so I tell her what's been brewing in my mind since Geoffrey gave me his decision.

The next morning, there's no question of the usual morning ride, so I send for Carew straightaway. When I tell him my intentions, his mien changes before my very eyes. It's as if I'm watching the apprehension, angst, even anger creep from his toes to the top of his head as his posture stiffens, his fists clench, and he struggles to keep a neutral expression on his face – something he doesn't quite achieve. Doing his best to overcome what must surely be raging inside, he slowly unclenches his fists before speaking. "Permission to be candid, sir?" Carew never asks, so I've no doubt he'd like to give me an earful.

"Always, Carew. I expect no less."

"Sir . . . with all due respect . . . that's completely foolhardy. To expose yourself and your son like that – after everything that happened yesterday and all the precautions we've taken – it's quite beyond the bounds of logic – certainly of prudence."

"But it's not beyond the bounds of love. What I intend to ask of Edward requires every drop of love and courage I possess. I can only do that in a place that has special meaning for us both."

"And yet you won't even tell me where that is."

"Which is what makes the place so special. I've not told anyone else where it is either, which means no one here could be bribed or coerced into revealing where it might be."

"That doesn't mean you couldn't be followed."

"I can't deny that. I'll have to be on my guard. And you have my word of honor that I'll take seriously anything that seems the least bit out of the ordinary. But we *will* go alone. And if I have to make that an order for the sake of your honor, I'll do that because I won't have anyone questioning your judgment when it's *my* choice not to heed your advice."

He looks first at his feet and then back up at his king – the man he's charged to protect. "That won't be necessary, sir. That's not how we do things between us."

"I know I'm putting you in a really uncomfortable place, Carew, and I don't like that any more than you like being there. When we return, I'll tell you what this has all been about. You'll need to know if things go as I hope they will."

Thus it is that Edward and I ride away from the stable alone, with Carew and Elvin watching our departing backs. And just as the first time I asked Carew to stay behind, I hear Elvin trying to reassure him. "Dinna' ye be fretting over-much now. I dinna' know if they be going to the hut or som'eres else, but Alfred, he know those woods like the back of his hand. And he have a special love for that lad – he never be taking him som'eres he couldna' keep him safe."

We take the left fork of the trail, riding nondescript mounts that no one would recognize. The sounds of the stream to our left and the birdsong in the canopy above are enough to make one forget that, five days to the east, men are fighting to preserve two kingdoms and there are two men in our cells who intended to do us harm. Edward seems to sense something serious is afoot. Why would he not, since he can otherwise barely move without guards ever-present? At the first sound of our horses' steps in the stream, a fox darts out of the hidden paddock and scampers away. "I hope we haven't disturbed a vixen with kits," says Edward as we dismount.

As a precaution, we unsaddle the horses and free them from their bridles to graze the lush spring grass along the stream bank. At least anyone chancing on the horses won't have an immediate clue that people are about somewhere.

"Let's have a look." We climb the bank and wander around, looking for other signs of animal life. Fortunately, the inside is deserted.

"Maybe she was just looking for a place to take her litter for a bit of exploring outside their den," says Edward, setting his gear down just inside the entrance.

I follow suit and gaze around before walking over to sit on the fallen log. Nothing ever seems to change here. The care my son has taken to ensure the opening doesn't become overgrown is evident. One end of the log has perhaps decayed a bit since the last time I was here. And though the thicket, from the outside, looks rather more dense, the vines still refrain from covering the opening at the top that lets the sun preserve the life within.

Edward sits cross-legged on the grass opposite me. "This must be important, Papa."

"I assume Geoffrey told you I offered him a safe haven until this business with the Teutons is finished."

"Aye. He said he decided against it."

"Did he tell you why?"

"Yes." His response is a bit . . . hesitant? . . . timid?

"And what do you think about his choice?"

"I think it was a hard one for him. It can't be easy to decide between what you *want* to do and what people think you *should* do – or even what maybe you yourself think you *should* do."

"It never is. And it wasn't easy for me to agree to his decision to remain here. I know we've talked about the risk someone might want to take me hostage, but I can't hide from you that you and Geoffrey are at risk too. A devious man like the Teuton king would certainly know he could get what he wants from me far more easily if he abducted one of you than if he just took me as his prisoner."

"I wondered if that was why you suggested Geoffrey go to the Peaks." His voice is quieter now.

"Well, it *is* important we send the message that our alliance with the Peaks is stronger than ever, but yes, I did think he might be safer there than here. I have to think about protecting the succession to our throne, no matter what happens. And it became far more urgent after we caught those Teuton spies yesterday. We were lucky this time. They were clumsy and easy to spot. But we can't count on always being lucky. Remember what happened to your grandfather. What could appear more innocent than a couple of stable boys? And yet they succeeded."

He looks up at the blue sky visible through the opening at the top of the thicket then down at his hands. "Are you going to ask me to go away, Papa? Is that why we came here?"

"I don't want to. God knows how much I don't want to."

"What if – like Geoffrey – I think I should stay here with you?"

"Truth be told, Son, this was a choice I didn't want to have to make. It's kept me awake more than one night. But yesterday's events brought me to the realization that perhaps it's what I *should* do. What I *must* do. And it was your mother who finally brought me some peace."

"How, Papa?"

"I thought about when she was forced to make the same choice during your Uncle John's reign. When my brother had dragged me off to war – hoping I'd get killed – and the sickness was raging through the land, drawing ever closer to the country manor. It was a heart-wrenching decision she had to make to protect your lives. To leave everything behind, knowing she might never see me again. To tell *no* one where she was going lest word get to John about how to find you. And I realized that if she could show that kind of courage – to protect your life no matter what it might cost her – then I can do no less."

"I was too young at the time to understand. It just seemed like an adventure."

"And that's exactly how she wanted it."

"At least it all turned out well in the end."

"Edward, God forfend anything should happen to me or to Geoffrey in this conflict. But should something dreadful occur, at least

I'll know you're safe and you're alive to pick up the pieces and carry on with what my grandfather and yours started."

"But where can I go that's truly safe?"

"To the Far Nordics. To Brandr. There's no one I trust more to protect you and to restore you to this throne should the unthinkable happen."

"How would I get there? Geoffrey says sailing from our port to Denis's kingdom isn't safe right now. How could sailing to the Far Nordics possibly be any safer?"

"It isn't. That's why I have something entirely different in mind." I describe Samuel's mission to him, ending with, "And I want you to go with him."

He looks at me quizzically. "Papa, if you trust Sir Samuel to keep me safe, why don't you just send me to de Courcy Manor to stay with Henry?" Samuel's second son is Edward's best friend.

"I trust Samuel as much as I do Brandr. But he'll be off on this mission, so he wouldn't be there to protect you."

And now he looks crestfallen. "Oh. I guess that's right." He comes to sit beside me on the log, and neither of us speaks for a very long time. Finally, he breaks the silence. "I really don't want to go, Papa. I don't want to leave you. But if it's what you think best . . . then I'll do as you ask."

I put an arm around his shoulders and pull him close. "Then take this thought with you. I love you. And I'll pray every day to every god I've ever heard of that this business is finished quickly and we can celebrate our reunion before this year's harvest festivals."

"Who will look after this place while I'm gone, Papa?"

"I know you want me to say I will, but I can't. I can't go anywhere without guards, and I'd never bring the guards here. But the animals will look after it – just as they did when we had to hide from your Uncle John. And when you come back, they'll welcome all the things you do that aren't so easy for them."

He rests his head on my shoulder momentarily, then rises and walks toward his horse's gear, his hands to his face – unwilling to let me see the tears he's almost certainly wiping away. "I suppose we'd best get back," he says, picking up his saddle, "before Carew thinks something's happened to us."

•   •   •   •   •

The next morning, I lean against the door of my dressing room and watch as Gwen says her farewells. "You and Samuel are going to have quite an adventure, I think." Somehow she manages to be cheerful despite the anxiety I know she feels inside. "You'll see a part of the world none of us have *ever* seen before, and I'll be counting the days until I can hear all about it when you come home."

"Will you, Mama?" Edward asks.

"Absolutely! The time will pass even more quickly for you at Brandr's court because there'll be so many new things to do, and who knows? You might even take a fancy to one of the young ladies of the court."

"Aw, Mama." My son looks embarrassed.

"You never know," says Gwen. "Anyway, Aunt Beatrix will be there to help with anything you need, and you won't have to cope with all the guards telling you where you can't go and what you can't do. It might be rather like a holiday."

"Perhaps."

"Now . . ." Gwen rises and Edward follows suit. "You take care of yourself and remember who you are, and we'll fetch you home just as soon as the danger is past." She hugs him tightly for a long moment then kisses his forehead. "I think the carriage is waiting for you and your father. And I have to go figure out how to keep Alicia from telling everyone she sees that you got to go on a holiday and she didn't and it isn't fair."

Edward finally manages a smile. "Good luck with *that*. Maybe you should get her some more dogs to look after."

"You know, that's really quite a brilliant idea. Alfred, maybe you could ask Brother Adam if he could come with some of his pups and distract her for a few days."

"Your wish is my command, dear lady," I reply, crossing the room to give her a kiss. "We should probably go, Edward. I suspect Samuel's already in the carriage."

We keep the curtains drawn for the entire trip to the monastery, having no wish for anyone to observe who might be inside, though the troop of guards accompanying us announces at full volume that it's someone important. Carew wouldn't hear of a smaller contingent, and I had no wish to argue with him after what I'd insisted on the previous day. None of us is in a talkative mood during the journey, but at one point Edward says, "I asked Geoffrey to look after Fortis for me, Papa, and I know he will. But could you maybe check on him now and then as well?"

"Happily. I rather suspect Elvin will give him some extra attention too."

When the carriage pulls through the gate at the monastery, half the guards take up position outside, watching the road. Warin is predictably astonished by all the military might but just as predictably good-hearted about its presence. "Carew seems to have outdone himself protecting you today," he chuckles when he meets us as we walk toward the main building.

"Carew's more on edge than usual at the moment," says Samuel, "after they captured two Teuton spies nosing around the castle a few days ago."

"As well he should be. Come. Let's go to my dining room. Frery's there waiting for us."

"Good," I reply. "I think you might want his help with what we've come to propose."

"Ah, scheming again, Alfred?"

Samuel laughs out loud. "When is he *not*?"

Once we're all seated comfortably around the hearth, we forego the usual pleasantries and get straight to what brought us here. The expressions on the two monks' faces grow increasingly somber as I describe the situation in the east and in Denis's kingdom, ending with the capture of the two spies and my growing concern over the Teuton king's interest in hostage-taking. "That they were so near the castle took the decision out of my hands, Warin. I've no choice but to take steps to protect the succession. And it's vital to get my message to my cousin about what the state of the war really is."

"Such a sad business that so many lives must be lost – have already been lost – to this conniving king," says Warin. "But how do you think we can help you?"

When I describe my idea for Samuel's journey, neither Warin nor Frery can suppress a smile. "So, Samuel," says Warin, "you're to become a monk once again."

"His idea, not mine," chuckles Samuel. "But in truth, I think he's landed on a good way to keep the Teutons from learning what we're up to. That said, I'm more than a little worried. I haven't used my Latin in years and am not sure I could put two sentences together convincingly."

Edward pipes up. "My Latin's quite good, sir. Maybe I can help out."

Over the course of the midday meal, Warin and Frery hatch their plan. Samuel will travel as a monk who's lost most of his hearing, Edward as an oblate accompanying him to a new posting. Samuel's feigned disability will allow Edward to do all the talking. Warin will provide a letter of introduction to the abbot of a monastery in the Far Nordics that the travelers can use as proof of the reason for their journey. As the plans take shape, Edward shows the first signs of cheerfulness I've seen in two days.

"The remaining question," says Frery, "is transport. Since you didn't arrive on horseback, I suppose they'll need two of our horses."

"I'm afraid that's right, Frery," I reply. "But I'll arrange for Elvin to send you some good, reliable replacements."

"Then, I think we have a plan," says Warin. "Leave it to us, Alfred. We'll see they have what they need for a successful journey. They can leave from here as soon as we get them properly prepared."

"I'm grateful, Warin." It's time for me to go. When I rise from my chair, so does everyone else. I embrace Edward. "Take good care of Samuel, Son. As your mother said, we'll fetch you home just as soon as it's safe." I break the embrace and turn to Samuel. "And maybe by the time you get to come home, your hair will have grown out some and Tamasine won't be so put off by your appearance." He smiles.

Warin accompanies me outside. "Your plan's a good one, Alfred. They should be safe. We'll see them on their way tomorrow."

"Thank you, Warin. But there's one more favor I need to ask."

"Oh?"

"Can you spare Brother Adam for a few days? Gwen is rather concerned about Alicia talking about Edward's so-called holiday around the wrong people. Knowing how outspoken my daughter can be, I think it's a valid concern. But if Brother Adam could come back with me – maybe bring a couple of his charges – and spend a few days working with her and her dogs, we think that might be enough distraction to take her mind off her brother's absence."

Warin laughs. "Tell Adam he has my blessing and that we'll take care of the kennel while he's away."

"Then I'll stop by the kennel to collect him and we'll be on our way."

Alicia jumps up and down with delight when Brother Adam alights from the carriage accompanied by Tilda and two of her six-week-old pups. "Well then, young lady," Adam says, "where shall we take these three to get them settled in?"

"Come with me." Alicia scoops up one of the puppies and beckons for Adam to follow her.

Gwen comes to my side and puts her arm around my waist, my own arm naturally falling around her shoulder as we walk slowly up the steps to the entrance of the castle. "How was he?" she asks quietly.

"I think he'll be just fine." We say nothing more until we're inside and starting up the staircase, still in our half embrace. "But a large piece of my heart will soon be traveling north."

"Mine too."

Geoffrey's determination to remain here took a lot of courage. So did his admission that he might be scared from time to time. But there's something I can do to help reduce his anxiety. When he wanders into my private reception room while I'm in the midst of Coliar's stack of papers, it seems now's as good as time as any.

Rising from my writing table, I make my way into the outer chamber. "I've finished about half of it, Coliar, but there's something I'd like to do with my son at the moment. I'll come back to the rest later."

"Very well, Sire. I'll collect what's finished in a bit. The rest can wait until tomorrow if you want to spend the day with Lord Geoffrey. Carew's asked for a few moments of my time, so I'll be off there now if you have everything you need."

"On your way then." Even better. No need for me to send him on some silly errand.

When Coliar closes the door to the corridor behind him, I return to where Geoffrey's waiting. "Tell you what, Son. There's one little thing I need to do. It won't take but a minute. Why don't you go on ahead to the old library? Light the candles and close the door so no one's tempted to join you, and I'll be there straightaway."

Once he's gone, I go into the bedchamber and check both dressing rooms. Satisfied that no one's around, I grab my tinder box from the shelf in my dressing room, release the hidden latch inside the hearth, and step into the secret passage, leaving the door ajar just enough to be able to see to light a torch. Those in the box look quite fresh, and the first one I try flares to life straightaway, without any priming. Placing it in the holder on the wall, I close the door completely, listening for the soft click of the latch that says it's secure. Then, torch in hand, I start down, counting the steps as I go.

At the level of the old library, I secure the torch in the holder on the landing and have a good look at the clothing hanging from the hook on the wall. Servants attire that looks to be about the right size to fit me and reasonably clean. Underneath it, on the same hook, another set of clothing slightly smaller. A recent addition. Fresh torches. Clothing for two. Whoever maintains this passage must have made the changes recently.

I release the latch on the door, its click so soft anyone inside might not notice if their attention was focused elsewhere. When I step through, Geoffrey jumps out of his chair and scurries backward until he's stopped by a wall of bookshelves. "Holy mother of God!" he shouts. I can only pray there's no one passing in the corridor. Regaining enough of his composure to lower his voice to normal speaking tones, he takes a step forward and says, "Christ on horseback! Where'd you come from, Papa? You could scare a man to death just appearing like that."

"Well, you said you might be scared from time to time since you decided to stay here." I can't wipe the grin off my face.

"But not by you. Come on, Papa. It's not funny."

"Actually, from where *I* stand it's quite funny." He shakes his head in dismay as I take a seat in one of the chairs in front of the hearth and beckon him to join me.

"So where *did* you come from?" he asks, calm finally restored.

"In the normal course of events, this would be something I'd have saved until later – perhaps until Edward came of age so I could show you both at the same time. But since we've already had a very real threat from those Teutons sitting in their cell, I decided it was time you learned one of the secrets of the castle.

"Have a look around this room. Walls entirely of stone. No windows. Have you ever taken note of just how thick the door is and how strong its hinges are?" His gaze follows my words. "That iron pole that holds the king's banner. Go grab it just below the banner and push it down and to the left."

He does as instructed and his eyes light up. "A barricade to keep the door from opening. I never would've guessed."

As he starts to raise it back into position, I tell him, "Let's just leave it down for the moment. We don't want anyone interrupting us." He returns to his seat.

"When this room was built, it had two purposes – to house the Treasury and to serve as a safe room for the king if the castle was under attack. When the Treasury was moved to its current location, my grandfather chose it for the library because it was the safest place in the castle from fire. But it still remained the king's safe room – and does so to this day."

"That still doesn't explain how you got here without coming through that door." He inclines his head toward the door to the corridor.

"What no one would realize unless they had the builder's drawings or took their own very careful measurements on this floor of the castle and the one above is that this room is directly beneath the king's bedchamber. And there's a hidden staircase that spirals around the chimneys from the king's bedchamber to the back of an undercroft, with an intermediate landing just outside this room."

"So you . . ."

"That's how I got here."

We spend the next hour exploring the secret passage, up and down from this level, though we don't emerge at the top lest Osbert or Robin or Letty might have returned. When I try to impress on him how important it is to count one's steps in case the torch should go out, he's dubious, so when we return to the library landing, I douse the torch without warning and his enormous gasp precedes a quiet, "Dear God in Heaven, I didn't know anything could be this dark."

"Alright now, let's go back down to the undercroft. I'll go first so I can catch you if you slip up. But count to five before you follow me so you have to make your own way down. Keep to the outer wall, where the steps are widest, and feel for the next step with your foot before shifting your balance. How many steps down?"

"Thirty-one. Wait, Papa. Where's the first step?"

"Feel the walls for the door into the library. Put your back to that and move to your right. Now I'm starting down. I'll see you at the bottom."

By the time he bumps into me when he arrives at the bottom, I've managed to find the box of torches and place one in the holder. Retrieving my tinderbox from my pocket, I strike the flint on the steel and the sparks bring the torch to life.

Geoffrey is trying valiantly to stop shaking. "I don't ever want to do that again ever in my life." He leans against the wall.

"So you understand, now, why you have to count steps even with a lit torch in your hand just so you'll know how to save yourself if the torch goes out."

"I think I'll always carry two torches."

I chuckle. "Not a bad idea. But count anyway. And try to have a tinderbox with you when you enter the passage. You could do it entirely in the dark if you were in such immediate danger there was no time to fetch a tinderbox. There's usually one on the floor beside the box of torches, but I choose never to count on that."

Releasing the latch, I peek around the door to be sure the coast is clear before we step into the undercroft. "Normally, this space is filled – like today – with things Matthias stores here. You don't have to worry about being seen while you wait back here in the shadows for your eyes to adjust before venturing farther out. There are also plenty of things that can be picked up as a prop so that, when you emerge into the courtyard, you look exactly like a servant going about their usual business. It's only for a celebration or big banquet of some sort that this place gets emptied out. That makes emerging from the passage riskier, but you're still way back in the shadows and unlikely to be noticed by anyone in the courtyard. Still, it's always wise to douse the torch before opening the door and to look and listen for sounds of anyone poking around in the undercroft before you actually step out."

When I show him the disguises that hang at the library level, he asks, "And not at the bedchamber level?"

"Grandfather told me there were several reasons. If the king could stay safe in the library until the danger was past, there'd be no reason for him to don a disguise at all. If time is of the essence to get to the safe room, then pausing to don a disguise would waste some of that precious time. And if the king *did* have to change his appearance, then better to leave the fine clothing where it couldn't easily be found rather than leave an obvious clue that the king was dressed differently in some way."

"That makes sense. But, Papa," he asks as we re-enter the library and resume our seats, "why no disguise for the queen?"

"Something I never thought to ask Grandfather. Perhaps someone thought it would be too suspicious for a man and woman to emerge from the undercroft together. Or maybe they just thought a queen would already have gone elsewhere – to a convent maybe – before the danger got so close."

"Or maybe no one thought a queen was worth caring about."

"Sadly, that's all too likely to be true."

"Maybe you should change that."

"Maybe I should."

I make him practice finding the hidden latch inside the hearth until he can do it reliably with his eyes closed. "It's in exactly the same place in the king's bedchamber, but it's most likely – for now at least – that if you ever need to access the passage, it would be from here, since your own room is on this level. I think we should agree that if there's ever a serious threat, you should come here and barricade yourself in.

I'll find you here the same way I did today, whether it's for safety or to let you know the danger has passed."

"That makes sense, Papa."

"There's just one thing, Geoffrey. Should there be knocking on the door – even if you hear my voice asking you to open the door or to come out – stay silent and do nothing. I will never come to you that way of my own accord, so you can be sure I'm under some sort of duress. If the knocking persists – and especially if it seems whoever's outside is trying to break through the door – make your escape. Be as inconspicuous as you can, but head for the monastery – on foot – by night if possible. Warin and Frery will protect you and, as soon as it's safe, they'll get you to the Lakes. From there you can go to Eirwen and her father. Should they be under attack, head for the Territories. If you can't get to Egon or Goron, then go to Korst. In fact, crossing into the Territories over the lowland border with the Peaks might be the safest route, so Korst might very well be your first destination."

Watching both his posture and his facial expression sag, I realize I may just be adding to his anxiety. "Don't misunderstand, Son. I'm not trying to scare you. It just seems wise for us to have a plan in advance should the worst happen. I'm not lying awake nights worrying about that, and neither should you.

"But the most important thing is that you never speak of this to anyone. Doing so could cost your life . . . or mine. It's *that* important."

He sits straighter – his confidence returning, the expression on his face now merely serious – and looks me straight in the eye. "I understand, Papa. You have my solemn word of honor."

I rise and cross the room to raise the barrier back to its usual position. "Come on. Let's go see the horses. I haven't spent any time with Regulus in the last few days."

As we step out into the corridor, Geoffrey says, "Thank you, Papa. I think I might just get a good night's sleep tonight."

Later, in our bedtime conversation, I tell Gwen about revealing the secret to Geoffrey. She's known about the passage since I had to use it to smuggle the contents of the library to the monastery during John's reign, and she saw the entrance from the king's bedchamber the night I used it to smuggle Denis out of the castle when he sought protection during the civil war across the sea. When I relate Geoffrey's suggestion that maybe queens should have disguises hidden in the secret passage, she smiles. "Then he'd be pleased to know I have that well in hand."

"Oh?"

"I had Letty acquire some servants' attire for me and for Alicia. She bought it in the market so no one would be suspicious. They're folded neatly away in my clothes chest."

"Why am I not surprised?" I chuckle.

"Seemed like it might be a good idea, if we should have to flee to the convent, to go there as penitents. Less likely someone would recognize us until we could get to Sister Madeleine."

"And have you mentioned this to Alicia?"

"You *ninny*. Do you think I've completely taken leave of my senses?"

Jasper's next dispatch arrives the following day.

Your Grace,

I can now report that we seem to have the enemy forces contained. The captains of the Peaks forces deployed south of the stream report no attempts to breach or even flank their line nor have they discovered any scouts looking for opportunities. There's still some risk of a reserve hidden somewhere in the north, but the Peaks captains have scouted extensively in that direction and found nothing to concern them. And I'm secure in the knowledge that we still have a large Lakes reserve hidden in the quarry should the situation change.

That means all the enemy forces are now concentrated directly opposite our main force. It's good to know exactly where they are, but it also means we're now facing them in greater numbers than ever before.

Four days ago, we launched a frontal attack. We gambled that they wouldn't be able to resist firing their cannon as soon as we were in range, so we sent a cavalry charge in the form of a wedge against their positions on the north side of the main road. The first four ranks were only eight abreast, so they could maneuver quickly. The remaining ranks lagged somewhat behind the first, intending to stay out of range of the cannon. Our gamble paid off. As soon as the lead ranks were approaching the farthest reach of the cannon, the firing crew sprang into action. The moment they touched fire to the fuse, our lead ranks wheeled right and left and were out of the way by the time the ball was sailing through the air. The following ranks allowed the ball to fall harmlessly then charged at full gallop while the leaders circled back to join them in the rear. We killed all those manning the cannon, wreaked some further havoc in their front lines, and then retreated quickly, with no loss of life – only a few minor injuries.

While they celebrated our retreat, we celebrated having learned exactly what we wanted to know, which was both the range of their cannon and how they were storing their powder. Imagine my delight to discover they had five casks of the stuff arrayed just to one side of the cannon, lined up as if they thought they'd be firing so much that they'd go through cask after cask of it in a single battle. Truth be told, Sire, I'm surprised that the Teuton king would have approved storing so much of it together on the very front lines, so I'm speculating this is something Gunnvor did on his own initiative.

In any event, we took advantage of the situation. That night – an hour after midnight – we sent a few longbowmen forward with a large pail containing hot coals from the cook fires and enough dried grass and small twigs to create a small fire inside the pail – small enough that the light of the fire would be hidden by the sides of the pail. But it was enough to light fire arrows.

The cannon position beside the border marker made it easy for the bowmen to know where the casks of black powder were. Because they were longbows, the men could also stay far enough away that they could easily flee if an arrow found its mark – which at least two of them did.

As soon as one cask exploded, it ignited the others, resulting in a colossal explosion unlike anything one could ever imagine. We could feel the ground shake even in the command tent. Sunrise revealed that the border marker and the cannon had been totally destroyed and bodies – or rather, body parts – littered the ground on the north side of the road.

I expected an angry reprisal, either from Gunnvor's men or from the Teuton camp, and we were prepared. In fact, I rather hoped for a headlong charge down the road and into the maws of our garrison cannons. But nothing happened. They didn't even clean up the carnage or the destroyed cannon position.

We've decided that the failure to clean anything up is intended to make it difficult for us to cross that part of the field. It's also painfully obvious that the Teuton king won't be drawn out and remains content to simply keep us pinned down here.

With that in mind, Your Grace, I've come to the conclusion that our only option is an aggressive assault. Our plans are ready. We need only make some adjustments in deployment. By the time you read this, we'll have launched our offensive. God grant that it goes favorably for us, but it will be a bloody business.

Jasper

Time passes slowly, with little to occupy my days besides anxiety – for Samuel and Edward, for Jasper's next dispatch, for what might be happening across the sea. Perhaps I should have taken the field anyway, despite Jasper's objections. At least I'd have something to occupy my mind. Right, Alfred, I tell myself – then you could've added anxiety about Geoffrey to all your list of worries.

Laurence's men take Gunhild away. Could Samuel be right? Would Laurence really have her done away with? Don't think about that, Alfred. Didn't you learn your lesson about getting too close to the details of that business?

Two days later, another dispatch from Jasper.

Your Grace,

We launched an assault on the enemy forces in the sector north of the road. With that cannon out of commission, it was a more conventional attack – at least until the other cannon was pivoted toward us. The following elements of our formation took some cannon fire until they were able to swing left, out of range.

Our cavalry charged through their lines then wheeled and charged back while the foot soldiers moved forward. The battle then became largely hand-to-hand fighting, with our archers holding their rear ranks at bay.

Oddly, the enemy never ordered a cavalry charge. Nor did the units on the south side of the road make any effort to come to the aid of those under assault. No one moved from the Teuton encampment.

We succeeded in moving their front lines back to the position of their rear ranks and set up our new forward position a hundred yards across the field from the enemy. We're now arrayed northeast-to-southwest across the road to keep all the enemy positions to our front.

I've sent word to the Peaks captains south of the creek to advance to join us, so we can continue to squeeze the enemy into an increasingly smaller space. For now, the Lakes men will remain in the quarry to respond should anyone come around the Peaks flank.

I'm now in no doubt that the Teuton king intends for us to do all the work, keeping the maximum number of their men fresh and rested while wearing us down, hoping we have little left to bring to Denis's aid. To counter that, I'm rotating units every few days, giving everyone a chance for some rest, and will not commit the reserves unless there's absolutely no other choice.

It is, however, my sad duty to report that we lost another two hundred men, including one of my senior captains, in the latest assault. Our best estimate is that the enemy lost three to four times that many. And it's my assessment that these were all Gunnvor's men, based on the fact that there was no real organization and the fighting was essentially every man for himself. Yet another reason to believe the Teuton king is saving both strength and skill for when he believes we've become vulnerable.

Jasper

I fold the page and add it to my collection.

Just after the midday meal, Brother Adam finds me in the library. It's become something of a habit to take refuge there in the afternoons, looking for something as a diversion, though some might question my current choice to read about Alexander's campaigns in Persia. At least it's not *my* war.

"Adam, I'm surprised to see you this early in the day." Typically, he joins us for our family supper, being otherwise occupied during the day.

"Well, Alfred, your lady wife has declared my mission a complete success, so it's probably best I return and relieve my brothers of the burden of doing my work in addition to theirs. Tilda and I will return to the monastery this afternoon. I merely wanted to say goodbye."

"Tilda only, eh? And the pups?"

"Alicia has agreed to raise them for me until the end of the summer, when she has to resume her studies."

I can't suppress a chuckle and he looks at me quizzically. "Somehow I think she'll spend most of the summer hatching a plan to keep them here even after she's back in school."

Adam smiles. "That wouldn't surprise me either. But truth be told, Alfred, she really has quite a knack with them – the young ones at least. Perhaps after all this fighting is over she should come up to the kennel, and we'll see if she has the same skill with the older ones. She's certainly done very well with her own two."

"You may have just hit on the bargain we can make with her when it's time to send the pups back to you. In any event, Adam, thank you for spending the time with her. Now let me arrange for a carriage to take you home."

"Gwendolyn already has that underway. I've only to fetch Tilda and then we'll be off."

Over supper, Alicia dominates the conversation with her plans for her two new charges. I wish I had such a pleasant distraction. And yet, at the same time, I wish I had news about what's happening across the sea.

Be careful what you wish for, Alfred. Cedric returns much sooner than expected. That can't bode well for the situation in Denis's kingdom.

"How did your fisherman know to look for you so soon?" The first thing I ask when I enter the commander's office.

"He didn't, Sire. But Denis wanted you to know the situation straightaway, so he wrote orders for one of their fisherman to take me into the waters where our own fleet often casts their nets, and luck was with us. A boat came alongside us, and the two were held in position with a grappling hook so I could leap from one to the other. The fishermen all laughed at this landman's anxiety about something they apparently do with ease. But I'll tell you right now, sir, I never want to do that again. Damn lucky I didn't end up at the bottom of the sea." Cedric shivers at the memory. "I am *not* cut out to be a seaman."

"Well, I'm grateful you took the risk, Cedric. So, what *is* the situation there?"

"Not good, sir. In truth, rather dire. By the time I got back, Denis's forces had already fallen back on Aleffe Manor. The commander told me it was much sooner than they wanted to, but they realized they were losing too many men and needed their cannons to balance the Teutons' advantage of numbers. The Teutons still seem to have an endless supply of reserves to replenish their ranks no matter how big their losses in any battle.

"Denis gave brief consideration to the idea of using Hedrek's forces to attack the Teutons from the rear but ruled that out pretty quickly. Hedrek would have to fight his way through the occupied Teuton border villages just to get in position to assault the main force and that might reduce his numbers to the point where they wouldn't have much real effect. Add to that those endless reserves, and Hedrek could have found himself surrounded and completely wiped out. In the end, they decided it was far better to leave well enough alone, since the presence of Hedrek's men along the border was keeping a thousand or more Teutons occupied and out of the main battle."

"Good decision," says Carew.

"They managed to pull off their repositioning with very few losses – except for the supplies they had to leave behind – and the array of cannons had the desired effect of halting the Teuton advance in its tracks. But Aleffe Manor is now under siege, and no one knows when the Teutons might launch an all-out offensive to try to take it – when they might calculate that however large the losses to the cannons might be, it's simply the unavoidable cost of taking the prize."

"What's the plan for defense of the manor?" asks Tobin.

"They don't have many options, I'm afraid. They have to make a stand at the manor. Once it falls, the path is open to the port." Every face in the room – mine included, I've no doubt – looks grim. "One thing they *have* done. Their commanders finally prevailed on Denis to leave the field. Yes, Aleffe Manor is a prize, but the chance to capture Aleffe Manor and Denis at the same time would be so irresistible the enemy wouldn't even count the cost. They sent a man disguised as Denis and accompanied by a dozen guards riding back toward the castle town as a decoy. Meanwhile, Denis himself and his guard captain – Crespin, I think his name is – disguised themselves as peasants and blended into the camp followers at the rear. Then, in the dead of night, they slipped away to the monastery. Everyone agreed he'd be reasonably safe there for the time being and that a longer journey in the open – either to the castle or the port – was just too risky.

A couple more guards were to follow in due course by the same route." He pauses, but no one speaks.

"They need our longbowmen, Sire. Even just a couple dozen of them firing from the roof of the manor or the windows of the topmost floor could do a lot to suppress the middle ranks of the enemy forces. Best, of course, would be our entire contingent, but I know Jasper can't give them all up. Beyond that, what they need is men – or a new assailant on the Teuton rear or eastern flank – something to change the balance of numbers. If we could divert their attention to a new threat, Hedrek might even be able to clear out the border."

"Surely, Carew, we can find a dozen or two longbowmen somewhere," I say.

"And if we did, sir," Carew replies, "how would we get them there? The route by way of Owen's cove wastes valuable time – the manor might have fallen by the time our archers got there. We'd have to use a direct crossing."

"What about Cedric's secret route?" asks Tobin.

"I don't want to reveal that," I reply. "It's far too valuable for getting Cedric in and out in complete secrecy." And it's almost certainly one of Laurence's most important infiltration routes, so I won't do anything to jeopardize that.

"Then we only have two options left," says Carew. "Use our fishing fleet or send a ship. Either one is risky since we won't be able to get word to the defenders of the port, who would undoubtedly attack first and ask questions later."

"I could go by way of the secret route and get word to the defenders," says Cedric, "but that, too, will take time."

"Is there any chance, Cedric . . ." I pause, uncertain if I should even suggest this.

"Surely you're not thinking about another transfer on the open sea, sir," he says.

"Well, if it were only, say, twenty men . . ."

"If it were only twenty men, that might work," says Carew. "But what about all their gear? They'll have to take boxes and boxes of arrows, and the last thing an archer wants is for his bowstrings or fletchings to get wet."

"I think," Tobin chuckles, "I'm hearing a hare-brained scheme being hatched."

"If twenty men can make a difference for Denis's commanders, then I think we have to find a way to make it happen, hare-brained or not," I tell them.

"Where are we going to find the men?" Carew asks. "I only have twenty longbowmen here, and I'd be foolish to give them up."

"So we get them elsewhere. I'd wager there are far more than twenty among the Peaks forces camped near the port. We send their twenty best, using our fishing fleet. Cedric, you said the fishermen laughed at your anxiety over crossing from one boat to another. Do you think they could manage to transfer the boxes successfully?"

"I really have no idea, sir."

"Well, we can always call off the operation if the fishermen say they can't do it."

"What if Jasper has been counting on those men at the port if he gets in trouble in the east?" asks Tobin.

"If twenty men are going to be the difference in whether Jasper wins or loses, then I'll order Carew to send his twenty from here. This is as bold – and as unexpected – as what we did to land Hedrek's army, gentlemen. It will work – I can feel it in my bones. And if we're careful, we might even be able to pull it off more than once and give Denis some real help to slow the Teuton advance."

Carew shakes his head slowly in resignation. "If you say so, sir." Tobin just grins.

"Alright, Cedric. I'm putting you in charge of this operation. I'll give you written orders to commandeer as many longbowmen as you need. That way you can use the same orders more than once if it looks feasible. And I'll send a message back to Jasper with his next courier, telling him we're stealing a few of his men."

"Not sure how much confidence I'm going to inspire in the archers, sir, looking like this." He gestures from his head to his feet. He looks scruffier each time he returns.

"I'm sure you'll figure it out," I chuckle. "And I'm sure you'll survive the leap between boats another time."

Cedric rolls his eyes. "If you say so, sir." Carew and Tobin laugh aloud.

"Maybe I can help in my orders. You have a quill and paper at hand, Carew?"

"Of course, sir."

As I take up the quill, another thought occurs to me. "And if you could send to Coliar for my seal, then Cedric can be on his way as soon as we finish here."

"I'll fetch it myself," says Tobin. "No point in tempting someone to mischief."

As I dip the quill in the ink pot then pause a moment to organize my thoughts before writing, Carew lights the flame under the wax warmer.

The bearer of this message is acting under my orders to assemble a group of archers for a purpose that he will reveal only to them and only at the appropriate time. His attire and appearance do not in any way diminish his authority. You are hereby ordered to comply with whatever request he may make and to maintain absolute secrecy about his presence, the nature of his request, and the manner in which you have fulfilled it.

Alfred Rex

I step away from the writing table and invite the others to read. "Will this be sufficient?"

"I think so, sir," says Cedric.

"There'll be gossip among the ranks, naturally, when twenty men go away," says Carew, "but that's unavoidable. That said, their imaginations are unlikely to venture anywhere close to the truth."

At that moment, Tobin returns. When he nods his approval of the message, I pour the wax and affix my seal. As soon as the wax is dry, Cedric folds the page and tucks it into his shirt. "Then I'd best be off, Sire."

"Just pay close attention on the crossing and in their fishing waters, Cedric," says Carew. "Make sure you're not being observed by a Teuton ship. And don't forget the Teutons might not be flying their colors. You have the advantage being in the smaller boats – if an enemy ship is near the horizon, there's no way they'll catch even a glimpse of you."

·　　·　　·　　·　　·

One might think the knowledge that we're trying to do more to help Denis would be reason enough for me to get a good night's sleep. But something else Cedric said keeps gnawing at my mind, making sleep impossible. "What they need is men – or a new assailant on the Teuton rear or eastern flank – something to change the balance of numbers."

Beyond the archers we're going to try to smuggle in, there are no more men I can send right now. Jasper's last dispatch reaffirmed that his progress is slow, complicated by the fact that the Teuton encampment won't budge and remains a constant deterrent to aggressive action against Gunnvor's forces on the south side of the road. Exactly the Teuton king's intention, I'm sure. By now, Jasper will have executed his plan to reveal his Peaks reserve and use them for a flank attack on the Teutons combined with a frontal assault by our own men. His worry is what it will cost. We've already lost substantial numbers, but he's trying valiantly to preserve our strength to go to Denis's aid despite the Teuton's obvious strategy to engender quite the opposite. Jasper had little choice, because doing otherwise merely postpones the time when we can declare victory in the east and turn our attention across the sea.

The losses weigh more heavily on me with each dispatch and each report from Cedric. And tonight, I have no alternative but to confront the choice that's been in front of me from the outset – the choice I've been avoiding in the hope I'd never have to make it. It's within my power to change the balance of numbers. But is it within my conscience?

When we wake the following morning, Gwen says nothing about my restlessness during the night, though she can hardly have failed to notice it. My morning ride does nothing to clear my head, and I find it hard to concentrate on my work, which includes several affirmations of sentences that haven't been reviewed by Rainard, so I need to read each one thoroughly. When I reach the end of the third one, I realize I have no idea what it was about – if the sentence even fits the crime – so I have to start over from the beginning. My mind seems unwilling to concentrate, wandering from the pages in front of me to the battlefield with Jasper – which takes me to an unsettling combination of anticipation and dread for his next dispatch. Even if he's succeeded in finally clearing out the Teuton encampment, his report will include the loss of many more men – ours and those of our allies.

And what of Samuel and Edward? Have they arrived safely in Brandr's court? Or have they been waylaid – or, God forfend, harmed in some way – on the journey? I've no idea, even, how long the journey *should* take, since no one's ever attempted it before.

Then there's Cedric's mission. Can he get the archers to their destination in time for them to make a difference? Maybe it *is* a hare-brained scheme. Something as ordinary as a summer rainstorm at sea could mean they'd have to turn back and wait for the weather to clear. Are the Teutons patrolling those waters? Cedric hasn't reported seeing ships on any of his crossings, but that doesn't mean they're not out there. And if they are, how long will Fortuna smile on us?

I've not told Geoffrey the news from across the sea. I no longer worry about his ability to keep secrets – after all, I've trusted him with the greatest secret of all. But he has enough on his mind thinking about the fight in the east, and I see it weigh on him every time he reads one of Jasper's dispatches. His young mind is tortured by the burden of sending men to their deaths in battle while desperately hoping for a faster victory here so we can rush to the aid of his friend. From time to time, I torture myself with the knowledge that it would be easier for him to bear if his brother were here.

With all the lords away on their estates, even ordinary footsteps echo in the emptiness of the rooms and corridors, the sound rebounding from floor to wall to wall much like the thoughts bouncing around in my head.

Oh, how I'd like to talk with Samuel! His words always seem to bring clarity to my thoughts. Of course, I've no one but myself to blame for his absence. And his mission is crucial. Brandr's actions could turn the tide of this entire conflict.

So could your own, I remind myself. But would it be wrong?

The draught of brandy I pour for myself after supper is twice as large as usual. Perhaps it will help me sleep. But as midnight comes and goes and my mind refuses to settle, it's clear even the extra brandy was insufficient to purpose.

Eventually, Gwen moves nearer and lays a hand on my chest, and I draw her close. "What's troubling you, Alfred?" she asks softly.

"Everything. But mostly the terrible waste of lives because of the ambitions of one man."

"Aren't you doing everything in your power to put an end to that?"

I don't answer straightaway. I've told her most of what happened in the forest two summers ago. But I've never broken my oath to the others who were with me. "Perhaps." I say nothing more for a very long moment. "Or perhaps there's one thing more I could do. I just don't know if it's moral." Another pause, but shorter this time. I don't want her to ask me directly what that thing is. "I just wish Samuel were here. He has a knack for helping me find peace with my decisions."

She strokes my chest as we lie together in silence, her closeness calming me far more than the brandy. At long last, she says, "You know, there are other places where you find peace."

"You mean Father and Grandfather's tombs? That's true. And yet, their voices in my head are fading with time."

"I think what you need is someone you can actually talk with. Someone who can help you with that question of morality."

"Warin?"

"Who better? As long as I've known you, he – and before him, André – have brought you through your darkest times."

I run my hand through her hair and kiss her forehead. Slowly, the questions in my mind recede, and we fall asleep in each other's arms.

●　　●　　●　　●　　●

The ride to the monastery is hardly relaxing, surrounded as I am by guards on high alert. Yet another reason to find a way to end this conflict and return to our usual way of life. Warin's intuition mirrors Gwen's. "I sense there's something troubling you, Alfred. Shall we retire to my study?"

"I'd be grateful, Warin. I mean no disrespect to Frery, but I think this may warrant the sanctity of the confessional, though I'm not looking for absolution – just guidance."

Somehow, the abbot's study seems to exude an air of solemnity appropriate to the gravity of my dilemma. The elaborately carved desk. Shelves filled with scrolls, ledgers, and holy writings. A simple, but elegant stone hearth. High windows that filter the sunlight to a soft glow. It feels like a safe place to unburden myself and find a path to the right choice. The moment we settle into the comfortable chairs before the hearth, I find myself eager to begin. "How much do you know about the current Pope, Warin?"

"Surprisingly little beyond the fact that his elevation to the papacy was most unusual. From archbishop to Pope? But presumably the cardinals knew what they were doing. It also seems he's highly circumspect about anything beyond the rituals of his office." He pauses, his brow furrowed. "Of course, there's that peculiar bit about how Hugo convinced him to launch the inquisition against you. I've never understood how that was achieved. And I find his decision to interfere in the current conflict rather puzzling . . . but perhaps that's because I disagree so strongly with his position."

"Suppose I were to tell you that I know the reason for both."

"Then I would be most curious indeed."

"I'm about to do something I've never done in my life, Warin. I'm going to break an oath I swore to the men who were with me at the time. Deciding to do that has caused me no end of turmoil, but I've come to the realization that you can't guide me on the larger problem without this knowledge."

"I believe this must be where the spirit of the confessional comes into play."

"This Pope has a secret that he'll do anything to protect. Hugo somehow learned the truth and used it to manipulate His Holiness to launch the inquisition."

"Presumably you learned this from the Teuton king at that meeting in the forest."

"Aye. Not only that, the Teuton told us precisely what the secret is. The Pope is not a scion of the family whose name he bears. He is in fact a bastard adopted into that family and has passed himself off throughout his life as a member of the Roman nobility. The Teuton king didn't say so explicitly, but I'm convinced the Pope is Teuton – most likely a cousin or even a half-brother of the king himself. How else would the king be able to force the Holy Father to call off the inquisition?"

"That's certainly one explanation, but might there not be others?"

"I'd have been willing to accept that possibility until the Pope intervened to prevent Denis's ally from coming to his assistance in the current conflict. There's no doubt in my mind that the Teuton king ordered the Pope to guarantee him a free hand in his fight with Denis – so he doesn't even have to consider the possibility of a second front in the south."

"That's a strong assertion, Alfred. And yet, based on what you've told me about the Teuton king, a credible one."

"And something I could use to bring a swift end to this conflict. But I struggle with whether it would be right to do so. Joining the ranks of venal men who manipulate Christ's vicar on earth for their own ends flies in the face of everything I believe about honor and morality. But so does the appalling waste of lives that's already happened and will only grow worse, just because of one man's ambition."

"You've made difficult choices before, Alfred. And in my observation, they've always been the right ones."

"But I'm not sure I've ever faced a choice where both options feel dishonorable . . . distasteful . . . immoral, even."

"Then tell me. What would be your motivation – what would be in your heart – if you were to reveal your knowledge to the Pope and try to compel him to lift his threat on the Kingdom East of Rome?"

"Saving lives. Giving a young man a chance to become the king I'm certain he can be. Giving his people a chance to embrace him and not fall into the mistaken conviction that *he's* the cause of their suffering. Preventing, I hope, another attempt to dismember or even overrun a kingdom that has survived for centuries."

"I hear nothing dishonorable or immoral in those motives. So why do you shy away?"

"What would it say about *me*, Warin, that I would stoop to the level of Hugo or that I would follow in the footsteps of the man responsible for all the ills currently befalling us? Who am I to threaten God's representative on earth? Is that not hubris beyond all measure?"

Warin doesn't answer straightaway – merely props his chin on his steepled fingers. At long last, he breaks the silence. "Do you remember, Alfred, your last visit with André? When you finally understood those truths about your Uncle Rupert."

"Aye."

"And do you remember what he told you? I know I do – I can still hear his voice in my head. 'You're right,' he said, 'that your uncle has it within himself to be ruthless if that's what is absolutely necessary. But that in no way changes the fact that he's a decent, honorable, thoughtful, wise, and compassionate man who cares deeply for his kingdom and who is worthy of your respect and admiration. It's the ability to be all of those things – even including the ruthless part – that makes a man suited to kingship. And when the good far outweighs the ruthlessness, that is what makes for an exceptional king.'

"Perhaps, Alfred, the real question you face is less about the choice of how to act than about whether you have it within you to be ruthless . . . and whether this is the right time."

Another long silence.

"There's something else that occurs to me," says Warin. "As I think back on your descriptions of those encounters in the forest with the Teuton king, I recall your saying more than once that he's always taking the measure of his potential adversaries. That the only thing he respects is strength. And that everything he does is purposeful. If that's true, then it was no slip of the tongue that he gave you the knowledge of how to manipulate the Pope. Perhaps even now he's waiting to see if you have the strength to use it. Perhaps the only way to hold him in check is for the strength of your resolve to match the strength of his ambition."

The silence resumes as I contemplate the truth of Warin's words. And in doing so, something else occurs to me. "Perhaps that was the secret Goscelin knew."

"I think, Alfred, that you've known the answer all along, but your honor to the oath you swore has stood in the way of your seeking affirmation. I'd wager not even your wife knows the entirety of what you've been contemplating."

"You know me too well, Warin," I chuckle.

He smiles. "Well enough. And that's precisely why you will always find sanctuary here, whether from the demons of the world or the demons of your mind." Then he adds, "Have you spoken with Rupert about your dilemma?"

"No. And now I wonder if maybe that's because I already knew what he would say."

"Let me offer you one other thought, Alfred. Unless this Pope is completely devoid of any moral compass, he may actually welcome a way out of the situation he finds himself in as a result of his ill-advised decision to lie about his birth. Find a way to release him from the hold others have over him, and there'll be no reason to threaten or to compel."

By the time we arrive back at the castle, my mind is made up. I find Carew alone in the commander's office. "Any idea where Tobin might be?"

"I gave him the afternoon off to spend some time with his family. He's only just left – wouldn't even be halfway to the town by now. I could send someone to fetch him back if you'd like."

"What I have to say, you both need to hear. And it's probably best if you hear it together."

While we wait for Tobin's return, I steer the conversation toward odds and ends – hope that Cedric has been successful, when we might next hear from Jasper, Alicia's frustration with only being able to ride her pony in the training arena, how Geoffrey's faring with all his mates and his brother away. "He asked me to arrange some practice swordplay for him, you know," says Carew.

"He hasn't mentioned that."

"I was happy to oblige. Talent like that doesn't need to get rusty. He didn't say it in so many words, but I'm pretty sure what he's thinking is that he needs to be prepared should the worst happen and he actually has to defend himself from intruders."

"I suppose I should be proud of him . . . and in truth, I am . . . but there's another part of me that's deeply saddened by the fact that he should even have to consider such a thing at his age."

Just at that moment, Tobin steps through the door. A crisp bow then, "Your Grace. The messenger said it was urgent."

"Relax, Tobin," I tell him. "It's just the three of us – take a seat. It's more important than urgent. And as I told Carew, something I think it best you hear together." I pause for a moment before proceeding.

"It's about the oath we five swore not to reveal what the Teuton king told us about the Pope's origins. I've come to the decision that I have to break it – that I have no choice if we're to end this war and put paid to the Teuton's ambitions once and for all."

The look that passes between my companions is intense – almost as if they're having a silent conversation, one man's mind to the other. It's Tobin who finally speaks. "Truth be told, sir, since Jasper's last report – and the news Cedric brought – we've been talking about how we might convince you to do just that. Not where we could be overheard, of course," he rushes to add, "but when we were sure no one was within earshot. We think that knowledge was a piece of the Teuton's strategy all along and that if you don't use it, he'll be convinced he has free rein to run roughshod over anyone and any place, anytime he pleases."

"And the sooner you do something, the better," Carew adds.

I wonder if the relief I feel is visible in my posture and my expression. "Then you'll be pleased to know I have a plan . . . though I suspect, Carew, you might be more than a little dismayed by what I have in mind."

Their next words come almost simultaneously. "Another harebrained scheme."

"I prefer to think of it as brilliant subterfuge." That gets a laugh from both of them.

"Very well, sir," says Carew. "I'll hold my tongue for the moment. Tell us first *what* you're going to do. Then maybe the risk will make more sense."

"A personal audience with the Pope."

"And what makes you think the Pope will grant *you* an audience?" asks Carew.

"He probably won't. But he'll almost certainly grant one to the Duchess of Lamoreaux, especially if it's requested by her father's cousin the cardinal."

Tobin's brow is furrowed. "So you're proposing to reveal the secret to her and hope she can persuade the Pope?"

"No. I have to speak to him myself. That's the only way to be certain he fully grasps the gravity of what's at stake. And this is where the subterfuge comes into play. From here to Lamoreaux, I travel alone as a peasant using one of Owen's fishing boats to cross the sea. I'll get Owen to captain the vessel, and there's absolutely no doubt he'll make sure his crewmen keep their mouths shut. From Lamoreaux, I'll travel as Lucia's manservant, riding inside her carriage to minimize the chances of someone seeing me. She'll arrange the audience with the Pope and take me with her on the day."

Carew looks thoughtful. "It's mostly a good plan. Well, except for that 'traveling alone' part. When you go, I go with you. As far as Owen's anyway."

"If you're gone that long, even the servants will know something is up and the gossip will begin."

"That's going to happen anyway once people realize *you're* gone," says Tobin.

"Which is why we need to put on a big show of Gwen and me going to the monastery in a carriage. I won't go, of course, but when Gwen returns, she'll put it about that I've decided to stay in seclusion there for a bit to contemplate how to bring the war to an end. I'll slip away in all the activity surrounding the queen's return."

"And I'll go with you." Carew is adamant. "Tobin will be in charge here, and he'll make it clear I've gone west to coordinate with Goron."

"And that's as far as you go. Once I'm behind Goron's lines, I'll be perfectly safe. Then you can return using the trail to the reservoir."

"Surely," says Tobin, "he'll be recognized at the reservoir, which means the rumors will just start there and spread east."

"He can stay close to the base of the low hills and circumvent the reservoir and village completely, joining up with the main road west of where the track to the reservoir branches off. And if you make that transit at night, Carew, it's very unlikely anyone will notice. Two men will disappear into the Territories, and neither will return on that route."

No one speaks for what feels like a quarter of an hour but is probably little more than two or three moments. I'm asking a lot of these two men who bear the responsibility for protecting my life. Finally, Carew breaks the silence. "You're not going to believe this, sir . . ." He pauses for effect. "But I think it's a risk we have to take. We can probably win in the east. But how soon and at what cost? Jasper's doing everything possible, but the longer we keep losing men in that fight, the weaker the forces we can eventually send to Denis's aid. Meanwhile, the loss of lives across the sea continues, and if they can't hold out until we get there . . ."

Tobin nods. "I agree."

"When do you want to leave, sir?" asks Carew.

"The day after tomorrow. I don't think we can get everything in place before then, but I don't want to wait any longer. And, Tobin, you're not going to be able to go home to your family while Carew's gone, so move them into the castle. Nurse can help with your daughter, and I'm sure the queen and Lady de Courcy would enjoy Sarah's company."

"Very well, sir," says Carew, "the day after tomorrow it is."

I rise in preparation for leaving and they both jump to their feet. "This was the easy part. Now I have to go tell my wife."

•   •   •   •   •

I don't know what I expected Gwen's reaction to be, but complete silence was *not* on the list. She sits with her hands clasped in her lap, her expression neutral . . . bland almost. I can't deny this is a lot to take in. At long last, she says, "And this is what Warin advised?"

"I wouldn't say that. All he did was help me see there was nothing immoral in what I knew all along I had to do – what's been on my mind since Jasper's last dispatch."

"Alfred, have you forgotten what happened to Harold when he ventured into another king's realm unannounced?"

"This is different. Denis knows what we learned in the forest and why I might choose this course of action. I'm trying to save his kingdom."

"Do you hear yourself, Alfred? That's exactly what Harold thought, but it didn't keep him from losing his life."

"Harold was meddling where he shouldn't have. I have an obligation to do everything I can to support Denis. An obligation we've spoken of openly. An obligation even the Teutons know about."

"What you say makes sense in my head, Alfred. It's just going to take me a while to convince my heart – or maybe it's my gut. And the day after tomorrow? I don't know if I can make my peace with it by then."

"I've waited too long, my love. Too many men have died – both here and across the sea. I can't wait any longer."

Rising from her chair in the sitting area of our bedchamber, she joins me on the couch and comes into my arms, her head on my chest. "And will you tell Geoffrey everything? I mean . . . in case the worst . . ." She can't bring herself to verbalize the rest of the thought.

"I've thought about that. And no, I'll only tell him I'll be away for a time, trying to put an end to the war. If the unthinkable should happen and he were to be kidnapped, he couldn't reveal what he doesn't know."

"But . . ." She pauses for a long time, as if reluctant to continue. At long last, she says, "But if . . . if you don't come back, Alfred . . . how will he know . . .?"

"Tobin and Carew were in the forest with me that day. They know everything. Neither of them will breathe a word of it unless it's absolutely necessary. But they can advise him. And so can Samuel when he returns." She clings to me and I hold her close. "But I *will* be back, my love. I have even more to come back for than when I was taken captive."

When I put my fingers under her chin and lift her head for a kiss, her eyes are glistening with moisture. I kiss her eyelids gently, then my lips find her mouth in a long, passionate kiss before whispering in her ear, "I *will* be back."

Carew and I watch from the barracks as Gwen's carriage approaches the sentry gates. When it passes inside, we start making our way on foot down the track that patrols use to access the road. With our caps pulled low in front, we keep our heads down and our gait unhurried. Carew feigns a limp, and I hunch my shoulders to appear both older and shorter than I really am. A nondescript satchel hangs from my shoulder, and Carew carries a cloth bag containing a loaf of bread and some dried meat. We both have daggers hidden in our boots. The satchel will go with me all the way to Lamoreaux – part of my disguise. Carew's well-worn pack is waiting with the horses, farther up the road, out of sight of the sentry towers. He'd bought a couple of sturdy horses from the stable in the town and hidden them, hobbled, in a small grove along with a couple of well-used but still-functional saddles and bridles.

Once we judge that the sentries have dismissed us as no threat, Carew drops his limp and we pick up our pace, arriving at the grove less than half an hour after leaving the barracks. With all the lush grass in the grove, the horses haven't wandered and we get them saddled and their hobbles off in no time. Carew slings his pack on his back and ties the sack of food to the front of his saddle, and we're on our way.

Though we're careful not to overtravail the horses, we take advantage of the long summer days to start out at first light and ride until almost sundown before making camp. Having decided on this course and knowing the journey all the way to Rome is a long one, urgency has replaced anxiety in my mind. When we pass the turnoff for Ernle Manor, I feel Juliana's presence there tug at my heartstrings, but we press on. By now we both look rather scruffy, with five days' growth of stubble and our clothes dusty from sleeping on the ground at night – just the look I need for the rest of the trip to Lucia's manor.

Neither of us has been particularly inclined to conversation up to now, but when we take to the fields to skirt the border village, Carew reveals his plan. "I don't know exactly how much farther it is to Goron's lines, so we should be ready. For this to work, we need to avoid the command tents and pass through the lines well off on the flank. Keep your cap low and your eyes down, and resume that old-man look you used when we left the castle. And let me do all the talking."

Within half an hour, the encampment is in sight. As we approach, a young soldier quickly grabs a mount and trots out to stop us. "What are you doing here? And where are you going?" he demands.

"My uncle," Carew inclines his head toward me, "came to fetch me home. My mother is dying and she begged to see me one last time."

"Then you should go that way," the soldier points north, "up to the main road so the sentries can pass you through."

"I don't have time for that. We may be too late already, and if we have to go the long way round . . ." Carew manages to sound desperate. "Please. I'm begging you. Just let us pass. We mean no harm. All I want is to grant my mother's dying wish."

"What is in that pack?"

"My good clothes. On account of I'm sure there'll be a funeral."

"And this man?" the soldier points to me.

"My uncle. Like I said, he came to fetch me. He doesn't hear so well – he's going deaf." And then he raises his voice almost to a shout. "You said we had to hurry, right, Uncle?" I nod. Resuming his normal volume, Carew adds, "Please, man. Please just let us pass. I promise you we'll be no trouble."

The young soldier looks us both over in silence then finally says, "Alright, follow me. I will lead you through. But you keep your mouths shut and your hands on your reins where everybody can see."

When we emerge out the other side of the camp, the young soldier stays on guard, watching us trot away. Carew turns to wave a thank you before we urge the horses to a canter and keep our backs turned. Once we've ridden far enough to be out of sight, we slow to a walk and Carew swivels in his saddle, checking to see if there's any pursuit. Satisfied there is none, we point our horses' heads northwest, angling toward the main road.

"Luck was with us back there," says Carew. "A more experienced man wouldn't have been so easy to convince. He'd have wanted to search my pack and your satchel at the very least. Might have insisted we go up to the main checkpoint."

"Well, that's why you picked the flanks, wasn't it?"

He laughs. "You know, sir, you might have made a pretty decent commander if the tables had been turned."

As the sun begins to lower in the western sky, we reach the spot where the track to the reservoir turns off the main road – the spot where we must go our separate ways. We rein the horses to a halt. "Are you sure you won't let me come with you to Owen's?" Carew asks.

"You've done your job, Carew. I'll be perfectly safe from here on. What I need now is for you to be back at the castle keeping my family safe."

He extends his arm and we exchange the warrior's greeting. "Godspeed, sir. Do what you have to do and get home as quickly as you can. We'll none of us sleep soundly until you do." And with that, he turns his horse's head and starts up the track as I urge my mount to the trot, heading west.

. . . . .

I waste no time getting to Owen's stronghold, all the while planning for how to manage my approach. I'm well known there, having spent almost a month as a prisoner in his tower while he and Ralf went off on some escapade having to do with a squabble among the western lords. But I really need to speak to Owen privately and enlist his help to cross the sea and to maintain the secrecy of my journey. Halfway down the hill, I dismount and lead the horse into the woods, hang his bridle on a branch, and hobble him so he won't wander far. Walking on toward the fortress, I resume my old-man posture and mannerisms.

As I'd hoped, a sentry comes out to stop me long before I get anywhere close to the entrance. "State your business or be on your way," he says.

"I need to see Lord Owen." I try to make my voice sound somewhat frail.

"And what business could the likes of you possibly have with my lord?"

"Just tell him an old friend is here and needs to speak with him. I'll wait." I point toward a big rock at the edge of the woods. "I'll be just over there. But tell him, please. Tell him an old friend needs his help."

Now I just have to hope the sentry actually does go in search of Owen and delivers my message rather than going back to his post and laughing with his fellow guards about the crazy old peasant and his silly claims. Patience, Alfred. You may have to sit on this rock a long time before they decide you're not going to leave and finally fetch Owen to do something about you.

As it turns out, the wait isn't all that long. When Owen emerges from the entrance, it seems – though I can't quite make out the words at this distance – as if he's chastising the sentry for not handling the intruder himself. And it appears the sentry might be trying to defend himself when he shakes a finger toward where I'm perched on the rock and draws his master's attention in my direction.

Owen storms up the trail, and I can see the fury on his face as he draws nearer. Gesticulating up the path, he shouts, "Didn't you hear my sentry tell you to be on your way? Off with you then."

I maintain my perch, willing him to come closer, waiting to speak until he's within earshot of a quiet conversation that won't be overheard by those watching from below. "I'm sure he told you I said I was an old friend." When he steps between me and the watchers, I remove my cap and add, "Sit with me, Owen. I need your help. But I don't need your people to know who I am." The expression on his face is priceless. I quickly don my cap while he clambers up to sit beside me on the rock.

"Alfred? Is it really you? You look as scruffy as when Ralf first brought you here . . . but maybe not as scrawny." He grins at his own jest. "What on earth brings you here alone and looking for all the world like some sort of ruffian?"

"Something exceedingly important that I can't do without your help. I think I've figured out a way to put an end to the Teutons' madness, but to do so, I have to get to Rome. And I have to do it in the utmost secrecy."

"And you need a way to cross the sea." Owen grasps the situation immediately.

"Aye. I do."

"Well, it is too late in the day to start now. But we can go at first light. I dare not invite you inside – too big a risk of someone recognizing you."

"I agree. I can easily manage another night's camping."

"Make your way down toward the docks, but stay in the woods. There's a little lean-to that we use for spare nets. You can stay out of sight if you stay behind it. But be ready to go as soon as there's any hint of dawn. I'll captain the boat myself, and the two men I'll bring for crew are completely trustworthy. If I tell them never to breathe a word of the journey, you can count on them to comply. Just stay silent, keep your cap down, and don't look at them."

"That won't be a problem. But there's something else I need to ask, Owen. When I return, it will probably be on one of our ships, but I don't want to sail any closer to my kingdom than this. Can you think of a way for me to come ashore here without having to swim?"

He furrows his brow in thought for a long moment. "The ship could lower a boat and you could row in . . . but if it's high tide, the rocks will be submerged and you would never find the channel. If you hit a rock, you'd be swimming anyway . . . assuming you survived the crash." He strokes his chin, thinking some more. "Have your ship captain heave to off my cove and run up your banner. I can post a lookout, and the minute we spy the banner, I will come out and fetch you myself. I assume you will want your return to be a secret too?"

"Aye, I think so."

"How long will this journey be? I would rather not raise suspicions by posting a lookout sooner than needed."

"Three weeks for certain. Possibly as long as four. I intend to travel fast . . . in both directions."

"Very well. First light in the morning. As soon as you see me, scurry onto the boat."

"Thank you, Owen. Oh, and there's a horse tethered in the woods about halfway up the hill. Can you look out for him while I'm away? I'll need him to get back home. And if I shouldn't return, he's yours. He's nothing special, but he's sturdy and reliable."

Owen hops off the rock. "You will return, Alfred. You always do. Now do you need any food for tonight?"

I pat the side of my satchel. "I'm set for tonight. But a sack of food for the journey onward wouldn't go amiss – just enough for three or four days."

"Alright then." He turns to walk out of the woods but looks over his shoulder to add quietly, "First light."

· · · · ·

I hardly sleep at all – merely dozing now and then – so anxious am I that I might miss the first hint of morning light. The moment Owen sets foot on the dock, I hurry down to join him and he tucks me away in the prow with the bag of food he's brought – which I quickly stow in my satchel.

"The crew will arrive momentarily, but before they do . . ." he says. "I was thinking last night. You'll need a horse on the other side. Do you have money?"

"Aye."

"And do you speak the language?"

"Well enough."

"Then this is what you should do. As soon as we dock, get off the boat. Use that old-man act you put on for my sentry. Don't speak to anyone. Don't look back. Just make your way straight into the town. Don't try to buy a horse there – people would remember and talk about a stranger coming off a fishing boat and buying a horse. There's a decent-size village about five miles south where you should be able to get a mount. Keep up the old-man act until you get well clear of the town. Once you're sure no one can see you, change your appearance completely. Push that cap to the back of your head. Maybe put the satchel on the opposite shoulder. Tuck that shirt into your trousers. Walk at a really brisk pace, like a young man who knows exactly where he's going and is in a hurry to get there. You should be safe then. And, Alfred?"

"Aye?"

"Don't pay too much for the horse. Chances are it will be a nag anyway."

Bootsteps on the dock send Owen scurrying to the mast to check the rigging. "Thank you, Owen," I whisper to his back.

On the other side, I follow Owen's instructions to the letter but can't avoid noticing one of the dockmen pointing at me and shouting to Owen, "Who's that?"

"Just some poor sod who claims he's trying to get to his family somewhere over here. I couldn't make out quite where he said they lived. Most likely some tiny village somewhere. Anyhow, didn't want him hanging around my dock, so I brought him across. Happy to see the back of him."

It's easy enough to find the road leading south from the market square. After about a quarter hour of trudging along like a worn-out old man, I spy a small copse of trees just off the right side of the road. Perfect. A quick survey of my surroundings to be sure no one's watching and I step into the shelter of the trees and quickly make the changes Owen suggested. God's beard, how good it feels to stand straight and stretch the muscles of my back and shoulders! Following a quick piss, I emerge from the copse buttoning up my trousers so any passerby will assume that was my sole purpose for being in the trees in the first place.

A gentle breeze keeps the air pleasant enough for quite a brisk pace, and I arrive at my destination in a bit over an hour. Fortunately, the stable is right at the north edge of the village, so I don't have to waste time looking for it.

"That mare over there is the only thing I have right now," says the stable master in response to my inquiry. "She's not much to look at, but she has a sweet disposition unless you run her too hard. If you do that, she has a dozen ways to dump you on your arse."

We walk over to where the mare is tied to a post near the water trough. She's chestnut all over – not even any white markings on her face – a bit sway-backed – and her dusty coat could use a good brushing. I look at her teeth to try to judge how old she might be then feel each of her legs from the hoof to where it joins her body. No heat, so she's probably sound. A quick check of her hooves reveals she was recently shod.

"How much?" I ask the stable master. We haggle for a bit – just for show on my part – I'd have been satisfied to pay what he asked, but Owen's words rang in my head. "I'll need a saddle too," I tell him.

"Don't have a spare. A man usually brings his own saddle. But you can have that bridle hanging over there. It was my son's. He left it here when he went off to live on the farm with his new bride. Guess he doesn't need it on account of he never came back for it."

I have a look at the bridle. It could use a cleaning, but the leather's not cracked and the stitching looks sound. "Alright, I'll give you a couple more coins for it." I retrieve a small purse from the pocket of my trousers and make a show of counting the coins into the stable master's hand – and an even bigger show of feeling around inside the purse as if there's nothing left in it. Best not to let anyone think I might be carrying money worth stealing.

"Now, do you have a brush I can use to clean up her coat?"

He produces a well-used but still functional brush from a basket on the floor, and I lead the mare outside to brush her down. Dust flies everywhere, so I take extra time making sure she's cleaned up enough that a rider on her back won't irritate her skin. Once the bridle's on, I remove the lead rope from around her neck and hand it to the stable master. It wouldn't normally be my choice to go without it, but there's no room for it in my satchel and, in any event, I do have another set of hobbles to keep her from wandering too far at night.

The stable master gives me a leg up, and I walk the mare around a bit to see how she responds. She seems compliant enough, so we'd best be on our way. Then a thought occurs to me. "Does she have a name?" I ask.

"Not that I'd know about. I just call her 'Mare.'"

"Very well, then, Mare, time to go."

We leave the village behind at a walk. But at this pace, it will take far too long to reach Lamoreaux. Alright, Alfred, I tell myself. You fancy yourself such good horseman. Let's see if you can stay on bareback. I squeeze Mare's ribs and she immediately responds with a trot – the roughest trot I think I've ever tried to sit. Despite my best efforts, I'm bouncing around on her back and in very real danger of bouncing off. I squeeze again, and she gives me a canter that's almost as smooth as Altair's. That's more like it. I wonder how long she'll agree to keep up the pace?

Quite some time, as it turns out. When she finally slows to a walk, I give her a good pat on the neck and tell her, "You and I are going to get along just fine, Mare." We continue until I'm certain she's cooled down sufficiently from her run then find a place beside a little stream and make camp.

Sometime after sunrise, I'm roused by soft nickers and Mare's muzzle nudging me awake. The grass all around has been closely cropped. I wish I'd thought to buy some oats from the stable master. Ah, well, can't be helped. I also wish I'd thought to choose a campsite with an old stump or something to serve as a mounting block. That can't be helped either. Best I can do is a rock beside the stream. It's less than a foot high, but with Mare standing in the stream bed, it's enough for me to sprawl across her back and then get my right leg over and into a sitting position so we can be on our way.

Avoiding Mare's trot entirely, a combination of walk and canter brings us to Lucia's manor late in the afternoon two days later – and to another challenge – this time to get past her guards. But I'm prepared for this one. Cantering up to the gate, I rein Mare to a quick stop and call out, "Hey – you there – open the gate. Message for the duchess."

The man takes his own sweet time about it, but I wait patiently, as any messenger would, and eventually ride up to the entrance where a servant emerges from the front door. Reaching into my satchel, I produce the message Gwen had prepared and sealed for me before I left home. "I'll wait," I tell him. "In case there's a reply."

Eventually, the servant returns. "My lady says I am to bring you to her. You can tether your horse just there." He points to a rail beside a stone trough filled with water. I tie Mare loosely so she can easily lower her head to drink. "Now follow me," says the servant.

Seated beside the windows in her spacious sitting room, Lucia shows no reaction until the servant leaves, closing the door behind him, and we hear his footsteps retreat down the corridor. Then she jumps to her feet, her expression a combination of surprise and delight, and crosses the room to give me a quick embrace. "My God, Alfred, it really is you beneath all that grime and shaggy beard."

She takes my hand and leads me to a chair opposite hers. "You're right about the grime, my dear. Maybe I shouldn't soil your nice cushions."

"Maybe you're right at that. Is it permissible to offer a king a seat on the floor?" We both laugh. "Better still, let's get you cleaned up. Gwen's message said only that you'd explain everything, but I think maybe that can wait until you've had a bath and some fresh clothes. Let me just call a servant . . ."

"Before you do, you need to know how important it is that no one know who I am. Too much is at stake for that to happen."

"Then you're simply my cousin. You've had a very long ride from my homeland bringing an urgent message. I think maybe it's best if we don't call you a servant because then there would be gossip about why I would give you a nice room."

"That should work. As for the fresh clothes, I have one change of clothes in my satchel, but there are other items in there that I can't risk losing so I don't want to leave it unattended. Can you arrange that?"

"Leave it to me." I follow her to the door where she calls for her steward. "Alphonse, this is my cousin." She makes for the staircase, the steward close at her side, as I bring up the rear. "I'm going to put him in the big corner room on the first floor. He's had a long ride, and I'm sure I don't have to tell you he's in need of a bath." At the top of the stairs she turns left. "And maybe you could get the servant to trim his beard and hair – tidy things up a bit." She opens the last door on the right, and we enter a spacious bedchamber. I lay my satchel on the bed and walk to the window, which overlooks the magnificent gardens at the back of the manor. "Oh, and Alphonse," she drops her voice conspiratorially, "my cousin's always been a bit of an eccentric. Prefers simple clothing and simple food. His family's always chided him for not dressing well, but it's just his way, so don't be put off by whatever he chooses to wear."

"Of course, my lady. Now, with your permission, I'll go get things underway . . . and see to his horse. May I ask . . . is riding bareback another of his eccentricities?"

I come to Lucia's rescue. "No, my good man, just an unfortunate bit of bad luck. I stupidly chose to have my horse swim across a river rather than going the extra mile to the bridge. The cinch broke midstream and I slid off the horse. Then I had to choose between catching up to my horse or trying to get to the saddle that was quickly washing downriver."

"Ah, I see," says the steward and makes his exit.

"Get your clothes out of the satchel, then give it to me," says Lucia. "I'll take it up to my apartment where I can hide it away." My task completed, she hugs the satchel to her chest and makes for the door. "When you've freshened up, join me in the garden. We can speak freely there without being overheard."

A half hour later – clean for the first time in over a week and with my beard neatly trimmed and hair properly combed, though a bit longer than I usually wear it – I find Lucia reading a book in a little pavilion at the center of the garden. "I must say, you look ever so much better." She closes the book and sets it aside. "You know . . . if someone didn't know you well, they'd be hard-pressed to be certain who you are, in those clothes and with the beard."

"You should see my imitation of an old man who's hard of hearing and doesn't get around as fast as he used to."

"Well, it's served you well if it's gotten you here in secrecy. Gwen's missive did say secrecy was essential. And I've burned her message, just in case you were wondering. So . . . tell me what this is all about and how I can help."

It takes most of an hour for me to bring her into the picture on the state of the war, what I've decided I *must* do, and how she can help me. Her expression grows first sad and then seriously determined as she listens. When I finish, she's silent at first, but it's clear she's thinking things through.

"It sounds like there's no time to lose, so we should leave tomorrow."

"Can you be ready so soon?"

"We'll leave just after the midday meal. That will give me time to pack and make the arrangements. We'll take the small carriage – it's not as comfortable as the large one, but with four horses pulling it, we can travel much more quickly. And my coachman will know where we can change horses so we can keep moving without having to worry about overtaxing the animals. The story that you brought an urgent message gives us all the reason we need to travel fast. And your being my cousin is a much better explanation for you to be traveling inside the carriage than the notion of a manservant being allowed to do so.

"That takes care of getting there. And when we arrive, I'll summon my cousin, the cardinal, straightaway. I don't really know why, but I have a feeling he'll be able to help us with more than just arranging the audience. Of course, you'll have to have much nicer clothes for the audience. You have to be dressed as a king."

"But I don't have time to wait for a tailor to make something suitable. I have a crown in my satchel and that will just have to suffice."

"Hmmm . . . it's a shame I gave away all of Charles's clothes. On the other hand, they were really much too flamboyant for you and for such a serious business. But I may have another solution. We'll have supper in the small sitting room in my apartment – the double doors to the left at the top of the second staircase. I should know by then if my idea will work. In the meantime, amuse yourself here in the gardens or walking around the grounds or perusing my little library. It's the door just opposite the room where you were first shown in."

"There's one thing I'd really like to do."

"Oh?"

"Do you think Alphonse could find me some carrots and show me to the stable? That horse I rode in was just an ordinary mare I bought in a village stable, but we seemed to form some sort of connection. I'd like to thank her for getting me here quickly before I leave her in her new home."

"Of course."

"And, Lucia . . . see that she's not misused. She has a really uncomfortable trot, but the rest of her gaits are nice and she's remarkably willing."

"You can count on it, Alfred."

When I join Lucia for supper, there's a rather elegant set of clothing arrayed on her bed. "Where on earth did you come up with that?"

She laughs softly. "Well, it isn't quite as fine as it looks, but I think it might just do – if it fits." She holds the shirt up to my back, checking the width of the shoulders, then holds the trousers to my waist. "You might have to cinch them up a little. And they're definitely a bit short, but since they'll be tucked into your boots, I don't think there'll be a problem."

"So where on earth did you come up with this?" I ask again.

"There's a troupe of mummers who play here and in the village rather frequently in the summer. One of their plays features a bumbling aristocrat who gets a lot of laughs. Earlier in the summer, they lost a couple of their members to a different troupe. They asked if they could leave their trunks of costumes and props here until they found some new actors or got their plays reworked for the smaller group."

"Fortune certainly seems to be favoring this venture . . . so far, at least."

"Now, let's go in to supper. It'll just be potage and bread. Simple fare for my eccentric cousin." She laughs and leads the way into the sitting room.

On the journey to Rome, we spend the nights in remote country inns – one night we even sleep in the carriage – to avoid Teuton spies. When we reach the Eternal City, Lucia takes rather sumptuous lodgings in a large house just across the river from the Castel Sant'Angelo. We have the entire first floor to ourselves. "Quite grand," I tell her when our host leaves after showing us around. "Unfortunately, what little money I brought with me was spent on my horse. I've only a couple of plain coins to contribute."

"Come now, Alfred. I'm a *very* wealthy woman. With my husband's fortune, my mother's, Charles's personal fortune, and the income from the duchy . . . I can *easily* afford for us to stay here in comfort."

She wastes no time sending a message to the cardinal, nor, it seems, does he, arriving less than half an hour later. The moment he walks through the sitting room door with his arms outstretched, Lucia brightens and calls out "Uncle Lorenzo!" as she hurries into his embrace.

"*Bambina mia!*" He breaks the embrace and holds her at arm's length. "You are more lovely than ever. And it has been far too long since you were last here." She seems about to offer some comment, but he waves her off. "Oh, I know it has only been two years, but at my age . . ."

Judging by the gray in his hair and the lines around his eyes, I would guess he's well into his sixth decade. But he stands straight and tall, with no hint of an old man's posture or halting movement. His countenance, however, is his most striking feature. Rarely have I seen such an expression of utter kindness and benevolence.

"And you have a guest," he says to Lucia.

"All in good time, Uncle."

He extends his hand to me, and I kiss his ring. "Eminence."

The cardinal crosses the room to a chair opposite where Lucia had been sitting. "May I, my dear?"

"Of course, Uncle." She resumes her own seat. "I'm afraid, Uncle Lorenzo, this visit isn't entirely one of pleasure. There's something of urgency and importance we must talk with you about, but I've no way of knowing – in a strange house – where listening ears might be lurking. Might we come with you back to your home?"

"Not a good idea, I'm afraid. In a cardinal's home, there are always spies. And one never knows if they belong to the Pope, a fellow cardinal, or some scheming nobleman . . . or even if all three are represented at once."

"Perhaps a nearby church then?"

"In Rome, my dear, even the churches have ears. But I do know of a place we can talk in complete privacy. There's what must once have been a lovely villa a couple of miles out in the countryside – it would have been much farther from the city walls in ancient times. It's a ruin now. The story is that, as the barbarians approached, the family fled to the city, thinking they'd be safer there. But, of course, we all know how that turned out. If your coachman could be troubled to take us there . . ."

"I'm sure he could, but isn't your own carriage already waiting outside?"

"If my carriage were to be seen leaving here with strangers aboard, tongues would be wagging even before we reached the Porta Aurelia. No, I'll dismiss my coachman and tell him I'll walk home. That's not unusual, so he'll think nothing of it."

• • • • •

When we reach the ruined villa, it's obvious why the cardinal chose this spot. Wherever we might choose to sit, we can see all our surroundings – no one could approach surreptitiously to eavesdrop. As we settle on the remains of what were once much taller walls, the cardinal says, "Now tell me, my dear, what's this urgent business that brings you and your companion here?"

"My companion, as you call him, Uncle Lorenzo, is actually King Alfred – my cousin from my mother's family. And, Alfred, though the cardinal is technically my cousin once removed, as a child, I could never figure out what that meant, so I've always called him Uncle."

"I'm honored indeed, Your Grace. Welcome to Rome. But why all the subterfuge?"

"It will soon become clear, Eminence. But first, let me ask you a question, if I may." He nods. "Do you play chess?"

"Now and then. But every day I play a game that is even more complex and filled with real risk. One with no rules, shifting alliances, frequent backstabbing, and, in the end, every man for himself." I look at him quizzically. "Church politics, my son. Not a game for the faint-hearted."

"Not unlike the game I've been forced to play against my will, it would seem, though my alliances are steadfast and my commitment to them resolute. It's the stakes, however, that trouble me deeply, involving, as they do, the lives of thousands of innocent men."

"Would I be correct in deducing you refer to this war that currently consumes three kingdoms?"

"More than three, Eminence. You'll recall I spoke of steadfast alliances."

"You did indeed. Yet I struggle to understand how I can be of any help in a military conflict that doesn't threaten the Church."

"Perhaps not directly, no. What I need is an audience with the Pope – an opportunity to speak with him face-to-face about joining forces to stop the madness."

"And why do you believe the Holy Father has any more influence than I might?"

"Because he's already interfered by preventing one of our allies from rallying to the cause."

"Our homeland, Uncle Lorenzo," says Lucia softly.

"If you know that," says the cardinal, "then you must also know that His Holiness is quite unlikely to grant you an audience."

"But would he be so reluctant to grant one to the Duchess of Lamoreaux?"

"Especially if you were to make the request on my behalf, Uncle. And then, on the day, Alfred could accompany me and make his case."

"I wish it were that easy, my dear. Most likely the Pope would have you removed from his presence straightaway for springing such a surprise on him. And without any doubt, his anger would be turned on me and I would lose any influence I may have for a very long time – perhaps even for the rest of my life. I doubt he would strip me of my appointment – the offence would not warrant such grave punishment – but there are other ways in which he can effectively banish me from the papal court."

"I'm sorry, Uncle. I'd never want to put you in that position."

"Think nothing of it, Lucia. But perhaps if I understood more about the nature of what you wish to discuss, Alfred, I might be able to help devise a means to achieve your goals."

I hesitate. Lucia is confident I can trust this man. And yet he, himself, has made it abundantly clear that the machinations of the Church hierarchy are not a trifling matter. Once I go any further, I've put my fate and that of everyone else involved in the hands of someone I've only just met and who is bound by a code I know nothing about. Is that a risk worth taking?

Lucia takes the decision out of my hands. "Tell him the rest, Alfred." She pauses, hoping, I suppose, that I'll speak. When I still hesitate, she adds, "If you don't, I will."

"Very well. What do you know, Eminence, about this Pope's background? Surely it's unusual for someone who's a mere archbishop to be raised to the papacy."

"Anyone who knows how long the last conclave lasted could reasonably guess that it was more contentious than most. So I can say without violating my oath, that we were all rather relieved when a candidate was proposed who was independent of the many factions vying for supremacy in the voting."

"And it would be my guess that the proposal was made by a Teuton cardinal."

"Surely you know, my son, that the secrecy of the conclave is sacrosanct." The faintest hint of a smile – one that never completely curves his lips – one that would easily be missed if you weren't watching for it – tells me I've struck a chord.

"What would you say if I told you the Pope is not a scion of the noble family whose name he bears? And that I have intimate knowledge of this from one who knows all the details of the matter."

It takes me by surprise when the cardinal relaxes and offers a broad smile. "Ah, that. Let me tell you a story, Alfred. When I was a seminarian here, my studies almost complete and waiting for my first assignment to a parish, the gossip of the day throughout Rome was Count Angellini's dismay over his lack of an heir. He had seven daughters but no one to inherit his wealth and title – though one wonders how much wealth would be left after providing seven dowries. That aside, the big news that summer was Angellini's adoption of a boy child. One couldn't go anywhere in society without hearing him boast of it. But by the New Year, Rome had moved on to whatever was the next scandal or scheme or high-profile marriage.

"Some twenty years later – having risen to become a bishop – I was recalled to Rome to serve as secretary to a cardinal who has long since passed into the next world. It was then I learned that the young adoptee had given up his title – passing it on to the eldest daughter's son – and entered the priesthood. We heard nothing more from Father Angellini for several years, and then he began a meteoric rise through the hierarchy to eventually become Archbishop of Gniezno in the eastern reaches of the Teutonic kingdom. It was from there he was plucked to be considered for the papacy."

"It sounds as if someone was pulling strings."

"That isn't out of the question." He pauses a moment before continuing. "There were three of us in the conclave who knew of the Archbishop's history. The rest were either too young or from a different country and wouldn't have been aware. We three were curious, I'll admit, about his adamant insistence on keeping the truth of his birth a secret. But the adoption was properly done – he was legally an Angellini – so we went along with him. After all, what harm could come from it?"

"I'm afraid a great deal."

"Then I think you should be more specific, my son."

"I'm sure you recall the inquisition launched against me a couple of summers ago."

"Of course. Quite a number of us thought it unwarranted, but the Holy Father would brook no dissent. And it all came right in the end."

"Ah, but do you know *how* it came right?"

"Patrasso concluded you were innocent of all charges."

"But not of his own volition. The outcome was ordered by the Teuton king."

"What leads you to that conclusion?"

"The king himself told me. He revealed who it was that coerced the Pope to launch the investigation. He revealed his power over that person and the action he'd taken against him. And he also told me the truth of the Holy Father's birth – that he was born out of wedlock and that the adoption by Angellini was arranged to protect the honor of the birth family. Which I've come to believe is the Teuton king's own family. The Pope is either a half-brother, a cousin, or a nephew of the king.

"In the case of the inquisition, the harm was no more than a temporary threat to my people's confidence in their monarch and has long since passed without ill effects. But I'm convinced beyond any doubt that, just as he ordered the end of the inquisition, the Teuton also ordered the Holy Father to prevent one of our allies from entering the current conflict. And the harm is happening every day in the form of loss of innocent lives in battles that should never have happened in the first place."

"That's quite a serious accusation, my son. And yet somehow it rings true. His Holiness consulted no one before issuing that proclamation. His privilege, of course. But in matters of such gravity, it is quite different from the usual practice of the pontiffs I've served."

We sit in silence for quite some time. Eventually, the cardinal asks, "And is it your intent, Alfred, to join the ranks of these men who threaten the Holy Father to achieve their worldly aims?"

"Not at all, Eminence. In fact, it was reluctance to stoop so low that held me back from pursuing this path sooner. But a very wise abbot helped me find an alternative that might put a permanent end to the madness."

"I'm listening."

"What we need to do is find a way for the Holy Father to free himself from the hold others have over him so he can truly act as Christ's Vicar."

We talk until the sun is nearing the horizon about how this might be done. Glancing to the west, the cardinal announces, "We should be getting back before night sets in," and we rise and make our way to the carriage. As we arrive back at our lodgings, Lucia says, "Join us for supper, Uncle Lorenzo. That will make your late return home more credible."

"You're quite the conspirator, my dear. And not only do I agree, but I'm also famished. This has been a most interesting afternoon."

Now there's nothing to do but wait. And worry. What if I've made the biggest mistake of my life by placing my trust in Uncle Lorenzo? What if, instead of a papal audience, we receive a papal condemnation? What if the Teuton king has a similar hold over others in the papal entourage as he does over the Pope himself?

And yet . . . the cardinal gave the impression of being a careful and thoughtful man. Someone who inspires trust. Someone keenly attuned to the highly charged political environment of the papal court and the risk that could be lurking in any act, any conversation. Or is this no more than a carefully crafted persona that allows him to play the game and survive?

My anxiety is only exacerbated by the fact that I've no idea what's happening in the two battlefields. No idea if Samuel and Edward have arrived safely in Brandr's court. No inkling of what Brandr will decide to do – or not do.

And yet . . . I know in the depths of my being that Brandr and the Pope are the keys to finishing this business once and for all and restoring the historical peace between Denis and his neighbor to the east. Brandr is free to act. The Pope is not unless a way can be found to release him from the man who, I now believe, has manipulated him all his life.

To pass the time, I let Lucia show me the sights of Rome. Oh, how I wish my pleasure in seeing places I've only read about wasn't tempered by this nagging anxiety! Set it aside for the moment, Alfred, I tell myself. No amount of fretting is going to change the pace of whatever's happening. And as the day goes on, Lucia's sunny disposition and her delight in showing me this city she seems to know so well become infectious. Over supper that first evening, she's full of ideas for what we can do the following day. "I only wish we had time to go further east – it's such a beautiful place, Alfred. The seacoast is breathtaking – one of my favorite places in the world. And I know the parts of my family who live there would make you so very welcome." She gives a little sigh. "But I suppose it's not to be this time."

"I'm actually sorry for that, my dear. Juliana could hardly stop talking about her enthusiasm for the places you visited on that trip with Richenda."

"Perhaps sometime when Gwen can come as well."

The following day, we decide to make our way to the summit of the Quirinal to see the city from the highest of its seven hills. The view is lovely, but the hill itself a bit of a disappointment. Once the summer home of emperors, it's now rather sad and neglected. What must have been magnificent homes for wealthy Romans have long since been stripped of their grandeur and pillaged for building stone. And as the day wears on, the anxiety I had suppressed seems determined to resurface. "Maybe we should return to our lodgings," I tell Lucia at midafternoon. "The cardinal might have sent us a message."

Alas, there is none and the servants report no one has called asking for either of us during the time we were away. Twilight is encroaching when hoofbeats in the street come to a stop below our windows and there's a sharp rap on the main door. In short order, one of the host's servants appears at the sitting room door. "Your pardon, my lady. This just arrived." Lucia crosses the room to take the message and opens it and reads while she returns to her chair. It must be short – she hands it to me straightaway.

My dear cousin,

My carriage will be at your door an hour before midday on the morrow. I trust you and your companion will be ready as promptness is among the virtues much to be admired in those who follow our Lord Jesus Christ.

Lorenzo

I refold the page and return it to her, my hand shaking a bit. "Perhaps we've gotten our wish."

"Perhaps we have at that."

As we finish supper, when the sounds in the street have abated, she casually opens a window above the alleyway on the side of the house. Then she pierces one corner of the message with her knife and touches the opposite corner to a candle flame, letting the ash fall into her wine glass. Once the ash has cooled, she pours what remains in the wine pitcher into her glass, swirls the liquid to thoroughly mix it with the ashes, and tosses the mixture out the window. Closing the window, she resumes her seat. "A complete waste of rather good wine," she says with a smile, "but necessary." I couldn't have chosen a better co-conspirator.

We're both ready long before the designated time. My mummer's costume may not be the best-fitting attire I've ever worn, but it's fit for purpose. Lucia's high-neck black gown, black lace veil that flows down to her elbows, and jeweled rosary hanging from her neck say she'd assumed, when packing her trunk, that we'd get our audience. I won't make that assumption until I'm actually on my knees before the pontiff himself.

At the appointed time, we climb into the carriage and sit side-by-side opposite the cardinal, who wastes little time with greetings as our conveyance gets underway. His brow furrows as he eyes my crown. "Perhaps, Alfred, it might be better for you to forego the crown . . . to present yourself simply as a faithful Christian desirous of the honor of being received by His Holiness."

"With respect, Eminence, I've no choice but to decline. This is part of the game *I* must play. The Teuton king gave me this card, to see if I would use it. It's vital that word reach him that I did so openly, as a crowned king – as his equal – and with no fear. And any others who might be in his thrall must be left in no doubt of my purpose."

"As you wish." He pauses briefly before continuing. "There are some things you should know before we arrive. The Holy Father is receiving us at the Lateran Palace, in the section where restorations since the last fire have been completed, though in my opinion they fall far short of the earlier magnificence of the place. The message he intends to send is that you are neither pious enough to deserve the holiness of St. Peter's nor of sufficient importance to warrant the honor of Santa Maria Maggiore."

"In truth, Eminence, I care not at all for whatever he wants to say about us – only that we succeed in our objective."

"A wise choice on your part, Alfred, but the message is at least as much for his entourage and the rest of the Christian world. Now, the Holy Father likes to hold his audiences precisely at midday, so we'll be arriving early. That's by design. We will be escorted first into an antechamber. Any number of people will pass through while we wait, some because it's the most convenient route to their destination and others for the express purpose of observing us and eavesdropping. It will be impossible to distinguish one from another, so any conversation we may engage in should be solemn and subdued and utterly irrelevant to our purpose.

"Because I requested the audience in your name, Lucia, it's most likely the Pope will address you first. Your role is to petition him for the outcome we want – not as a demand or even a request but as a plea on behalf of our countrymen. When he addresses you, Alfred, your role is to plant the seed that there's a way for him to free himself from the clutches of the Teuton king and any others who may seek to manipulate him. Plant the seed only, my son. Refrain from trying to convince him of its merits, no matter how tempted you may be to do so or how important you believe it to be. That task is for others."

"Others?" I ask.

"Two other cardinals will join us just as we're to be shown into the Holy Father's presence. These are the men I mentioned who share my knowledge. They were parish priests here when I was just a seminarian, which means they're approaching the age at which cardinals must withdraw from active participation in the papal court, so there's little risk to them in undertaking the task. If they fail and are relieved of their current duties, then they simply retire from the scene a bit sooner than expected. Neither of them has any concern about that possibility. *They* will be the ones to steer the Pope's thinking." Left unsaid is what I perceive as their additional task – to protect Cardinal Lorenzo from recrimination if things should fall apart.

The carriage slows and finally comes to a stop. "One last thing," says the cardinal, "before we exit. If the room in which we're received has a gallery, do not deceive yourself that we're alone. It's quite easy – especially in priestly garb – for a man to disappear into the shadows of the gallery yet still hear every word spoken below."

As the cardinal moves to descend from the carriage, Lucia grasps his arm. "One thing I only just thought of, Uncle Lorenzo. What's the proper protocol to express appreciation for the audience?"

"Today, my dear, I think the less said the better. You need do no more than kneel for his blessing. If he gives it without further comment, I believe we can infer that no offense has been given and that your gratitude is assumed."

We follow the cardinal up the steps to an entrance door, where it's obvious we're expected. The door opens as we approach, and a man in simple priest's attire bows and gestures toward the corridor. "The staircase is to your left, Eminence. Your escort is waiting there to welcome you." Lorenzo offers a slight tip of the head in acknowledgment but doesn't speak or break his stride. At the foot of the staircase, a bishop bows slightly and greets his superior with "*Dominus vobiscum.*"

"*Et cum spiritu tuo.*"

"Please come this way." The bishop falls in step beside the cardinal as we ascend the stairs. "The Holy Father has chosen the Garden Room to receive you – a more intimate setting, don't you think, than the vast reception rooms."

"A lovely room indeed, with its windows overlooking the rose garden," says Lorenzo.

"We have prepared a comfortable seating area for you to await the summons to his presence."

The "comfortable seating area" turns out to be three luxurious chairs arranged around a rather large, low table at the intersection of two corridors. Quite a busy intersection, it turns out, with all manner of clerics coming and going from all four directions. The chairs have been arranged to make it impossible to carry on a hushed conversation, so we opt for no conversation at all.

At long last, the bishop returns and escorts us farther down the main corridor. When he stops in front of elaborately carved double doors, two cardinals join us from where they had been waiting on the opposite side. The bishop looks momentarily flustered, raises an eyebrow to Lorenzo, who merely nods, and then knocks three times on the door before throwing them both open and stepping into the room to announce, "Your visitors, Holy Father." Once all five of us are inside, the bishop backs out into the corridor, pulling the doors closed as he does so.

To our left, a beautifully decorated crucifix hangs on the wall above what appears to be a small altar. The cardinals turn to it, genuflect, and make the sign of the cross. Lucia and I follow suit, then turn to see the Pope occupying a throne-like chair set on a low platform on the opposite side of the room. The cardinals kiss his ring in turn, each of them saying quietly, "Holy Father," then move to stand along the side wall on the Pope's left. Lucia and I kneel before the pontiff, heads bowed.

"Rise, my children, and be welcome." He stands to extend his hand first to Lucia and then to me for the ritual kissing of the ring, then resumes his seat. "Pray tell, my daughter, what brings you to seek my counsel on this day?"

"I come to seek your benevolence, Holy Father, for the people of my homeland."

"I believe your homeland is now the Kingdom Across the Southern Sea, as you are a duchess of some importance there. I am aware that their army is at war, but I have heard nothing of any dire straits the ordinary people might be experiencing."

"Your Holiness speaks the truth. And yet I still think of the land of my birth as my first and dearest homeland and of all the people there as my first and dearest family in Christ. They suffer under the weight of the edict that threatens them with excommunication. They have no control over the actions of their rulers, so they live in constant fear of being separated from the body of Christ for something they did not do. I come on their behalf, Holy Father, to plead that you might find it in your heart to lift this weight and offer them reassurance of God's love and mercy."

"You have a kind heart, my child. But there are times when God must show men the correct path to his love and mercy, even though the instruction may seem stern."

Lucia says no more. She's played her role.

"And you, King Alfred. Are you here on the duchess's behalf? Or do you come with some other motive?"

"I believe I can say with a clear conscience, Holy Father, that my motive is to support the duchess. But I also believe I am in possession of knowledge that she may not possess."

"And what might that knowledge be, my son?"

"I know the truth, Holiness, that you are at pains to keep secret from the world lest it diminish you in the eyes of men. The secret that men use without compunction to compel you to do their bidding."

There's no missing the anger – fury even – that flares in his eyes. "And you come here to threaten me with that knowledge?" And there's no mistaking the tone of his voice.

Before he can call for someone to throw us out, I hurry to reply. "Far from it, Holy Father. I come to give *you* the knowledge that the man who also knows this secret has not been circumspect in protecting your interests. He has told me. Who else might he have told? And if he has told others, is there not the danger that they might have even more unwelcome demands as a condition for keeping the knowledge to themselves? My plea, Holy Father, is that you extricate yourself from their clutches so that you're free to act only with God's guidance and not to satisfy the whims of man."

While I've been speaking, the choler has left his expression though the set of his mouth remains rather stern. "And how do you propose I do that?" His tone now borders on the sarcastic – as if I'm completely naïve to suggest such a thing.

"Are we not taught that our Lord said 'And ye shall know the truth and the truth shall set you free'? Might it not also be equally true that 'ye shall *tell* the truth and the truth shall set you free'? If you yourself reveal the secret of your birth to the world at large, Holiness, then it is no longer a weapon to be used against you. Instead, it's a beacon of hope – that even the lowly can be raised up through God's grace."

No one speaks. No one moves. It seems, almost, as if no one breathes. For a very long time. Finally, the Pope says, "Your words merit contemplation, King Alfred." He rises from his seat – the cue for Lucia and me to kneel for his blessing. To each of us, he offers the papal benediction sign with his right hand, accompanied by the words "*Benedicat tibi Dominus et custodiat te.*" Then he makes the sign of the cross and adds, "*In nomine Patris et Filii et Spiritus Sancti. Amen*" and resumes his seat. Lucia and I rise as Cardinal Lorenzo joins us, and the three of us leave together.

As we approach our waiting area, a cardinal emerges from the corridor to the right. A face I recognize. Patrasso. "It came to my attention that you would be passing here today, King Alfred," he says. "A perfect opportunity for me to tell you that I bear you no ill will." Before I can offer any response, he adds, "*Dominus vobiscum,*" and continues on his way, leaving me no option but to reply, "*Et cum spiritu tuo.*"

"That was unusual," I tell the cardinal.

"In due course, Alfred." His way of reminding me these walls have ears.

Once we're in the carriage and well away from the papal precincts, an enormous smile breaks out on the cardinal's face. "You did *very* well, my children."

"Do you really think so, Uncle Lorenzo?" Lucia's tone is hopeful.

"I can't predict the outcome, my dear, but you gave my colleagues everything they need to guide the Holy Father's contemplation. And, Alfred, I would have thought you to be of a decidedly more secular bent but your words and manner were those of a deeply pious man."

I can't suppress a small chuckle. "I learned a bit during the inquisition, Eminence. But I suspect those closest to me would say I was just making it up as I went along."

"Then I highly approve of your *ex tempore* skills."

"What was that business with Cardinal Patrasso?"

"Ah, yes. You may have concluded from your experience with him that Patrasso is either mean-spirited or exceedingly dogmatic. In truth, what he is, is ambitious. One who would very much like to sit on Peter's throne. So every assignment he takes, every relationship he cultivates is designed to ingratiate himself with those who may one day hold his fate in their hands. I believe today was his first step toward dispelling whatever animosity you may harbor toward him."

I shake my head in disbelief. "I cannot even imagine how you keep up with all the nuances of your world."

It's Lorenzo's turn to chuckle. "I won't deny that it can be daunting at times."

"So what do we do now, Uncle?" asks Lucia.

"We wait. For as long as it takes. I cannot come to you again until the outcome is known, but once it is, I will be the bearer of the news."

We bid him farewell when the carriage stops in front of our lodgings. I suspect neither of us will sleep soundly until we see him again.

Time crawls. It's as if the hour glass has become clogged and the grains of sand are struggling to find a path to the other side. Were I back home, I'd at least have the library to distract my thoughts. Don't delude yourself, Alfred. Yes, you'd sit in the library, a book in your lap, looking at the words but not really concentrating. Eventually, you'd return the book to its shelf and prowl the corridors or go riding in the woods. And when none of that makes the sand flow any faster, you'd wind up back in the library, a book in your lap, gazing out the window more often than at the page.

It seems a shame to be here in this city and not visit the booksellers' stalls. They're bound to have volumes I'd find nowhere else. But neither of us is inclined to venture out lest we miss a visit or a message from the cardinal.

Lucia does her best to keep our spirits up, regaling me with her expectations for the coming grape harvest. "The weather has been perfect this year, Alfred. It's not unusual to hear my winemaker muttering 'Please, God, no last-minute rain before the harvest' while he's checking the fruit. But what's really exciting is that we've just tapped the first barrel from two summers ago, and it promises to be a remarkable vintage. The monks of St. Didier are clamoring for it, so in a few more years, they may have some brandy as fine as those casks I sent to you and Rupert after Charles died."

But despite her best efforts – and mine to be a good conversationalist – we both lapse into anxious silence after each attempt at cheerfulness. Neither of us is hungry, so we forego the evening meal and douse the candles not long after sundown. The next morning is overcast, which does nothing to improve our mood. As midday approaches, Lucia says, "Enough of this. I'm going out for a stroll. Care to join me?" She knows I won't let her go alone.

Two streets away we find a little neighborhood tavern and stop in for a meal. We're offered a local wine, which is quite delicious, and something curious called *vermicelli* over which has been drizzled olive oil infused with herbs and garlic. A plate of thin slices of a hard cheese with a slightly nutty flavor – *Parmigiano Reggiano*, the innkeeper calls it – and a bowl of olives round out the meal.

When we emerge from the tavern, the sun has broken through and dispelled most of the clouds. "Think we should take that as a good omen?" I ask Lucia.

"Well, if it is, we'd best hurry back to our lodgings."

But we arrive to learn there's been no visitor and no news. An hour later, just as I'm about to declare how foolish my earlier comment had been, a knock on the door and footsteps on the stairs send a frisson of excitement up my spine. Excitement or dread? Even when the cardinal steps through the door, there's no way to know which, as his expression gives nothing away. "I thought perhaps you two might wish to see St. Peter's before you leave," he says.

It's but a short drive across the river and down the Via Cornelia to our destination. When the carriage comes to a halt, the cardinal says, "Before we go in, I have something for you, Alfred." From a leather pouch on the seat beside him he retrieves a small wooden box, elaborately carved and painted, and extends it to me. "The Holy Father wished you to have this."

I take the box and admire it from all sides before opening it. "This is quite lovely." Inside, a simple rosary with perfectly round wooden beads lies on a red velvet lining. And in the lid, an inscription – *Et cognoscetis veritatem et veritas liberabit vos.*

"I'm given to understand," says the cardinal, "that the inscription is a very recent addition."

"Does this mean what I think it does, Eminence?"

"Lorenzo. Though you may be from the other half of Lucia's family, we are no less family. And yes, it does. His Holiness made two announcements at the end of this morning's mass, both of which I think would be to your liking."

"I cannot thank you enough, Lorenzo, for everything you've done."

"A kind sentiment, Alfred, but I deserve very little credit. Your words and the counsel of two wise and patient men are what led the Holy Father to his decision. If I were to speculate, however, I think he may have actually welcomed a way out of his dilemma.

"Now . . ." He opens the door and descends from the carriage, offering Lucia a hand to step down. ". . . let me show you the basilica. I think you'll be quite impressed by the *Navicella*, in particular. It was eight years in the making and quite a thing of beauty."

On the drive back to our lodgings, Lorenzo returns to our previous topic. "I've been assigned to deliver the document rescinding the Pope's earlier edict against my homeland. However, my calling, and particularly my position in the Church hierarchy, make it inadvisable for me to engage in conversations about war." He turns to Lucia. "But if you should wish to accompany me, my dear, to renew your acquaintance with those to whom I deliver the Pope's message, I would be more than delighted to have your company. And who better to bring them news of the current conflict than someone with connections to three of the ruling houses involved."

"It would be my pleasure, Uncle. When do we leave?"

"Would tomorrow midmorning be too soon?"

"Not at all. Alfred, you should take my carriage back to the manor. I can hire one when it's time to return home."

"A generous offer, Lucia, but if I return to the manor without you – if I even return at all, for that matter – it will completely dismantle our ruse that I'm your cousin sent to fetch you here. In any event, I can travel much more quickly on horseback. I just have to find some way to acquire one."

"Then let me buy you a nice one – and a decent saddle. He was riding bareback when he turned up at my doorstep, Uncle."

"Sound and reliable is enough – better even. Nothing flashy that people would remember seeing. Have you any idea where we might find one, sir?"

Just at that moment, the carriage comes to a stop in front of our lodgings. "Send your coachman down with the money, Lucia. We'll take him to a suitable place, and my own coachman will see that he gets a fair deal."

Lucia alights from the carriage and hurries to the door, the cardinal calling after her, "Remember, my dear, midmorning tomorrow."

"I'll be ready, Uncle."

I step down from the carriage then turn back to the cardinal. "Take good care of her, Lorenzo. And I very much hope we meet again."

"As do I, Alfred. As do I."

As I approach the port, my mind is racing. This will be the trickiest part of my journey so far – nothing I can do but make it up as I go along. My senses have to be on high alert. A bit of Fortuna's favor wouldn't go amiss either. At the edge of town, I ask a pedestrian for directions to the docks. "Just follow this street to the market square. Then turn left on the road that runs in front of the church."

Once there, I dismount and lead my horse along the quay until I find our two ships at the far end. Tying the horse to a rail beside what appears to be a large warehouse, I approach the man leaning against a bollard near the bottom of the gangplank of the first ship. "Any idea where the captain might be?" I ask him.

"On board. Most like, he be in his cabin seeing to the log entry."

Without another word, I dash up the gangplank and onto the deck. "Wait! Ye canna' just go on board ship 'thout being invited," the man shouts after me. By the time he reaches the deck, I'm already descending the ladder that leads to the cabin area. Making my way quickly to the stern, I knock twice then open the door of the captain's cabin and step inside to find him seated at his tiny desk writing in the log.

He looks up immediately, angry at the intrusion. "What in God's name do you think you're doing, seaman? You can't just barge in here like that."

But the moment he looked up, I realized luck was on my side. This captain has taken me and my family across the sea several times. I only hope he recognizes me in my current attire and beard. He looks puzzled at first, then recognition dawns and he jumps to his feet. "Holy Mother of God! Your Grace! What the . . . how in the world . . . what are you doing here?"

"Calm yourself, Captain. It's a long story. But right now, I very much need your help."

"Whatever you wish, Sire." He suddenly remembers to bow.

"As you were." I take a seat on his cot, there being no other chair in the tiny cabin. "I need you to take me home – well, at least part way home. But it's vital none of the seamen learn my identity. I'm just a messenger with orders for you to give him transport. That said, I don't want to be seen, so I'll need a cabin that can be locked from the inside."

"You can stay here. I'll share with my lieutenant – do my sleeping when he's in charge on deck. That's how we always do it anyway. And I'll bring your food myself."

"Thank you, Captain. There's one other thing I need you to do. Be sure the knight captain in charge of the troops here knows you'll be back. And while you're at it, the horse I rode here is tied up just across the quay. Give him to the troops to add to their spares. Now, how soon can we get underway?"

"As soon as I can get the rest of my crew back on board. That'll take an hour or so. But at least it's early enough in the day, they won't all be drunk out of their minds."

"Sorry to press you, Captain. It's just that time is of the essence."

"Think nothing of it, Sire. The crew could actually use the discipline of being at sea once again. Permission to go see to things?"

"Aye."

As he leaves, he adds, "There's a key in the door this side, and the only other one is around my neck." I quickly lock the door behind him.

And once again, there's nothing I can do but wait. At least this time, though, the motion of the ship and the sound of the water against the hull provide constant reassurance that we're making progress. I gave the captain his instructions when he brought my supper the first night at sea, so when we heave to and drop anchor just after sunup one morning, my eagerness to be back on land once again is at a fever pitch. Which makes the wait until the captain unlocks the cabin door seem far longer than it really is. "Fishing boat's alongside, Your Grace," he says. "Time for you to go."

"I'm really quite grateful, Captain. One day, I'll tell you the whole story. And with any luck, that day isn't too far off."

"It's been my honor, Sire. Just see you get the rest of the way home safely."

I sling my satchel over my shoulder and go up on deck, where a rope ladder has been hung over the side, extending almost to the water. Climbing down, I begin to understand Cedric's unease at leaping from boat to boat. I pause just above the fishing boat's gunwale and toss my satchel to the fisherman waiting below – given what's inside, I'd be devastated if it somehow went to the bottom of the sea. After a moment studying the gap between the two vessels, I push myself off the ladder, clearing the gunwale and landing rather unceremoniously on the deck of the fishing boat. As soon as I'm on my feet and obviously uninjured, Owen raises sail and turns toward shore.

Before we reach the channel, he gives the tiller to one of his men and joins me in the prow. "Just like before, when we dock, you scurry into the woods and be on your way. I tethered your horse up the hill, more or less where you left it, saddled and ready to ride, and there's a bag of food tied to his saddle – assuming the critters haven't gotten to it. One of these days, I want to hear the story behind all this."

"And I'm just as eager to tell you. If things work out as I hope they do, that day will come sooner than you think. In the meantime, thank you, my friend – for everything."

He returns to the tiller to pilot the boat through the channel. With the ebbing tide, I finally get a glimpse of a few of the rocks that guard this cove. Owen once called them monsters. Monsters they are indeed!

. . . . .

I've already decided to take the path to the reservoir and avoid trying to negotiate Goron's army once again. But the thought of crossing into my own lands – having no idea what might have transpired during my absence – brings a certain amount of apprehension. It's unlikely I'd be recognized in my current state if I avoid the towns and larger villages. But what if Teuton spies or hostage-takers have learned I was never at the monastery – or worse yet, gotten wind of what I've actually been up to? Armed with nothing more than a dagger in my boot, I'd be no match for even a couple of renegades intent on malice. So when I reach the road that leads to Egon's fortress, I turn my horse's head north.

Nearing the smithy, I finally have the inspiration for how to get Egon's attention without drawing attention to myself. I stop, dismount, and walk straight to where the blacksmith is busy shaping a horseshoe at his anvil. "I wonder if I could get some of your help, my good man."

He hammers the hot metal twice more then douses it in a barrel of water before looking up and asking, "What kind of help do you need?" He looks me up and down, then squints his eyes to stare at my face, clearly trying to make up his mind about something. I let him take his time. Finally, he asks, "Lord Alfred? Is . . . is that you?"

"It is indeed, my friend, and I really do need your help. But I don't want anyone else to know I'm here. Is there somewhere private we could talk?"

"Tie your horse just there," he points to the rail where another horse stands waiting for new shoes, "and come with me." At the far back of the smithy we come to what appears to be his living quarters. He invites me to sit at his table and produces two mugs of ale. "Now tell me what you need."

"I need to speak to Egon, but in private, so none of his men know. Do you think you could get him to come down here?"

"Can I tell him who it is what wants to talk to him?"

"That seems the best way – just be sure there aren't others within earshot when you do."

He downs what remains in his mug in a single swallow then gets to his feet. "You wait here. I will not be long."

In less time than I expected, Egon strides into the smithy's quarters, gives me the once-over, and exclaims, "What on earth, Alfred? I am rather amazed the blacksmith even recognized you. Not sure I would have if you had just wandered into my courtyard."

"It's rather a long story, but quite an interesting one. I've been on a journey – in disguise, as you can see – and I'm headed home. But I've had no news for over three weeks, so no idea what might be waiting for me across the border. Is there any way I might convince you to ride with me and allow me to masquerade as your squire? I'd feel much safer being with someone well-armed."

"You need not ask twice, my friend. Would I be correct in assuming that you are eager to be on our way?"

"If it isn't too great an inconvenience."

"Then give me a half hour to prepare. Would I also be correct that we will need some food for the journey?"

"You would indeed. I've just about exhausted mine."

"Very well. I shall be back as quickly as I can."

While he's gone, the blacksmith attends to my horse, brushing down his coat, giving him oats and water, and checking his shoes before re-saddling him for the journey. Egon returns wearing sword and dagger, his pack bulging. I hope it's mostly food, but it wouldn't surprise me if there were also more weapons inside. "Here," he tosses me a bit of cloth. "It occurred to me that if you wear a tunic bearing my livery, it would make our ruse even more believable." I pull the tunic over my head, sling my satchel over my shoulder, and mount up.

There are no secrets between Egon and me, so when we ride in open country with no chance of being overheard, I tell him the entire story of my journey, from the difficult decision to use my knowledge to what happened in Rome to my hope that by now, Denis's ally has opened a new front at the Teutons' rear. Just talking about it all lifts an enormous weight from my shoulders and reminds me how much I've missed Samuel's steadying influence.

When I finish the tale, Egon says, "I am most impressed, Alfred. And yet, I wonder why Samuel has not been with you on this journey." Which leads me to tell him of Samuel's mission to Brandr. By the time the castle is in sight, Egon knows more than anyone else about my strategy to defeat the Teutons. "If the Teuton king is as astute as you believe him to be," says Egon, "then he will soon know that in you, he has met his match. More than his match, I would say."

The guards let us pass without question or challenge. Presumably because they recognize Egon from prior visits. But I can't help but wonder, in the current circumstances, if that's comforting or worrisome. When I see Geoffrey dashing out the entrance as we cross the inner courtyard, I get my answer – someone had obviously rushed to tell him there was an important visitor to be greeted. "Welcome, Lord Egon," he calls out as we dismount and hand our horses over to a nearby guard. "Had we known you were coming, we'd have been better prepared to receive you."

"Ah, Lord Geoffrey, in these treacherous times, it is sometimes best if a man does not announce his movements in advance. But it has been far too long since I paid a visit."

Geoffrey glances at me briefly . . . then does a double-take. As he's about to speak, Egon intervenes. "Perhaps, Lord Geoffrey, it would be best if we go inside."

My son looks my way once again, but then turns to precede us up the steps and into the entrance hall. No sooner is the door closed than he says, a bit tentatively, "Papa?"

"Aye, Son. But Egon's right. Best we say no more until we're upstairs. Would you be kind enough to show us to the private reception room?" It's obvious Geoffrey's about to burst with questions, but he makes straight for the staircase and dashes up, leaving Egon and me in his wake, hard-pressed to keep up with his youthful energy.

As we pass through the outer chamber, Coliar glances up from his writing table, ready to deter anyone who shouldn't be in these rooms without invitation – and does his own double-take, completely unable to prevent his jaw dropping. "Your Grace? Is it really you?"

"Come inside with us, Coliar, and your questions will be answered." He follows us into the inner chamber and closes the doors while Geoffrey dashes across to open the bedchamber door, shouting, "Mama? Mama, come quick."

We hear movement inside and then Gwen steps through the open doorway . . . and bursts into laughter. "Oh my God, Alfred! I've never *seen* you so shaggy." She crosses to where I stand, obviously intent on a welcoming hug, but stops just short and holds me at arm's length. "Or so filthy either." She leans forward to give me a quick kiss.

"And Egon." *He* gets the welcoming hug and a kiss on the cheek, which seem to put him at a bit of unease. "You brought him home to us. I'm forever in your debt."

"He is quite a pleasant traveling companion, my dear," says Egon then gestures to my attire. "But his skills as a squire leave something to be desired."

Gwen laughs again, and from the bedchamber doorway comes, "That be on account of he never be properly trained, m'lord." Osbert steps tentatively into the room before adding, "And he be a right mess too."

"I can't argue with that, Osbert," I tell him. "And I rather suspect it's going to take more than one bath to remove all the grime."

"The sooner you get started cleaning him up, Osbert, the better," says Gwen. "Coliar, ask Matthias to arrange one of the finest rooms for our guest. And since he's without a squire, Osbert, do you think young Robin might know enough by now to assist Egon while he's here?"

"I be thinking mayhap so. But mayhap ye also be needing to tell him how ye be wanting things done, m'lord, since he only be in training a few months. I bring him to ye as soon as Matthias get ye settled."

As I make my way toward my dressing room, I hear Gwen issuing more instructions. "Once you've taken care of our guest, Coliar, send for Carew and Tobin then arrange for some wine and nuncheons in my sitting room. As soon as our travelers get refreshed, we'll gather there to hear their tale. And that includes you, Coliar."

When Osbert reaches to take my satchel, I hold up my hand. "Not just yet." Reaching inside, I remove the only two items left there. The crown, I hand to Osbert. The leather pouch containing the little carved box I take back into the bedchamber and place in the center of the small writing desk that was once my father's. "Now . . ." I give Osbert the empty satchel. ". . . it may no longer be suitable for anything but burning, but it served me well. These clothes, on the other hand," I add as I start shedding my filthy garments while the kitchen boys fill the bathtub with steaming water, "I'm certain are beyond any hope of ever being clean again."

Osbert laughs and shoos the kitchen boys out of the room. "Now ye just sit there and soak, m'lord, while I be taking young Robin off to Lord Egon. And mayhap by the time I get back, ye be shed of a layer or two of dirt."

An hour later – clean for the first time since leaving Rome – clean-shaven for the first time since leaving home – I join the others in Gwen's sitting room. I'm not sure I've ever seen such a broad smile from either Carew or Tobin. They both jump to their feet to bow and offer me the warrior's greeting. Instead, I embrace each of them in turn, royal protocol be damned. These men have suffered in silence for weeks, knowing what I've been doing and how much danger I might be in. "Welcome home, sir," Tobin says quietly as we all take our seats.

"So, Papa," says Geoffrey, "I thought you were at the monastery."

"As did I," Coliar adds. "As did everyone, so far as I can discern. Even in the town, the only gossip has been wondering why you were staying there so long in the middle of a war."

"Exactly what you were supposed to think," I tell them. "In fact, if people still think that, then it seems I've managed to pull this off."

"Pull what off, Papa?"

Gwen returns from the sideboard with a glass of wine for me. "Patience, Geoffrey," she admonishes him.

I sip the wine and take a moment to savor it. "Now *that* is worth coming home for." Everyone – even Coliar – laughs. "So, Geoffrey, this is the short version of the story. The details will have to keep until the war is over. In truth, everything I'm about to tell you has to remain secret until then, but those of you who've been so anxious deserve to know a bit more than you do now.

"Even before all this started, Denis and I have known something that had the potential to change the course of the war."

"So why didn't you use it straightaway?" Geoffrey asks.

"Because to do so felt like I'd be lowering myself to the level of weak and venal men like Hugo, who manipulate others to get what they want. But as I watched the growing loss of innocent lives both here and across the sea – and among our allies as well – I finally came to the conclusion that, no matter how distasteful it might be, if it wasn't immoral, we had no choice but to reveal what we knew. And Warin helped me see a path.

"Denis couldn't do it. Where he is – in the middle of a battlefield and a hotbed of Teuton spies – he'd have been followed and captured as soon as he set out on the journey, no matter how convincing his disguise might have been to ordinary people. So the task fell to me. But it had to be done in utter secrecy.

"My supposed seclusion at the monastery was merely a ruse to explain my absence from the castle. During that time, I've traveled to Rome, had an audience with the Pope, and made my way back." Geoffrey's jaw drops, and both he and Coliar are at pains to suppress an audible gasp. "Thankfully," I add, "since I had no idea what might be afoot here, Egon agreed to be my protector for the last leg of the journey."

"For which we are exceedingly grateful, my lord." Carew raises his glass to Egon.

"What else, Papa?" Geoffrey asks.

"I think we'd best leave it at that for now. And even that has to remain a secret. As far as the world outside this room is concerned, I've just returned from the monastery as on other occasions when I've spent time there. But I *will* tell you everything in due course, Son." Geoffrey nods his understanding. "Now, what news of the war?"

"Jasper's dispatches have become far less frequent," says Carew.

"A sure sign he's had his hands full," Tobin adds.

"Aye." Carew again. "The operation to clear out the Teuton encampment was successful, though not without casualties, as you can no doubt imagine. The last we heard from him, the Peaks reserve was now part of his main force, and they were advancing into the Eastern Kingdom. Since he'd managed to squeeze Gunnvor's army and whatever Teutons remain with it into far less territory, he's facing a much narrower front, with the enemy unable to achieve any flanking maneuvers, but apparently they're putting up considerable resistance, even fighting in retreat."

Silence settles over the room, but not in my mind. Was Lucia able to convince the rulers of her homeland to open a new front in the south? Or, with the threat of excommunication lifted, did they merely heave a sigh of relief and decide that staying out of the fray was the safest and wisest course? There's no way to know until we hear from Cedric again.

Then Gwen reaches into her sleeve and produces a folded page. "This arrived at midmorning, Alfred. I puzzled over it for a while, trying to decide what to make of it. Is it legitimate? Or was it written under duress? And either way, what to do in your absence? I'd just made up my mind to talk with Tobin and Carew when you and Egon rode into the courtyard." She hands me the message.

Your Grace,

Your presence is required here straightaway. In royal regalia. Accompanied by a full troop riding as an honor guard. Come as quickly as you can.

Jasper

I hand the page to Tobin, who's sitting nearest, and they pass it around.

"Interesting," says Carew. "I see why you were cautious, My Lady. It's rather terse for Jasper, especially if his intent is to convince you to come, sir. That said, if he wanted to get the messenger on his way immediately, he wouldn't waste time writing a long missive."

"No way to know, really," says Tobin.

"And yet," I tell them, "I have reason to believe it might be just the sign I've been waiting for."

"Sir?" asks Carew.

"There's no way to be certain without going there, but my gut tells me that's what we do. Can you be ready to ride at first light tomorrow?"

"As you wish, sir."

"And Egon, it's your choice, of course, since we can't be sure this isn't a trap, but my gut also says you might enjoy coming along."

"Then it would be my pleasure to trust your gut yet again."

"What about me, Papa?"

"Let me think about it. We'll talk after supper."

•　　•　　•　　•　　•

Before joining Gwen for the night, I make my way to Geoffrey's room. He's laid his pack on Edward's bed alongside the fine sword that Egon gave him as a birthday gift a couple of years ago. "Looks like you could be ready to go in no time at all."

"If you say yes, Papa."

I hate what I'm about to do, but there's really no other choice. "Unfortunately, I'm going to disappoint you." He sits down hard on his bed, completely crestfallen, as I settle on Edward's bed opposite him.

"Why, Papa?"

"Because if this is a trap – if I were to be captured or – "

He cuts me off. "Don't say it."

"If the worst should happen, then it's absolutely vital that you be here where you can be crowned straightaway, before anything can be done to prevent it."

"But what if it's not a trap? What if your gut is right? Lord Egon certainly seems willing to trust your instincts."

"I understand. And I know how much you'd like to be part of things if Jasper really has secured a surrender. But there's one other thing I have to consider. If the Teuton king is still on these shores, then I have to leave him and his retainers in absolutely no doubt that *I'm* the one who's beaten him at his own game. There can be *nothing* to distract his attention from that. And you would most definitely distract him. It would be the first time he's laid eyes on you, so he would push aside the fact that I've defeated him and turn his mind to studying you and what kind of a young man you might be. That's just how he is. But what's needed now – if there's to be a long-lasting peace – is that he be unable to stray from the thought that *I* have the strength to thwart his ambition."

Geoffrey looks down at his feet. "It sounds like there's not much chance I could talk you into it."

"I know you're disappointed. You've shown such courage through this whole messy business. But we can't let our guard down before we're absolutely certain it's time. And it won't be time until we can go to Denis's aid and put an end to Teuton ambitions there as well."

He looks up to meet my gaze. "But you *will* tell me everything about your secret journey, won't you?"

"Every last detail, down to a nondescript mare that turned out to be my best friend."

Finally, a smile. "Then I guess I'll just have to be patient a little longer."

Once we're well out of sight of the ferry landing, Carew calls a halt and we dispense with the all the formal regalia. Banners are furled, caparisons removed, ceremonial saddlecloths carefully folded, all stowed in the wagon with our food, tents, and extra weapons, should they be needed. My coronet goes into Osbert's pack. Osbert had insisted Robin accompany us as part of his training. "On account of how it not be often a young squire get to see how this be done afore he be having to do it fer real." Logic I couldn't argue with.

At Gwen's suggestion, we'd ridden to the port and across the river in full regal trappings. "It will raise people's spirits to see you decked out for celebration rather than armed for war," she'd said during our bedtime conversation.

"Might that not be putting the plough before the oxen?" I asked.

"Mightn't it give people a reason to be hopeful?"

"What if it's false hope?"

"You didn't sound like it was false hope this afternoon."

"Maybe I'm just trying to temper my own hopefulness."

She smiled and squeezed my hand. "Well, *I'm* going to remain hopeful. I'm tired of war and ready for our son to come home." And then she turned a bit melancholy. "At least we know he *will* be coming home."

As we rode through the town, people came out of shops and houses to wave and wish us well. And when we reached the port, it was clear the news of our coming had arrived well before us. People lined the streets and crowded around the ferry crossing, where we had to summon the ferry from the other side. With the exception of a couple of young hooligans who tried to pick a fight with the guards – and who were quickly removed by the sheriff's men – those who turned out were friendly. The most common questions, of course, were "Is the war over?" and "When is my son or husband or brother or father coming home?" How I wish I could have replied "Yes" and "In a few days." But everyone seemed satisfied with "Soon, I hope" and "Not long now." Gwen was right, of course. It was hope that they longed for.

Even allowing for the pace of the wagon, we can travel more quickly without all the regal trappings. It's a joy to be riding Altair again. Which reminds me that Regulus is long overdue for his first ride. I too am ready for Edward to come home. Ready for both my sons to finish training their colts alongside me. Ready for a time when getting dumped on my arse by a young horse unaccustomed to a rider is the greatest threat I have to face.

The journey takes half a day longer than usual. Jasper's forces are now well inside the Eastern Kingdom. At the border markers, the sights leave no doubt of the brutality of the fighting here. A stump of stone on the left side of the road no longer mirrors its twin on the right. Chunks of metal lie here and there, remnants of the cannon blown apart in the explosion. Ahead and to the left, spaced well apart in the field, piles of bones – all that's left of what must have been enormous funeral pyres – all that's left of men and animals fallen in the field, friend no longer distinguishable from foe.

The smell of burning bodies comes to me unbidden – a memory from John's terrible war that I'd long ago put out of my mind. The horror of war, it seems, never truly leaves anyone who's survived it, and more memories come rushing back. The sounds of pounding hooves and clashing arms and men and animals in agony. The sights of flashing swords and flying arrows and the utter chaos of hand-to-hand combat . . . and of blood – everywhere – on weapons, in the grass, in the mud, on the living and the dying and those maimed for the rest of their lives. And the smells of sweat and of blood and of fear and of death – the smells that penetrate your nose and your mouth and your hair and your clothes and linger long after the battle is done and the funeral fires are nothing but ash and bones.

I shake my head sharply to dispel the memories as we make our way slowly through the vestiges of what happened here. Carew notices and calls for a canter, and the grim sights are soon behind us. Out of sight, but never completely erased from memory.

At the first glimpse of Jasper's camp, Carew calls a halt and we break out the ceremonial trappings once again. We advance at the trot until we reach the supply wagons, where camp followers line each side of the path that's been cleared for us. A hopeful sign indeed! Jasper would never have created such easy access to his rear if he felt under threat.

We emerge from the wagons to find knights assembled in ranks on both sides of a wide avenue leading to what appears to be the command post at the opposite end. The cheers that erupt in the ranks are quickly taken up by the rest of the camp as two men on horseback ride toward us from the opposite direction. Jasper and Evrouin meet us halfway. "Welcome, Your Grace," says Jasper as he and his deputy bow from their saddles. Then without another word, they wheel their horses around and lead us the rest of the way to the command tent.

Where I get my next sign that hopefulness might not be misplaced. All the formality, I now realize, is for the benefit of those watching, primarily those watching – but not cheering – from the camp facing us across a swath of meadow.

As Egon and I dismount and give our horses into the care of Robin and Osbert, Jasper greets us once again. "If it please Your Grace," he offers another slight bow and a gesture of his hand toward the tent, "may I invite you and your companion inside to partake of some refreshment."

There, I'm completely taken aback. "Samuel! Brandr!" I rush to embrace each of them in turn. No need for formalities now that we're inside.

"And Egon," says Samuel, "how is it you come to be here?"

"It is a long story, my friend, but perhaps one best told by Alfred when the time is right."

Mugs of ale are already waiting for us on a camp table. Jasper's clearly had his scouts out monitoring our progress. Good scouts. I wasn't even aware of their presence. Then again, I wasn't on the lookout for them. Something tells me the same can't be said for Carew or his hand-picked guards.

"The more pertinent question," I say after taking a long draught of ale, "is how is it *you* two come to be here?"

"We have a surprise for you," says Samuel.

"Come," says Brandr and leads us to what appears to be Jasper's personal tent. There, on a camp stool with his hands tied in front of him and one leg shackled to the stool, is a man with black eyes and a scar on his left cheek who sits fully erect the moment he catches a glimpse of me. "We caught him trying to escape across the sea to join his fleet and lead them in an attack on Denis's port."

"From what we've been able to piece together," Samuel picks up the story, "he recently got word that a substantial force had crossed his southern border and was advancing quickly to join up with Hedrek for an assault on the Teuton rear."

My spirits soar. Lorenzo and Lucia succeeded. How their countrymen were able to move so quickly is a question for another day, though perhaps they were already considering ignoring the papal threat. Suppressing a huge grin is one of the most difficult things I've ever done in my life, but I *will* not allow the Teuton king to see such emotion. The glee can wait until later.

"Rest assured, Alfred," says Brandr, "that my fleet has the straits blockaded and this one's" – he gestures toward the man on the stool – "ships cannot escape to the open sea." I wonder what inspired Brandr to use that phrase in reference to the Teuton. It will not go unnoticed that this is precisely how he referred to Charles during our first meeting in the forest.

"Sir Jasper, would you please have someone release this man's restraints?"

"But, Sire, isn't that too dangerous?"

"You've searched him for weapons, I trust."

"Indeed, Sire. And confiscated them."

"Don't assume you found them all unless you stripped him of all his clothing." The Teuton's enigmatic half-smile – the one I've seen more than once – tells me I'm right. "So do what you must," I continue, "to confine him and prevent escape or risk to your men. But he'll do me no harm while we're speaking, so the restraints are surplus to need." Jasper looks doubtful, but signals for one of the guards to do as I've asked. The Teuton shakes out his wrists and adjusts his position on the stool but says nothing.

"An army crossing your southern border," I address my nemesis. "I wonder how that came to be."

"And *I* have been wondering if you possessed the courage to use the tool I gave you or if you'd allow your sense of honor and dignity to stand in the way. I see now that we are quite alike."

"Hardly. This tool, as you call it. You've used it entirely for your own ends. To manipulate men – one man in particular – to do your bidding. To act in ways that further *your* ambitions at the expense of others. Ruthless. Cunning. But hardly honorable or moral. I, on the other hand, used the knowledge for the benefit of others. To save lives by bringing this fighting to an end. To preserve two kingdoms. Even to show the Pope a way to free himself to follow God's guidance rather than your orders. He lifted his sanction on the Kingdom East of Rome of his own free will – not because of any threat from me. You've heard their armies moved in support of King Denis. What you probably haven't heard is that the Pope has made a public declaration of the truth of his birth."

Only someone watching closely will have noticed the subtle shift in the Teuton's demeanor – the slight drop of his shoulders, the pressing together of his lips, the hardening of his gaze. He remains erect on his stool, silent in the face of my revelations.

"So, no," I conclude, "we are not at *all* alike. And you have *seriously* underestimated my determination."

Not wanting to engage in further conversation with this man until I know more about the military situation, I slowly turn and leave the tent, accompanied by Egon, Brandr, and Samuel. Behind us, Jasper gives instructions for constraining the prisoner before making his own way back to the command tent. Having made his dispositions of the guards, Carew also joins us.

Over a fresh mug of ale, I ask Brandr, "So how did you manage this?"

"We were with Hasten when he got word that the Teuton fleet was leaving port and headed for the straits. Our fleet was standing to, just off the Southern Nordics harbor, awaiting my orders. The stop there was originally intended as a courtesy call to let Hasten know what we were up to. Our plan was to sail to Denis's port and blockade it to prevent a Teuton landing and to provide protection for your transport ships when you began moving forces across the sea.

"So we quickly altered our plans and diverted enough ships to completely blockade the straits. Hasten's fishing fleet spied the Teuton king's ship on course for the straits and slowly began encircling it, tightening the noose as it got closer to shore and keeping it from escaping while Thorvald and his men boarded her. Thorvald brought her into port, placed the Teuton king in the brig of his own ship, and we set sail straightaway for these shores, along with the remaining four ships of my fleet. The crew of the Teuton ship is locked up in a jail in the Southern Nordics port. And, of course, Hasten's fishermen will remain vigilant on the open sea."

"And once you made landfall here?"

"Luck was with us," says Brandr. "There wasn't a single Teuton ship in port. Presumably, those that transported the warriors here had returned to their home port to await further orders. So no one impeded our disembarking."

"Surely you didn't come through the enemy encampment."

"We didn't even consider it," says Samuel. "The Peaks forces sitting on Gunnvor's right flank provided us with an escort. It was rather the long way around, but it seemed preferable to trusting our captive to guarantee us safe passage."

Jasper picks up the tale. "Luck was with us too. We had just finished moving the command post forward in preparation for the next push against our retreating enemy when these two arrived with their prisoner. Everyone in the front lines on the other side had a good view of their erstwhile commandant in restraints and under guard. Word must have spread quickly through their camp, because just a half hour later, they charged across the meadow. Not an organized assault, mind you. More of a crazed mob lashing out at whatever was in their path. No doubt they thought they could overwhelm the guards and free the prisoner.

"Our knights rode them down easily, and the archers quickly suppressed any further notion of mounting an attack. We spent the remainder of the day finding and collecting the rest of their leaders. Gunnvor and his cronies are being held in a makeshift prison in the rear, shackled and chained to one of the large supply wagons. They're going nowhere."

"It's been quiet on the other side since then," says Evrouin. "The scouts report some men walking away during the night, but not yet in great numbers. It's as if they're just waiting for someone to tell them it's over and they can go home."

"And we think the man to do that is already with us," Jasper resumes.

"Oh?" I ask.

"The morning after we rounded up Gunnvor and the others, I was busy preparing messages to you and to the commander of the Peaks forces waiting near our port when there was a huge commotion all along our front line. A carriage accompanied by a full honor guard pulled to a stop in front of the command tent, and an old man wearing a coronet descended slowly and surveyed his surroundings. Things were quite awkward. We had none of his language, and neither he nor any in his entourage had even the simplest words of Latin. The tension was rising when Lord de Courcy came up with the notion that the Teuton king might be able to help."

"Well," says Samuel, "if he'd been ordering the battle tactics of Gunnvor's forces, it stood to reason that he must have at least a modicum of the Eastern Kingdom tongue."

"We used him to calm the situation. Told him to convey to our visitor that we would send for a translator. I wasn't about to trust him with anything more than that. God only knows whether he would translate our words faithfully or use the opportunity for his own ends. We made space for the Easterners just beyond Evrouin's tent. The king seems content to keep to himself for now, spending most of his time in his tent but taking a stroll once a day where he can be seen by those across the meadow. I venture to say that's why there's been no further aggression from that quarter.

"In any event, his arrival meant that my messages took on a greater sense of urgency. I'd already completed the one to the Peaks commander – orders to set sail straightaway to go to King Denis's aid. It remained only for me to dash off something to you and compose a message to Abbot Warin asking for Brother Nicholas to come in haste. I hope you'll forgive me for my terseness, sir, but there was no time for long explanations. Getting the courier on his way was the priority."

"No need to fret, Jasper. Since I already knew something might be brewing across the sea, there was far less reason to be suspicious of what might be afoot here. But if you have a look in the wagon that accompanied us, you'll see Carew was taking no chances."

"Just doing my job, sir." Carew nods in my direction, a broad smile on his face. Having heard everything about the situation here, he can now relax – well, at least as much as he ever does on these missions.

"So when do you expect Brother Nicholas?" I ask.

"Soon," says Jasper. "The courier that brought the message to you went straight on to the monastery. Allowing for the fact that a monk is likely less adept as a horseman than you are, sir, he'd be at least a full day behind you, assuming he started his journey at the same time you did."

"And the departure of the Peaks forces?" Egon asks. "We saw no evidence of that when we passed through the port."

"Most likely you were there before they arrived. As you know, my lord, it's no small feat to break camp and get organized for a sea voyage – especially with a force as large as theirs."

"Then, if I may, Sir Jasper," says Egon, "I would like to send a message to Goron. Since it appears the fight here is completed, it seems safe for him to relax his vigilance and send some of his forces to join the Peaks in going to support young Denis. It will be his decision, of course, but he needs to know the situation here. Perhaps you might allow me to avail myself of your paper and ink and one of your fast couriers."

"It would be my pleasure, Lord Egon, though I don't know how many forces Denis will actually need now that he has support from his allies in the south."

"Indulge me, Sir Jasper. There is much to be gained from showing our solidarity with our friends from the Peaks after what the Teutons contrived to do at Korst's mine. Even if it turns out that Goron's men never actually engage the enemy, the gesture is important."

"Now, sir," Jasper turns to me, "would you care to greet the Eastern king? He and his entourage will have observed your arrival."

"It's getting late in what's been a particularly eventful day, Jasper. And, truth be told, I really prefer to greet him when we can actually converse. I think I'll follow his lead and retire to my tent for a quiet supper with Samuel and Brandr and Egon. If Brother Nicholas hasn't arrived by midday tomorrow, then we'll have to sort something out."

• • • • •

What an army eats is predictable. Potage and ale or porridge. The only thing that changes is the makeup of the potage. But tonight is different. There's bread that isn't horribly stale and wine – at least in our tent.

And the potage is thick with meat, lentils, and carrots. "The minute Jasper dispatched his courier to you," Samuel explains, "he sent a wagon to Peveril Castle for supplies and organized a hunting party of his best archers. He already had two kings to entertain and knew there'd be three once you arrived. The bread was fresher a couple of days ago, but at least it hasn't gotten so hard it might break a tooth."

"The hunting party came back with three stags and a boar," says Brandr, "so I suspect even the foot soldiers are getting better fare than usual."

We eat in companionable silence until our bowls are empty and I can't bear the restraint a moment longer. "What news of Edward?" I ask.

Brandr and Samuel look at one another and chuckle. "We've been wondering how long it would take you to ask," says Samuel.

"He's quite well, Alfred," says Brandr. "When we left, he was enjoying all the pleasures of my court – in particular, I think, of one of Arnora's nieces who's staying with us for the summer."

"Though he gets quite embarrassed," Samuel chimes in, "when I tease him about spending time in her company."

"She's really a lovely girl," Brandr resumes. "Not at all like her aunt. And everyone likes her, which aggravates Arnora immensely. She's complained to me more than once that the girl doesn't show the proper dignity for the royal court. I think we both know what dignity means in Arnora's lexicon. I must admit though, Alfred, that I was never so surprised as when Samuel and Edward turned up on my doorstep. And Samuel disguised as a monk, no less!"

It's Egon's turn to chuckle. "Not the first time he has done that. I think perhaps it is Alfred's preferred disguise when sending his friend on secret missions."

I glance at my friend. "Well, at least it looks like his hair is growing out well enough that his wife won't be put off by his appearance when he finally gets home."

Brandr and Egon both look quizzical. "The last time I adopted this disguise," Samuel explains, "Tamasine wouldn't share my bed unless

I wore a cap to cover my missing hair. Said she could never lie with a monk – even if it was all pretense."

"How was the journey, Samuel?"

"Interesting. You were right about the transport ships, Alfred. There were three in port offloading mountains of wood when we arrived, so securing passage was easy. But we did see some evidence of young trees just beginning to develop into forests, so perhaps the lessons in forestry that Brandr's tried to teach are starting to take hold."

"I do hope so," says Brandr. "Our need to supply their fuel every year is starting to put a strain on our own resources, vast though those may be."

The conversation pauses when a camp follower comes in to collect our empty bowls and deliver another pitcher of wine. When she leaves, Samuel brings us back to the serious matters at hand. "So what are our next steps, Alfred?"

"We settle things here first. We can't take the risk that if we divert our attention across the sea, a new fight might erupt here and Jasper would have his hands full all over again. This meeting with the Eastern king is crucial. That's why I don't even want to begin that dialogue without a translator I can trust. I just hope their king can – and more importantly, wants to – control what's left of Gunnvor's army. For all we know at the moment, he's annoyed at our invasion and angry that Gunnvor couldn't hold us at bay."

"If that were the case, why would he have chosen to stay here – in our camp – rather than across the meadow with his own people?" asks Samuel. "It looks to me like he's sending them a message."

"I hope you're right. But I have to be on my guard that it might not be that at all." Brandr and Egon nod their agreement. I take a sip of wine. "I really must remember to compliment Peveril on his cellar. I certainly didn't expect *this* in the middle of a battlefield."

"Nor I," says Brandr. "So, Alfred, once things are settled here?"

"If I can prevail on you, Brandr, I'd like all of us to take the Teuton king to face Denis and to call off his armies. You too, Egon, if you wish to join us."

"That's why we're here, Alfred," says Brandr. "We'll sail with Thorvald and my other ships will follow. My fondest hope is that those ships can be part of transporting your men and those from the Peaks and the Territories back home."

"And I will decline your kind offer, my friend," says Egon. "It is essential in these matters that Goron be seen to represent our interests."

"Then all we can do for now is to see how things lie with the Eastern king," says Samuel, downing the remainder of the wine in his mug. "And the sooner I find my bed, the sooner it will be morning and the sooner we'll find out." He rises and makes for the tent flap, followed quickly by Egon.

Brandr lingers, dividing what remains in the wine pitcher between my mug and his. "I'm always impressed with your ingenuity, Alfred, but sending Samuel through the Northern Kingdom was brilliant. We knew some of what was afoot. Hasten's spies reported the massing of the Teuton army on Denis's border. They'd also seen a few Teuton ships headed west rather than south from the straits. The fishing fleet tracked them to the middle of the Northern Sea before turning back, so we suspected some connection to the Eastern Kingdom but didn't know what. Which left us in a quandary over the right action to take. Once Samuel filled in the rest of the details, it was much easier to see how we could help Denis in ways that wouldn't be available to you."

He pauses for a sip of wine. "Hasten sends his greetings, by the way. He is, of necessity, playing the role of neutral party once again, but he has high hopes that sending the Teutons home in defeat will subdue their ambitions . . . for a time at least."

"I share his hope . . . but with great caution. Nothing I know about the Teuton king gives me any insight into whether his reaction will be to lash out against us or to turn his sights elsewhere."

"An unavoidable problem, I fear, when dealing with men who are both ambitious and cunning. Samuel told me your thoughts on just what a long game this particular man has been playing. If you're right, he may view this as only a momentary setback. Best we pray to all the gods we know that he has other irons in the fire to occupy his attention." Nominally a Christian, Brandr believes there's nothing to be lost – and perhaps something to be gained – by appealing to the old Nordic gods as well.

"I . . . I simply don't have adequate words to thank you for protecting my son, Brandr. When Geoffrey decided his duty lay in staying with our people . . . On the one hand, I was enormously proud of him. On the other, I'd have breathed ever so much easier if he'd taken refuge with his betrothed at the Peaks court."

"You could have sent him there anyway."

"Aye. But what would that have taught him about the art of kingship?"

Brandr chuckles. "Raising future kings is not for the faint of heart." He raises his mug. "To our sons!" I join him in the toast. "In any event, Alfred, I don't require your thanks. You'd have done the same for Thorbrand."

"Without question. How are the young couple faring?"

"Quite well. Margery's surrounded herself with some lovely young women – her solution, I think, to staying out of Arnora's way. And she's welcomed my mother into their little gatherings. Arnora whines at me from time to time that Margery's setting up a separate court or that Mother should be attending her own gatherings instead. I can't help but be amused that Arnora had no use for Mother until someone else made her welcome."

"How is Aunt Beatrix, by the way?"

"Showing her age more than she would like. But Margery's company has been a blessing for her."

Later, as Osbert is removing my boots before we settle into our camp beds, I ask him how young Robin is faring. "He be right beside hisself fer certes, m'lord. In all his life, he never see a battlefield or so many knights all in one place or so many kings. I be having to remind him to be closing his jaw . . . that it not be proper fer a squire to an important lord to be gawking about all the time. But it be just the first day. So I be thinking once he be here fer another day and it all not be so new, he be just fine."

"I'm sure you're right, Osbert. It's quite a lot to take in for a young lad who's only ever known village life. Do you plan to take him with us when we cross the sea to Denis's kingdom?"

"Nay, m'lord. That be too much all at once. So I be sending him home with Lord Egon."

"What makes you think Egon's not crossing the sea with us?"

"On account of all those lords do things together, and most like Egon not be wanting the others to be feeling left out."

"You are quite an astute observer, Osbert. I'm impressed." And as I pull the blanket over me for the night, I'm also curious about what he might have observed about Goron increasingly taking the lead on behalf of all the Territorial lords. At least I know I can rely on him not to voice those observations unless he knows I'd approve.

I spend the early hours of the following morning wandering about the camp, talking with knights, archers, foot soldiers, and camp followers. Carew and Evrouin are never more than a few steps away. I tried to convince them I'd be perfectly safe on my own, but to no avail. "It's good for the commanders to be seen as well, Sire," Evrouin pointed out, "so we can stop two gaps with one bush." I could hardly argue with that.

As the sun is nearing its zenith, a commotion near the command tent draws Evrouin's attention. "I'd best go see what's up, Sire," he says.

"Why don't we all go?" I suggest. "If we're lucky, it might be Brother Nicholas arriving."

And indeed it is. "I came as quickly as I could," Nicholas is telling Jasper when we enter the tent. "But I didn't want to overtax my horse. She's not used to such long journeys."

"Nicholas, you're the most welcome sight I've seen today."

The monk turns at the sound of my voice. "Then it's a good day for me as well," he replies.

"Has Jasper explained what we need?"

"Aye, he has."

"Then as soon as you've refreshed yourself, I'd like to get on with things." Brandr, Samuel, and Egon – who'd apparently spent the morning with Jasper – nod their agreement.

"Sir Jasper's already given me a mug of ale, sir. I need nothing more at the moment."

As we make our way to the Eastern king's tent, Nicholas explains the protocol. "I'll stop just inside the tent flap and introduce myself as the translator everyone's been waiting for then request permission for all of us to enter the tent. You should step inside one at a time so I can introduce you – you first, Alfred, since you're his nearest neighbor. He'll expect no deference from his fellow kings, but a nod of the head from the lords would go a long way toward assuring him no one is trying to run roughshod over his sovereignty. Sir Jasper, if you can bring yourself to do so, a deep bow would be what he expects from a military man."

The arrangements inside the tent provide a good indication that members of his entourage have been observing the hierarchy within our ranks. Two chairs with arms, similar to the one he occupies, sit nearest him, at right angles to his position so he can easily converse with his fellow monarchs. A stool directly adjacent to his chair is obviously meant for Brother Nicholas. Three additional stools facing him provide seating for Samuel, Egon, and Jasper. Guards stand at attention along three sides of the tent.

The king's long grey hair, which brushes the tops of his shoulders, and his extremely thin physique suggest someone old and frail. But the straightness of his posture when he rises to receive us and the intensity of his gaze reveal a strength that's not to be trifled with.

Formalities complete, I begin with, "We're honored that you choose to make your camp among us. I want you to know, first and foremost, that this fight was not of our choosing and that our presence on your soil is only to secure the surrender of those who came against us." Nicholas wastes no time in translating my words.

"I have no tolerance for this uprising either, which is why I have come to help put a stop to it." His voice is strong, like that of a much younger man. Old he may be. Frail he is not. "We knew of Gunnvor's plot to overthrow me and were preparing to quash it when the Teutons landed and went to join him. We were also aware that you were using his sister as some sort of go-between, but to what end, we could not work out."

"We learned of Gunnvor's scheming from his sister. I have no tolerance for upstarts like him whose ambitions exceed their good sense. We were trying to find a way to get word to you that we were prepared to be of assistance if that was needed to defeat the plotters. But we did not trust the sister to carry that message. Once we learned of the arrival of the Teutons, we knew that Gunnvor was being used to further their ends, though what the Teuton king might have promised in return, we can only guess."

"I have no doubt it was my throne." He pauses before continuing. "I am given to understand that Gunnvor and those who plotted with him are now your prisoners. As is the Teuton king. Perhaps they should be brought here to face the consequences of their actions."

Jasper looks to me. "Sire?"

"I don't disagree with my fellow monarch, Sir Jasper. Have them brought here, if you will." It's then that I notice five more stools placed side by side in the open area on the opposite side of the tent. Clearly, the Eastern king intends to be in charge of these proceedings. So long as we get what we need, I'm happy to allow him that. After all, it's *his* kingdom that's been invaded by two foreign forces – four, if you count the Peaks and Lakes as distinct from us.

Nothing further is said until Jasper's men return with the prisoners, Gunnvor and his cronies with their hands shackled behind their backs, the Teuton king with his hands tied in front of him as an acknowledgment of his status. As each of the cronies takes a seat on a stool, an Eastern guard moves to stand immediately behind him. The Teuton king is allowed to sit alone. Jasper motions for his own men to wait outside.

The Eastern king rises and walks slowly from one end to the other of the seated prisoners, not deigning to look at his own countrymen but pausing to briefly study the Teuton. When he returns to his chair, his next words are addressed to me. "A pathetic lot, are they not?"

Knowing I need the Teuton for other purposes, I refrain from joining in my fellow sovereign's condemnation, asking instead, "How do you propose we deal with them?"

"Those four are mine," he gestures to Gunnvor and the three others. "They will be made an example of. A lesson to any other who might consider being so bold as to challenge their king. Their lands and titles are already forfeit and their families attainted. The land will be given to men whose loyalty is beyond question. And those men who are now my prisoners will be taken to my dungeon to await their fates. Him," he points to Gunnvor, "I have already decided will be executed. His sister as well if I ever find her."

"His sister has already been dealt with. She was held briefly as my prisoner before she was banished to a place from which she can't return. She'll never be a threat to either of us again." Wherever she is – whether in the convent Laurence spoke of or in the next world as Samuel believes – I'm grateful that's already a fait accompli.

"Him," he now points to the Teuton, "I have no use for. You are the one he has harmed, so it is you who should decide his fate. I only want him out of my sight and out of my kingdom."

"I have no disagreement with your dispositions, especially since I need him to end the other part of this conflict."

He speaks to his guards, who take the four prisoners out of the tent, and I nod to Jasper for his men to take custody of the Teuton. When we're again alone, the Eastern king resumes. "I will this afternoon take command of the rabble on the other side of the meadow. From there, I intend to march them to my castle to sort out those who have been complicit with Gunnvor from those who were merely conscripts. To that end, Sir Jasper, I require you to withdraw your forces along the rabble's flank as quickly as possible and then to remove all of your army from my lands."

Jasper says nothing, wisely not acknowledging an order from a foreign king, and I speak up quickly to minimize the awkwardness.

"Sir Jasper and I will discuss an orderly withdrawal to our own territory. We have no wish to remain here now that the hostilities are over and you've taken charge of your own people. I do agree, Sir Jasper, that it would be a good idea for you to send a fast messenger to the captain of the flanking force, ordering them to stand down and pull back from their current position."

"As you wish, Sire," says Jasper.

"And then, King Alfred," the Eastern king resumes, "it is my wish that we return to our previous way of existence. Neighbors who leave each other alone."

"May I offer one suggestion?"

"I have no wish to discuss alliances."

"That is your privilege. My suggestion concerns the woodlands and meadows in the south of your kingdom. I've been given to understand that many decaying corpses of men and animals still remain there. I ask that you allow us to clean up the meadow. And once that's complete, we'll leave and return it to nature." He stares at me, wondering, I'm sure, what ulterior motives might be behind my request. "It was because of us that the Teutons despoiled the wildness of the place. It seems only right that we should restore it to its natural state. There are wild places like that in my kingdom as well, and I would be dismayed if they became places of rot and decay." But, of course, I *do* have ulterior motives. This may be our only chance to learn precisely what lies in that part of the world.

He continues to stare at me in silence. At long last, he says, "I will accept your offer. But do it quickly and then be gone."

"I too have a request," Brandr says.

"Very well. What is it?" The Eastern king's tone and his expression are both of annoyance.

"You know that four of my ships are, at present, in your harbor. May we have permission to traverse your lands to take our prisoner to those ships? We'll then depart immediately for the Kingdom Across the Southern Sea and have no need to return." Thank you, Brandr, for thinking of this. The last thing we need is to be waylaid or attacked on that journey.

"Permission granted. And to ensure no one interferes with you, one of my guards will bring you a safe-passage before the day is over." He rises. "I believe our business is finished and that this war is at an end."

Our cue to leave.

Back in the command tent, Jasper brings Evrouin into the picture, ending with, "So you see, all your time spent these last few days on withdrawal plans wasn't wasted effort. I'm sure the king and his entourage will be decamping to the other side of the meadow this afternoon. But I want to observe their departure before we begin our own. That said, I need to get word to the Peaks commander on the flank to pull back and not impede their progress. Who's your fastest courier?"

"I'll have him here by the time your orders are ready," says Evrouin as he heads out the tent flap. Jasper sits at his camp desk and, in no time at all, is pouring wax and sealing his message.

Once the courier is on his way, we can all relax. "That was a most intriguing encounter," says Egon.

"Pretty clear," says Samuel, "that he was just biding his time, letting us do all the work of mopping up his rebels and sending the Teutons packing."

"Well," Jasper chuckles, "I'm not sure we sent any of them packing, Sir Samuel, except to St. Peter's Gate. Unless they're cowering in that rabble he's taking to his castle, they're lying dead somewhere in the field. Neither Gunnvor nor the Teuton king showed any interest in collecting their dead. We've burned many of them, but I've no doubt there are plenty more rotting in the fields."

"Brother Nicholas, I'm once again in your debt," I say. "We'd never have gotten through that without you."

"There's no debt, sir. I'm happy to be of service. Truth be told, I never dreamed when I was growing up, always going back and forth between our two villages, that knowing both languages and the customs of both kingdoms would ever be so important."

"Do those two villages by chance share a clapper bridge? A bit north of where the stream turns east?"

"The very same, sir."

"Any idea what happened to those villagers, Jasper? I'm sure they would've been in the path of the Lakes forces as they pushed Gunnvor's cronies away from the border."

"Not specifically, Sire. Any villagers along the border who fled into our lands would've been encouraged to seek refuge at the quarries."

"Do you think you could spare some men to go with Brother Nicholas to the quarries to see if any of his people are there and then to help them get resettled in their village? They'll need food and building materials and some chickens and a cow or a few goats to get their lives back on track."

"Consider it done, Sire."

"I'd be ever so grateful, sir," says Nicholas, "but I don't know if Father Abbot can spare me from my duties."

"Don't fret about that, Nicholas. I've no doubt Warin will consider it another opportunity for you to serve your fellow man – especially when he receives my message that I've encouraged you to do just that. Get your people started putting their lives back together, and then it will be time to return to the monastery."

• • • • •

That night, as I lie awake with Osbert snoring softly in the other camp bed, my thoughts return to the encounter with the Eastern king. Is he truly the hard man he presented to us? A harsh ruler whose demands might have pushed Gunnvor and the others to rebellion. Or was he compelled to take control of the proceedings because he felt outnumbered? Not just by the imposing size of the foreign armies on his soil but also by the number of kings and great lords arrayed opposite him.

With no need even for bargaining, we got everything I wanted. How does that square with the man who insisted on dominating the proceedings? And then I think back to Samuel's remark about him letting us do all the work.

Perhaps, at his core, he's merely a kind-hearted, unassuming man, ill-suited to cope with the brewing rebellion – an easy target for the likes of Gunnvor – and utterly unprepared to deal with foreign intervention. Perhaps his pride prevented him from asking for help – or perhaps he simply didn't know how. If he *is* of such a temperament, it would explain the ease with which Charles was able march through his kingdom to invade ours so many years ago. Perhaps his unwillingness to engage further with us reflects a sense of shame that we had to do the work for him.

How I wish we could have spoken directly, without the awkwardness of Nicholas's translation! Had that been possible, I might have been better able to judge his true nature. As it is, I can only speculate . . . and wonder . . . and be grateful to Laurence that, despite all the turmoil involved, he now has an asset to help us learn more about this heretofore opaque society.

·   ·   ·   ·   ·

The following morning, we depart to three different points of the compass. Egon and Robin ride west, Robin in possession of my letters to Warin and to Gwen. I had to suppress a smile as I listened to Osbert give Robin his instructions. "Now, when ye be back at the castle, first thing be to get Lord Egon settled. After that be done, then ye go in search of Letty and ask her all nice like to be taking ye to the queen. Mayhap it be she say she be giving the letters to the queen fer ye. But it be *yer* job to be sure fer certes those letters be in the queen's hands. So ye tell Letty, all nice like again, that the king give you a message fer the queen and say ye should be telling her yerself. Mayhap ye have to wait a bit if m'lady be busy. Ye just do what Letty say. Then when ye see the queen, ye tell her the king be all safe and he say the fighting be done and the army be coming home soon. And dinna' ferget to be giving her the letters."

Brother Nicholas has acquired quite the entourage for his journey northwest. Half a dozen knights, just in case they should run into any trouble along the way. A score or more of archers and foot soldiers whose homes are somewhere in the vicinity of the quarries. A large wagon laden with food and a couple dozen camp tents, in anticipation that the villagers will need some sort of shelter while they repair their homes and outbuildings. Even a couple of spare horses to give the villagers some transportation and some help with the spring ploughing. Nicholas seems overwhelmed by the generosity. He's just the right man, I think, to inspire those people to rebuild their familiar little world.

While Carew sees to the preparations for our own trip east to the waiting ships, I take Jasper aside. "There's something I want you to do, Jasper, as the army withdraws from the field."

"What might that be, Sire?"

"It will go against your inclination to be the last to leave, but I want you among the first to go home. You and Evrouin. Let the garrison commandant deal with stragglers and tying up any loose ends at the rear. I want you to lead your army home in triumph. God knows you've earned it."

"It's a generous gesture, Sire, but I really don't need the glory. We did what we had to do. And now that it's done, it's more important to me to see that no one and nothing gets left behind."

"That's why you're a good commander, Jasper. But there's more to my request than generosity. The people need a show – they need to *see* that we've triumphed over everything that was arrayed against us. And what better show than the commander and his deputy leading the victorious army home, banners flying. There are so very many who won't be coming home. The pain of that, for those who loved them, will be unbearable for a time. But if they can see with their own eyes that we've soundly defeated the enemy – that their loved ones fought for something important – then maybe it will be just a bit easier for them to make some sense of their personal loss."

Carew clears his throat from a respectful distance and I glance his way. "We're ready when you are, sir," he says.

I hold up a finger, signaling I'll join him momentarily. "Make it a good show, Jasper. And tell the queen to prepare for a big celebration when I get home."

"As you wish, sir. Now best you be off. The sooner you put a stop to the war across the sea the happier we'll all be."

As we make our way to where Altair stands saddled and awaiting his rider, Carew explains his dispositions. "Until we're well clear of that rabble, I want both you and King Brandr well protected, so this is the formation. Lord de Courcy and I will ride in the lead. Immediately behind us, you and King Brandr will ride single-file with guards on both sides and a row of guards behind you. Next comes the Teuton king, surrounded by guards, then the squires and the remainder of the guards. We're leaving the wagon behind – packs only for the rest of the journey. There'll be food on board the ship, and at Denis's encampment, there'll be both food and shelter." While I check Altair's gear before mounting up, he finishes with, "Everyone's assembled, sir, just waiting for us to take our places in the formation."

We ride across the meadow at a walk, giving Carew and Samuel an opportunity to survey the camp on the other side. There's no more activity along the front line than we saw yesterday, so we can only assume the Eastern King is somewhere in the rear giving his orders. About five yards from the line, Carew calls a halt. Are we going to have to plough our way through rows and rows of men who seem to have nothing to do but sit on their backsides?

Then somewhere off to our left, someone barks an order and the men in front of us slowly and reluctantly move to make a path – a path that's barely wide enough for us to pass through. Carew waits until the path is about five horse-lengths long then turns in his saddle and shouts, "At the gallop . . . *now*!" He and Samuel charge headlong into he path, the rest of our formation hot on their heels. On both sides, men scramble to get out of the way of the flying hooves, any reluctance o stir themselves now transformed into frantic efforts at self-preservation. No one has a moment even to consider putting up a ight.

Carew maintains the pace until we're well clear of the camp and he's certain there's not a reserve lurking off the rear that could take us by surprise. Once he's satisfied the road ahead is clear, he calls for a rot and then quickly slows to a walk to allow the horses to cool down. Turning in his saddle once again, he invites Brandr and me to become the second rank. The guards around us adjust their formation so that only the Teuton is still surrounded.

"That was rather exciting," says Brandr. "But I must admit, it's as lose as I want to come to an all-out cavalry charge. It must take normous courage to ride like that into the teeth of armed men determined to make short shrift of your time on earth."

"What it takes mostly, Sire," says Carew, "is training."

"And really good horses," Samuel adds with a chuckle then turns erious. "Those who survive – man and horse alike – are those who've aken to heart the lesson that hesitation will be their undoing."

For the remainder of our journey, we maintain a fast pace. Not only do I want to reach Denis as quickly as we can, but I worry about the length of time we've held the Teuton king captive. Once we're on board ship, I insist he have some time on deck with the caveat that he not be allowed access to the ship's railings. It seems unlikely he would choose to throw himself into the sea. From what I know of him, I'd wager his curiosity about what I intend to do with him surpasses any thought of self-destruction. Unless, of course, he's contemplating denying me the opportunity to determine his fate. Since it's impossible to know, it's essential to take no chances.

Even sailing into the prevailing westerlies, Thorvald manages a rapid passage to Denis's port. On our last night at sea, I retire to my cabin to compose a message to Denis. There are things he must know things he must do – before our arrival if my plans are to succeed.

My dear Denis,

The threat on my eastern border has been suppressed and the fighting is at an end. By now, the Peaks reinforcements should be with your army. I hope their presence, combined with the new advance from the south, has altered the battlefield dynamics in your favor.

Once your southern ally joined the fray, you no doubt deduced what I've done. There was no time – nor even any way – to consult you in the matter, so I had no choice but to presume you would have no objection. I look forward to telling you the full story of that adventure as soon as we see the backs of those who've dared to invade your kingdom.

And to that purpose, we'll be with you about a day from when you receive this missive. Carew is with me, as are others you'll be pleased to see. The Teuton king is in our custody, and it's my intention that he put an end to the hostilities.

But there are some things I need you to do before we arrive. We'll go straight to Aleffe Manor, so get safely back there straightaway. Send out scouts or post lookouts to ensure you have advance knowledge of our arrival. Then ride out to meet us as we approach the manor. In full regal attire, surrounded by an honor guard flying your banner – and on the tallest horse you have available. The Teuton's big grey isn't with us, so you'll be the most commanding presence of all. It's our turn to stage the tableau.

It will all be over soon.

Alfred

The moment we're alongside – even before we're fully moored – one of Thorvald's men is over the side, swapping a purse full of silver coins for the horse of the nearest mounted man and pausing only long enough for directions to the monastery before galloping away with my letter in his satchel. The other three Nordic ships stand to off the port guards against any unwelcome arrivals, though if Brandr is right about his blockade, they'll see no action. The rest of the afternoon is spent offloading the horses in preparation for the onward journey.

We spend the night on the ship. I'm unwilling to disembark the Teuton king in a town that's likely teeming with his agents until the very moment we can put him on a horse surrounded by guards and ride away. But on the morrow, it will suit my purposes very well for those agents to see him captive and begin to spread the word that it might be wise to leave town while they still can.

We depart an hour before midday. It's roughly a day's ride to Aleffe Manor, so the time reflects a compromise between my desire to arrive there in early afternoon and Carew's to keep the pace up lest we fall prey to an ambush along the road. We camp for the night in an open meadow, far away from any trees or even hedges, denying cover to anyone who might be tempted to sneak up on us during the night. The moon is with us too – just a day past full, giving the sentries ample light even until dawn begins to tinge the eastern horizon.

An hour past midday on the following day, as we approach the lane leading to the manor, it's time for the spectacle to play out. Carew calls a halt and signals to a guard to remove the restraints from the Teuton's wrists. We then adjust our own formation to place him in the front rank so he misses nothing, Samuel and Carew ride either side of him with Brandr and me on the flanks – an arrangement Carew insisted on. "Should he try to make a run for it, Sire," Carew had said, "you and King Brandr can veer off and make way for the guards to charge in pursuit." When Samuel agreed with Carew, I had little choice but to acquiesce, though it wasn't quite the image I'd hoped to present.

Despite having had little time to organize things, Denis has managed exactly what was needed. When we turn into the lane, his entourage begins a measured pace toward us. Somewhere he's found a solid black stallion that appears to be at least sixteen hands high, its coat gleaming in the sunlight. The guards who ride with him are all mounted on greys, some almost white. Their formation is two rows of seven abreast, three guards either side of Denis, the middle one on each side bearing the king's banner. The image is striking. Even better than I'd dared hope.

They stop where a track leaves the lane to skirt around the main grounds of the manor. When we come to a halt opposite them, just short of the track, Denis says, "Gentlemen, I invite you to join me at my command post." His formation wheels onto the track then re-forms into a column two abreast. As they do so, Denis raises his voice to add, "May I suggest proceeding at the trot. We have some distance to cover."

Even at the trot, it's at least a quarter of an hour before we reach the rear of the encampment, where we have to slow to a walk, and almost as long before we come to the command tent at the edge of the empty field separating the two armies. There, Denis and his guards dismount and enter the tent. We follow suit. Carew gives instructions for our guards to wait outside, though he, himself, follows me into the tent. The only men inside, other than the guards, I take to be Denis's commander and deputy.

Camp stools have been arranged in a circle with a large gap nearest the tent flap. The Teuton is given the center stool, with Denis and me at each end, facing him. "Perhaps, Commander," Denis addresses one of the two men I've never met, "you would repeat for our guests the report you gave me this morning on the progress of the fighting here."

"With pleasure, Your Grace. As I told you, the reinforcements who recently joined us have made a considerable difference. Over the past two days, we have pushed our opponents a mile or a bit more away from their previous position. The pause today to accommodate these visitors is but a brief lull. When the fighting resumes tomorrow, I have no reason to doubt that we will continue to advance.

"As you know, Sire, I received word this morning that the army of the Kingdom East of Rome has connected with Lord Hedrek's defenders along the border and that the Teuton border troops are putting up no resistance but are, instead, fleeing to the interior. Lord Hedrek reports they will be in position by now to launch an all-out assault on the Teuton rear guard."

"Thank you, Commander," says Denis. "Gentlemen, the dynamics of the fight may be taking a turn, but victory is far from assured. And I've long since grown exasperated and annoyed at the senseless bloodshed and the number of lives expended just to keep my kingdom intact." He pauses briefly before adding, "This fight is *not* of my choosing."

Brandr and Samuel glance my way and I shake my head ever so slightly. What's needed now is silence, and none of us should break it. A gentle breeze lifts the tent flap then drops it against the tent wall with a little slap that wouldn't normally be noticed. Outside, a group of foot soldiers pass by, laughing among themselves. From somewhere in the distance comes a shout, presumably orders being given. The whinny of a horse is answered by another and then another. We all take great pains studying our boots.

At long last, the Teuton asks, "Why have you brought me here?"

"To order an end to the hostilities," I reply.

Denis understands instinctively this is his moment to speak. "To take your armies *out* of my kingdom." He pauses for effect then adds, "And keep them out."

"And why would I do that?"

Brandr touches Denis's arm and gives him a barely perceptible shake of the head. It's my answer that matters most, and I've chosen my words carefully. "Because your gamble hasn't paid off. Because you lost hundreds and hundreds of men in the ill-fated partnership with Gunnvor – all to no avail. Because the young king has risen to the challenge to defend his lands. Because your army is in serious disarray – in retreat here and under threat from the rear. And because your fleet is not coming to their rescue."

"And what if, once I take command, I reorganize and launch a new assault?"

"I think you already know that would be ill-advised. The forces closing in on your flank and your rear are far from battle-weary. You've heard what fresh reinforcements here have accomplished in just a day or two. And if your spies have been telling you the truth, you also know we have significant additional reserves, ready to take the field, who have yet to wield a sword or swing a flail. It's time for this to end."

The silence in the tent is profound. Time slows to a crawl as the Teuton contemplates his next words. At long last, he looks directly into Denis's eyes, searching for something – some reaction perhaps. Denis returns the gaze and doesn't flinch. He learned his lesson well that day in the forest.

In due course, the black eyes seek me out. "If I do this, will those who have invaded my lands from the south and west withdraw?"

"As soon as we can get word to them."

"And what assurance do I have that you will not then turn on us in revenge – with all those fresh troops you speak of?"

"You have my word of honor. And I think you know that can be trusted."

"What about the boy king?"

"He's no longer a boy."

Denis recognizes it's his turn. "You have my word of honor as well. What I want is not revenge but to live in peace with the boundaries of my realm intact."

Another long pause and then, "Very well. Let us put an end to this."

"There's one other thing I require," I say.

"Require?" asks the Teuton incredulously.

"Call off your hostage-takers. Wherever they may be lurking."

And there's that enigmatic half-smile once again. Perhaps he was hoping I wouldn't think of that. That half-smile guaranteed the peace during Denis's regency. I suppose it will have to suffice for now.

The Teuton rises from his stool. "And now I may go?"

"My honor guard will escort you to your troops," says Denis, rising as well. Samuel and Brandr follow suit.

"There's just one more thing." Rising from my own stool, I reach into my pocket, withdraw the amulet, and hold it up by its chain. "Have you ever seen this before?"

The black eyes flash – the first sign of emotion I've ever seen from this man – but he recovers quickly. "Where did you get that?"

"From the body of a man found dead in a collapsed barn after a winter storm over a year ago. The same collapse that killed my mother and the First Lord of my realm."

The Teuton's shoulders fall ever so slightly at the word dead. "And where is this man now?"

"Buried somewhere in a pauper's grave. We could never work out who he was or find anyone who knew him."

The amulet sways gently from side to side on its chain, sparkling now and then when it catches the sunlight streaming through the open tent flap. The Teuton can't take his eyes off it. At long last, he turns his gaze back to me. "That piece is one of a kind. There is no other like it. It belonged to my son – not my heir – my second son. He was sent to your land to immerse himself in your society. To ingratiate himself with important men. To become one of you." He pauses to glance at the amulet. "And to take your throne if you had made the wrong choice."

It takes all my self-control to keep my expression and my voice neutral and my words measured. "Yet in the end, it was all for nought." I fancy I see a sadness in his eyes that's never been there before.

He opens his hand. "May I take it with me?"

I take my time, carefully coiling the chain in my hand and laying the amulet respectfully on top of it before returning it to my pocket. "I think I'll keep it for now." He lowers his hand to his side and his gaze to the ground. "But perhaps someday in the future – when I'm confident of your intent to live in peace and mutual respect alongside the heir to Goscelin's legacy – perhaps then it will find its way back to you."

He squares his shoulders and offers me an almost imperceptible nod of the head – nothing anyone could consider as deference, but an acknowledgment nevertheless. "You have proven yourself a worthy opponent, King Alfred." He turns to Denis. "And I think perhaps you show some of Goscelin's perspicacity." He turns back to me. "Is there anything else?"

"You're free to go." He looks all around one more time then makes for the tent flap as I add, "The debt has been paid."

We watch from outside the tent as Denis's guards escort the Teuton king across the meadow, five abreast and slightly behind. Midway across the field, the guards pull up and observe as the Teuton covers the remaining distance alone and is rapidly swallowed up in the camp. The sounds of a cheer begin but are quickly silenced. In their camp, at least, there's no cause for celebration.

Denis is busy giving orders. "Your fastest courier, Commander. Instructions to Hedrek and the others to withdraw immediately behind our borders. No one goes home until we're confident the Teutons are in full retreat, but they're to stay within our territory."

"And our own army, Your Grace?"

"Follow them. At a respectful distance. But leave them in no doubt you intend to see they cross the border and go home. No one to raise a finger against them. But if they turn to fight, leave them in no doubt that we'll slaughter every last one of them if that's what it takes to make this kingdom whole again." He pauses for a moment. "But somehow, Commander, I doubt that will be necessary. The Teuton king knows he's met his match for now. And his army's in too much disarray at the moment to do much of anything but go home and lick their wounds."

As the commander bows and hurries about his business, the rest of us can finally greet each other as friends. Denis rushes to embrace

Brandr first of all, an enormous smile on his face. "I suppose our friendship's no longer a secret," he chuckles. "And Lord de Courcy!" He embraces Samuel. "I'm sure there's a story behind your presence here, and I want to hear everything. Shall we return to the manor?"

Denis leads the way with Crespin at his side as we all mount up and fall somewhat haphazardly into a column, guards intermingled behind us. "Where on earth did you find that impressive horse in the middle of a battlefield?" I ask Denis.

"Remarkable, isn't he? He's actually a product of our draught horse breeding program but much too high-spirited to ever settle comfortably into the traces, so we put him in training as a destrier. Even though he's not fully trained, my commanders insisted on bringing every available horse into the field so they had plenty of spares. But having ridden him, I think I might just keep him for myself."

"Truth be told, Your Graces, my lord," says Crespin, "the king's had a soft spot for that horse from the day he was foaled. I'm pretty certain he's never going to be a war horse – unless he's the king's war horse."

Denis urges the big black stallion to a canter, and we're all hard-pressed to keep up with those long legs, but the race, as it were, makes for a pleasant ride back to the manor. A messenger must have galloped back from the camp ahead of us, because wine is already poured and waiting when we shed our weapons and make our way into the drawing room. Denis waits until we all have a glass in hand then raises his. "To the folly of false choices . . . and to the best friends any man could ever have."

We talk the rest of the afternoon, over a remarkably good evening meal, and long into the night about everything that's led us to this moment. At one point, Denis suggests a grand state visit here to celebrate. "A chance to acknowledge what we've accomplished together," he concludes.

"And quite possibly bankrupt your Treasury," Brandr chuckles.

"Maybe you should set that idea aside for the time being," I say. "That progress you've been wanting to make? Now's the perfect time. Visit your nobles, yes, but spend time with your people. Show them your compassion. Let them know you share the pain of their losses. Help them understand what it was all for. And the sooner you do it, the better. Nothing will bind their loyalty to you more firmly."

"Alfred's right," says Brandr. "And don't make it all about loss either. Let them be part of the victory as well. Not grandiose banquets but more intimate celebrations they can really feel part of."

"There's someone else you need to thank," I say.

"Oh?" Denis asks.

"The Duchess of Lamoreaux. Without her help, I could never have gotten an audience with the Pope. Nor, I think, would her countrymen have responded so rapidly to the rescinding of the Pope's threat had she not personally encouraged them. Without her, we would both still be slogging it out on our respective battlefields for who knows how much longer. Lucia may be my cousin – mine and Brandr's – but she's a jewel in your court."

"I've known she was special," says Denis, "from the moment she gave me her own coronet for my coronation. That was a gesture very few could have made had they been in the same position. Until Uncle Charles died, there was little I could do for her because she was still mistrusted by both factions. But of late, when she's come to court, the welcome is genuine. I think, though, that my gratitude to her will have to be a private matter. To reveal her role in ending the war would expose *your* role, Alfred, in intervening with the Pope. And just as we decided after that day in the forest that what we learned was best kept secret, so it seems to me that what you did with it is also best held closely among the very few of us who know why it was necessary."

"That shows remarkable wisdom, Denis," says Brandr.

"I agree," I reply. "With both of you." I've always thought this young man would make a good king. Now I believe he'll make an extraordinary one.

As we drain the last drops from the brandy decanter, I return to practicalities. "I've no choice but to ask, Denis, if we might prevail on your hospitality for a few more days. I'd hate to get back home only to learn that the Teuton has done something stupid and I have to come back to remind him of his commitments."

"You're welcome for as long as you'd like, Alfred. All of you."

"Should I send word to Thorvald," asks Brandr, "to dispatch one of our ships to bring Edward home?"

"Probably best to wait a few days . . . give the Teuton time to get messages to his agents that hostages are no longer required. We can send for Edward at the same time we set sail from here."

And with that, we all drain our glasses and go in search of our beds. It's been a momentous day. Will I finally sleep well tonight?

Osbert greets me with, "There be someone here what be wanting to say hello, m'lord."

As he shuts the door I turn to find my visitor on the other side of the room. "Cedric! What a nice surprise! And look at you – all cleaned up and looking like a proper knight again."

Cedric bows. "Aye, Your Grace. As soon as I heard what happened, I went in search of Carew to find out if it was really true. Osbert was still seeing to your horses, but when he finished, he helped me get cleaned up and the servants here found me some clean clothes and . . . well, here I am. Carew says I shouldn't be needed here any longer and can come home with him."

"Indeed you can, Cedric. We're staying a few more days to be sure the Teuton king keeps his word, but then we'll be headed home. And with no leaping between fishing boats to get there."

"I'm grateful, Sire."

"It's I who's grateful, Cedric." I extend my arm and we exchange the warrior's greeting. "And I intend to see you're properly rewarded, so start thinking about which one of those foals you'd like to have."

He grins. "I'll have a look once we're back home. But for now, I think I'll just go get a good night's sleep in a real bed for a change."

I suspect Cedric falls asleep the moment his head hits the pillow. Soldiers have a knack for that. Not so for me. Perhaps it's the release of knowing it's finally over . . . for now, at least. My mind relives the events of the day, from the first sight of Denis and his guards to watching the Teuton king disappear into the crowds on the far side of the meadow. A momentous day. And none too soon. We'll never know exactly how many lives were lost . . . lives cut short too soon . . sacrifices that shouldn't have been required. Was I wrong to wait so long before acting on my knowledge of the Pope's secret? Don't torture yourself with that, Alfred. Had you acted sooner – before the Teutons had already expended so many men – the outcome might have been quite different.

Will the peace hold? For now, I think, the Teuton is painfully aware that he's met his match. Will the knowledge that I have his son's amulet be enough to guarantee his good behavior? And when do I return the last connection he has to that son? Don't go down the path of sentimentality, Alfred. You know the Teuton is a calculating, conniving creature who gives no thought to using people for his own ends – including his son. What you took as emotion when he saw the amulet may have been nothing more than anger that it was in your possession – that his son had failed in his mission.

And yet, I'm convinced what I saw was as much as he would ever expose of real human feeling – of sorrow – of loss. So the amulet will be returned to him one day. The question isn't if but when – and how to know when that day has come.

I roll onto my side, plump the pillow, and pull the covers over my shoulders. And as I drift off to sleep, I hear my father's voice in my head, "Trust your instincts, Alfred. You will know when the time is right."

Three days later, a messenger arrives with news that the lead elements of the Teuton army have crossed the border. "Our commander sees no signs," Denis tells us after reading the dispatch, "of anything but a continued orderly retreat. He'll set up camp on the border for a full week before starting to send some of our forces home."

"Much like what we did when Charles came against us," says Samuel. "We reduced that camp to a small border force pretty quickly, though."

"Do you have enough spies," Brandr asks, "to keep an eye on what they're up to?"

"Father's networks should still be intact," Denis replies. "Or should I say Mother's?" he adds with a chuckle. Nominally, the Duke of Aleffe is responsible for Denis's intelligence gathering, but it's widely believed that it's actually the duchess who's running the show.

"Then I suppose it's time for us to leave," I tell him, "so you can get that progress organized and see to your people. We'll leave it to you and your commanders to decide when it's safe for Hedrek's army and the Peaks forces to start making their way home."

"And two of my ships can remain to help with the transport," says Brandr. "Just remember they'll have to leave before winter sets in and our waters freeze."

"I'm grateful, Brandr – for everything," says Denis. "And rest assured your sailors will be home long before the ice arrives."

· · · · ·

We arrive at the port to find all the Nordic ships docked. "We decided," Thorvald tells us, "since we didn't have enough ships for a full blockade, that the best way to forestall any landings here would be to occupy as many of the berths as possible."

"Good strategy, Captain," says Samuel.

"Though you'll be pleased to know," I add, "that hostilities are at an end and the Teutons are on their way home."

"The best news a man could have hoped for." Thorvald smiles broadly. "Come aboard – all of you." His gesture includes Carew and all the guards.

While Samuel and I head for the prow to watch the loading of the horses, Brandr disappears below with Thorvald. They re-emerge just as the last horse is being settled in the hold. "This is where we part company, my friends," says Brandr.

"Surely you can come stay with us at least through the harvest festivals," I reply. "There'll be plenty of time then for you to get home before winter."

"As delightful as that sounds, I need to take the news to Hasten. He needs to know as soon as possible what's happened so he can be prepared if the Teutons should start looking in his direction. And we need to come to an agreement on when to lift the blockade. I suspect we'll wait until the Teuton fleet starts returning to port, but it may take some time before those orders reach them."

"I rather suspect the Teutons are going to be hard-pressed for food this winter," says Samuel. "They'll likely have expended their stores feeding the army. And, of course, with so many men conscripted to fight, there won't have been many left to tend the crops. As long as

Hasten can keep them supplied with fish, I doubt he'll be a target for them any time soon."

"I hope you're right, Samuel," says Brandr. "Now, Thorvald is going to take you home. Then as soon as he can get the hold cleaned out from the horses, he'll set sail to fetch Edward home. He'll winter over with you this year, Alfred. I hope the Teutons remain quiet, but I'll sleep ever so much better knowing there's a way for you to get word to us should they get up to any mischief."

I embrace my cousin, then hold him at arm's length. "My gratitude knows no bounds. Without your help . . ." I leave the thought hanging in the air. Brandr knows the strength of our alliance and of our family bonds. He claps me on the shoulder, exchanges the warrior's greeting with Samuel, and hurries down the gangway to board the ship in the next berth.

"So when would you like to depart, Sire?" Thorvald's voice brings me back to our own ship.

"How soon can you get underway, Captain?"

"My crew is ready." He turns to make his way to the stern, quietly issuing instructions as he goes. Sails are raised, moorings released, positions manned . . . and in short order, we're making our way to the open sea.

During the voyage, Samuel regales me with the story of his and Edward's journey through the Northern Kingdom. "Did you get any sense of what the people are like?"

"Only that they mostly ignored us and went about their business. Come on, Alfred, you know yourself how impossible it is to get any feel for what men are like if you can't converse with them."

"All too well. That awkward conversation with the Eastern king that wasn't really a conversation at all. I honestly don't know if the man is a tyrant or timid."

"Either way, that's not something we have to concern ourselves with at the moment."

· · · · ·

When we finally disembark, I find myself impatient with how long it takes to unload the horses. Is it impatience to get home myself or impatience for Thorvald to get underway and bring Edward home? Both, I finally decide. It's time for life to get back to normal.

Life may be getting back to normal sooner than I'd expected. As Samuel and I ride into the inner courtyard, the guards veer off and make straight for the stables. Gwen and Geoffrey stand patiently at the bottom of the steps while we hand our horses into the care of the waiting groom. She comes into my arms for a hug, and I pick her up and swing her around in a circle as I've done so often before on such occasions. "It's over," I tell her, placing her back on her feet. "It's finally over."

"And I couldn't be happier." She plants a quick kiss on my lips followed by another on Samuel's cheek. "Tamasine has gone to help your father bring the children back to court. She said he would undoubtedly chide her that he was quite capable of doing it himself."

"That he would." Samuel grins.

"I think she just wanted something to do once she knew you were safe and would be home soon. They should be back any day now." She locks one arm in mine and one in Samuel's, and we climb the steps with Geoffrey following behind. "Speaking of being back," she continues, "I sent word to all the lords as soon as I read your letter, Alfred. And yes, before you ask, that includes Simon and Mary. I swear, Lord Montfort must have foresight. He was here before my messenger even returned. Estrilda and the children are here. Laurence will join them in a few days, as soon as he's gotten the arrivals of the returning armies underway."

"Same thing he told us," says Samuel. "And we could see the army gathering on the opposite side of the river, getting organized for the ferry crossing. The lead elements might arrive here as early as tomorrow afternoon."

"Thank goodness Richard and Avelina are already here," says Gwen as we step into the entrance hall. "At least they won't be delayed waiting for all the soldiers to cross."

"When is Edward coming home?" asks Geoffrey.

"Captain Thorvald will leave tomorrow or the next day to fetch him," I reply. "He wanted to get his hold thoroughly cleaned out after transporting the horses before he set sail again."

Geoffrey's face lights up. "That's the best news I've had in weeks!" Then, realizing what he's just said, he adds, "Not that I'm not pleased you're home, Papa."

I reach up and tousle his hair. Maybe it's time for me to start just clapping him on the shoulder. "Don't worry, Son. I miss him too."

The following day, just after the midday meal, the sentries shout out news of the army's approach. We rush to the parapets to watch the arrival – as impressive as I'd hoped it would be. Flag bearers lead the column, Jasper and Evrouin right behind them. Foot soldiers and archers next with mounted knights bringing up the rear. There'll be many more arrivals like this before all our men are home and similar arrivals in the Lakes and the Peaks. I hope all those have the same pomp and ceremony attached.

Over the next few days, the rest of the court returns. Rainard and Juliana are the last to arrive. When the carriage door opens and Juliana alights, I rush to embrace her, only to be rewarded with a small but unmistakable punch in the gut. I break the embrace and hold her at arm's length as she laughs. "Looks like someone's decided to spoil my surprise," she says just as Gwen rushes down the steps to join us.

"What surprise?" asks Gwen.

"We, my love, are going to be grandparents."

"This little one," Juliana touches her belly, "seems determined to make his own announcements that he's preparing to join the world." She laughs again while her mother smothers her in a hug.

By now, Rainard has descended from the carriage and I'm able to offer him a quiet "Congratulations" as mother and daughter make their way toward the door.

When Edward arrives, accompanied by Thorvald, on the tenth day after Samuel and I rode into the courtyard, my little world is finally complete again. The court dinner two nights later is perhaps the most joyous I ever remember.

· · · · ·

The following morning, Geoffrey and Edward accost me while I'm pulling on my boots. "We've decided today should be the day," says Geoffrey.

"What day?"

"The day all three of us ride our new mounts for the first time," Edward explains.

"Why not?" The sun is shining and anxiety is far from my mind this morning, so it should be a good day for a first ride.

We stop by the kitchens for apples, and when I ask for a sack of flour, Edward says, "We won't need that, Papa. Mervyn Lightfoot's been keeping them in practice with having their saddles on and weight on their backs."

At the stable, we brush down our horses in their stalls then move them into the corridor for saddles and bridles. None of them put up a fuss. It's clear Mervyn or Elvin or both have been working with them in our absence. I let the boys mount up first and walk their mounts the length of the corridor and back. When I step in the stirrup to let Regulus feel the weight, he seems comfortable with the process, so I swing up into the saddle. His ears turn backward and he flicks his tail as if asking, "What's this all about?" But he walks calmly from one end of the corridor to the other with his ears mostly pointed forward, only the occasional flick of one ear back in my direction. When I dismount, he shakes his body all over as if he's just had a dust bath then stands calmly as I ask the boys, "Are you ready?" They both nod like small children being asked if they'd like a sweet cake.

Elvin and Mervyn come along as we lead the horses out to the arena. The first ride in a wide open area is always a bit nerve-wracking for horse and rider both, but if it goes well they'll have confidence in the training yet to come.

Edward doesn't hesitate. He stands in front of Fortis, one hand on his cheek and the other stroking his nose. "You can do this, boy," he says quietly to the horse. "I know you can. And it's just the beginning of all the adventures we'll have together." Then he walks calmly to the horse's side and mounts slowly – no sudden or unexpected motion to startle or frighten. A gentle squeeze of Fortis's ribs and they take their first tentative steps along the fence. Halfway down, Edward lays the reins across Fortis's neck, and they turn around and walk back, Edward speaking soothingly to the horse the entire way. By the third time doing this, Edward decides to move away from the fence and cross the arena. Fortis goes willingly, and they actually return at a trot. The little colt born in the middle of a storm is going to be a magnificent mount.

Geoffrey goes next. His grey is a bit more hesitant when asked to try the open arena, but Geoffrey shows uncommon patience, letting the horse figure things out at his own pace. Perhaps it's just as well we didn't have first rides earlier in the year. The maturity Geoffrey gained during the war is shining through in how he deals with his horse's uncertainty.

Finally, it's my turn. Regulus has been watching, so he knows what's to come. He stands calmly as I mount up then takes his first tentative steps along the fence, ears flicking back and forth, alternately listening to my voice and scanning for what's in front of us. A dozen steps down the fence and he turns, of his own volition, toward the middle of the arena. Has he been watching that carefully? A dozen more steps and he kicks his hind legs high into the air, requiring me to practically lie flat to shift my weight enough to get his hind feet back on the ground. And the minute I'm off balance in that direction, he rears up and paws the air, forcing me to suddenly and very awkwardly shift forward. Just as I'm afraid he's going to tip over backward, he shakes me loose and I land on my back in the dirt.

Geoffrey and Edward roar with laughter. Elvin and Mervyn conceal their chuckles behind their hands. And Regulus turns toward me, paws the ground twice, and snorts. "I be thinking," says Elvin, unable to mask a big grin, "mayhap he be telling ye he not like ye leaving him alone fer so long." Then Regulus walks up and nudges me gently with his muzzle, acting for all the world like he wants to help me get up. Shaking off the surprise of being dumped so thoroughly, I comply. I'll be ready for you next time, I tell him in my mind. You won't get away with that twice.

I take his reins and lead him back to where the others are waiting, shake some of the dirt off my clothes, and mount up again. When I squeeze his ribs, Regulus walks calmly halfway down the fence and once again turns on his own into the open arena – and this time he behaves perfectly – so I take him on another circuit, this time asking for the turn before he makes the decision for himself. It seems Elvin was right. He just had to make his point.

Back with the others, I dismount and declare success for all of us. First rides should end on a high note for horse and rider as well. Pretty sure I'm going to have a sore back tomorrow, but it's been a delightful morning. Over the next week, the colts progress more rapidly than any I've ever trained. Did the extra time allow their minds to mature? Or did Mervyn Lightfoot do more with them than he's letting on? It hardly matters, since the most important thing is growing my sons' confidence in their own abilities.

·   ·   ·   ·   ·

Working with the colts has taken the place of my usual morning ride. When I return from the latest session, Coliar waylays me in the outer chamber. "This just arrived, Sire." He hands me a sealed letter. "The messenger said no reply was required." The seal is not one I recognize, so I open the missive straightaway and read while I walk to my writing table.

My dear Alfred,

I write to tell you of my joy at the cessation of the hostilities that were raging when first we met. There are many here who share my pleasure but who, for reasons you will undoubtedly comprehend, must remain nameless. One in particular commends your success as God's approval of the paths you both chose.

I am also particularly grateful to you for enabling the opportunity for me to spend many days in the company of my lovely cousin. Now that she is no longer in the shadow of her sometimes daunting mother, she has become quite a remarkable woman who is worthy of all the good fortune that has come her way.

Lucia has invited me to spend an extended period on her estate during the coming spring, and I find myself quite looking forward to the pleasure of some time away from the intensity of life in the papal court. I am also keen to meet the young king of whom she speaks so highly. She has further promised me the opportunity to greet another of her aunts, who I'm given to believe is quite a remarkable Mother Abbess and who has been Lucia's guide in some of her most troubled hours.

Nothing would give me greater pleasure, Alfred, than to see you as well during my visit. I sense from our brief encounter that you are the sort of man with whom I could have quite wonderful conversations on any number of topics unrelated to either of our callings. Perhaps you would also bring your wife and children. It is long since time that I became acquainted with the rest of my dear Lucia's family.

Yours in Christ,

Lorenzo

When I show the letter to Gwen during our bedtime conversation, her face lights up. "That's a wonderful idea, Alfred. I've never been to Lamoreaux, though I've heard it's quite beautiful."

"I've only been there during moments of extreme stress, so I hardly know what the place is really like."

"I do hope Lucia invites us."

"I suspect if Cardinal Lorenzo has anything to do with it, she will."

Gwen snuggles close and lays her head on my chest. "Then Lamoreaux in the spring it shall be," she proclaims.

Planning ahead like this . . . perhaps life really *is* getting back to normal. But that brings to mind another thought – the advice I gave Denis. Perhaps that's advice I should take as well. "What do you think of going on a quick progress this autumn? If we leave right after the celebration banquet and don't linger anywhere, there should be enough time before the cold weather sets in to stay."

"I think that's a brilliant idea, my love. It's been far too long since we've been out among the people. Your grandfather would be appalled at how long it's been."

I chuckle. "He would indeed. And we'll take the children too."

"Alicia as well?"

"Why not? She's old enough to start learning about her duty as a princess."

"And about how to control her tongue." Gwen laughs.

"You know, I've been thinking of late that her outspokenness might turn out to be part of her charm. And this is as good a way as any to find out. I'll put things in motion in the morning."

I take my beautiful wife in my arms and we snuggle deep under the covers as another thought occurs to me. There's someone else who should go. Someone who's already given me a piece of his mind about being left behind but has been impeccably well-behaved ever since. Yes, Regulus, you can go too.

Author's Notes

The building known as the Lateran Palace dates from the Roman Empire and was originally the home of a family of administrators in the service of early emperors. It came into the possession of the emperor Constantine through his second marriage and was later gifted to the Bishop of Rome in approximately the fourth century CE – the precise date is unknown. From that time, it became the papal residence and ceremonial center. Until the eighth century, it was called the Lateran patriarchate.

Extensive additions and embellishments under Popes Hadrian, Leo, and Paschal led to the adoption of the term palace when referring to the edifice. It was restored after a major fire in the tenth century and then further embellished in the early thirteenth century to a magnificence that led Dante to describe it as beyond all human achievement.

Despite restorations after two fires during the Avignon papacy, the Lateran Palace never regained its former grandeur. And when the popes returned to Rome, they established their residence briefly in Trastavere, then at Santa Maria Maggiore before finally moving to the Apostolic Palace in the Vatican. Pope Sixtus V had the old Lateran Palace destroyed in 1586 and built a smaller building there, which has had many uses since then and today houses the residence of the Cardinal Vicar of Rome and the offices of the Vicariate.

The building we know today as St. Peter's Basilica is the second edifice of the same name built on the site of St. Peter's burial. Its construction was begun in 1506 and completed 120 years later.

The original St. Peter's Basilica is the building that would have been there in Alfred's time. This nineteenth-century drawing (public domain image) depicts what Old St. Peter's is believed to have looked like.

The *Navicella* mosaic, which Cardinal Lorenzo mentions when he takes Alfred and Lucia to visit St. Peter's, was completed over a period of eight years (1305-1313) and apparently occupied an entire wall above the entrance to the arcade. Since it faced the courtyard, it can't be seen from the perspective of this drawing. Sadly, it was destroyed during the construction of the new basilica.

While the legend still circulates that Marco Polo discovered pasta in China and brought it home with him to Italy, it is far more likely that it came from the Arab world or North Africa at a much earlier date. A ninth-century dictionary compiled by an Arab physician mentions string-shaped food made from semolina and dried for storage. One theory is that this type of pasta was introduced into Sicily at about that time. Pasta almost certainly came to Italy via the active and extensive Mediterranean trading economy of the era. From the thirteenth century onward, references to various forms of pasta appear with increasing frequency throughout Italy.

Parmigiano Reggiano cheese is believed to have been created in the Middle Ages in the Italian province of Reggio Emilia. There is certainly documentary evidence from the thirteenth century of its existence in more or less the form that we know it today, so it would have been well known in Rome at the time of Alfred's visit.

In earlier volumes of the series, I've not made reference to the destrier. In point of fact, the destrier was a specific type of horse, known for its particularly powerful hindquarters that allowed it to coil for a leap, stop suddenly, spin or turn quickly, and perform other maneuvers not within the capabilities of other horses. Two breeds – the Andalusian and the Friesian – are believed to have been the most common types that had the proper musculature and strength to be trained as destriers. Thus, not even all war horses were destriers. Alfred's beloved horses were certainly not. It seemed appropriate, however, for Denis's tall, black mount to have been unusual among the horses that might otherwise have been available to him – hence the reference to the animal having been chosen for training as a destrier.

This novel is a work of fiction that tells the story of what might have been in a world that doesn't precisely correspond to the one we know. Readers will note similarities with northern Europe, but my decision to fictionalize the setting was a matter of practicality for my characters. European history from this period and its major actors are too well known for it to be plausible that a different set of kings and nobility might actually have existed.

I began this series as an allegory of modern times, and the allegory is still there for readers who care to look. Since then, however, so many readers have commented on how attached they've grown to Alfred and the people around him and how eager they are to discover what happens next. For a novelist, such remarks are truly heartwarming, and I'm deeply grateful that the characters I've come to love also touch the hearts and minds of my readers. I'm also grateful for all the readers who've chosen to come along with Alfred on his journey.

About the Author

Pamela Taylor brings her love of history to the art of storytelling in the *Second Son Chronicles*. An avid reader of historical fact and fiction, she finds the past offers rich sources for character, ambiance, and plot that allow readers to escape into a world totally unlike their daily lives. She shares her home with two Pembroke Welsh Corgis who remind her frequently that a dog walk is the best way to find inspiration for that next chapter.

Other Books by Pamela Taylor

Second Son Chronicles

Second Son

My Father, My King

Pestilence

Upon this Throne

Shadows

The Weight of the Crown

Destiny

A Feeling in the Bones

Note from the Author

Word-of-mouth is crucial for any author to succeed. If you enjoyed *The Burden of Choice*, please leave a review online—anywhere you are able. Even if it's just a sentence or two. It would make all the difference and would be very much appreciated.

Thanks!
Pamela Taylor

We hope you enjoyed reading this title from:

BLACK ROSE
writing™

www.blackrosewriting.com

Subscribe to our mailing list – *The Rosevine* – and receive **FREE** books, daily deals, and stay current with news about upcoming releases and our hottest authors.
Scan the QR code below to sign up.

Already a subscriber? Please accept a sincere thank you for being a fan of Black Rose Writing authors.

View other Black Rose Writing titles at
www.blackrosewriting.com/books and use promo code
PRINT to receive a **20% discount** when purchasing.

Printed in Great Britain
by Amazon

43655912R00142